NAMED

THEY CALL HER GIRL, *I CALL HER MINE*

M. L. MARIAN

EPIGRAPH

Smother me with these thighs, wife.

— JEDIDIAH SHAY

INTRODUCTION

The Shay family has a tradition, one inspired by the story of the Roman soldiers and the Sabine women.

When a Shay sees the woman meant for him, he's not above a little...ahem...*persuasion* to convince her they belong together.

Hot loving every night.

Forced cuddling.

Steamy kisses.

Happily ever afters.

This is what it means to be a Shay.

This story has a bit of sweet bite to it with themes that may be disturbing to some readers. For a content warning, please visit the author's website at mlmarian.com.

1

GIRL

Rubbing a hand over my swollen cheek, I numbly stare at my closed bedroom door, flinching when my father drunkenly stumbles upstairs and into the room across from mine. It's nothing new, really, him striking me for some imagined transgression. Whether he's drunk or sober, I'm nothing but a useless woman to him.

A burden to begrudgingly care for.

A body that takes up precious space.

I wonder how quickly he'd consider me a burden if he suddenly had to cook his own meals and clean his own house. Or if he woke up outside, face-down in the mud because I wasn't there to drag him home from the saloon like I did tonight while all the men stood there and laughed at us.

Maybe that'd be a good thing, though, if I weren't here.

Maybe he'd suffocate in that mud.

I pause for a moment, envisioning that imagery.

I wouldn't mind.

Oil lamp in hand, I quietly step to the small chest of drawers by my bed to see how bad the damage is this time.

Looking in the chipped mirror that shows fractured sections of my face, I grimace. It's bad, but not as bad as it has been in the past. Maybe the bruise will last only a few days this time instead of a week.

The girl in the mirror has such tired, hazel eyes. She's pretty enough, with dark hair that has a bit of curl to it, but exhaustion and the marks of abuse add a darker layer to her comeliness. I trace over my reflection's swollen cheek, stopping when I reach the high-necked collar of her dress, and make a promise to her—to *us*.

Whatever it takes, I'm going to leave Springwell. As soon as the hidden stash of money in my mother's old dress grows big enough, I'm on the first stagecoach out of town and headed to Hope's Stand to catch a train.

I place the lamp down and open the top drawer of my vanity, lips twisting in frustration when it catches. Stubborn, stubborn thing. Finally, it squeaks open and I hold my breath, silently praying my father didn't hear that. He shouldn't have, as soused as he is, but sometimes he surprises me. When I don't hear angry footsteps, I reach for my nightdress and carefully unfold it, revealing a black book that belonged to my mother, God rest her soul. A young widow with a toddler and no immediate family or means of income, she had no choice but to marry the man who threatened to take her to the poorhouse if she didn't.

Dead husband barely cold in the ground, Temperance Irons became Mrs. Clarence Crowley, bravely preparing herself to submit to this new, unwanted husband. And the toddler? That was me. I now had a father who tolerated me, at best.

Clarence Crowley wasn't the softest of men, nor the most religious. So much so that he refused to let his meek, Puritan wife keep her Bible. But Temperance Irons was nothing if not resourceful, so she made do with this book instead. Every night after kissing my forehead and tucking me in, she'd sit in the firelight and write, all while I watched her until my eyes could no longer stay open.

Now my fingers brush over the letters on the front of the cracked leather cover as my lips futilely try to form the word.

D-I-A-R-Y.

I wish I knew what she'd written inside. I know the shapes are pictures for sounds, but I don't know how to put them together. Even if I did, it would only be in my mind. My hand moves from the book to my neck, the faded silver scars hidden under my collar reminding me of why I don't speak now.

I was only five years old when my mother died, and it was at the graveside ceremony when I realized she wasn't coming back. I cried inconsolably, holding onto my father's leg for comfort. Comfort that came in the form of heavy fingers digging into my shoulder, silently warning me to be quiet.

I cried as the minister spoke big words I didn't know the meaning of, telling me, my father, and his sister that Temperance Crowley was now received into the hands of God. Then at the first thud of dirt atop the wooden casket, I was pushed into my pinch-faced aunt's skirts as my father headed back to the saloon.

My crying didn't stop that night, either.

Not until my father stopped it for me with a dull knife to my throat, threatening to cut out my voice if I made another noise. I wet the bed in fear, the acrid aroma mixing with the foul smell of whiskey on his breath as he hovered over me, but I didn't cry anymore.

Not until the next night.

And then I learned that my father was indeed capable of keeping a promise.

Every night for a week, a burning, stinging cut on my neck would wake me, just as my nightmares woke my father.

On the eighth night, I didn't make a sound.

Not even when the nightmares came.

Thirteen years have now passed, and I haven't made a sound since. It's been so long that I don't know if I can.

And I won't even try because I value my life more than my voice.

———

"GIRL! GET YOUR LAZY ASS UP AND GET OUT HERE." AT THE expletives and banging fists that follow, my eyes fly open and adjust to the bright sunlight streaming in my upstairs window.

Too much sunlight.

I've overslept. Probably because of the blow to the face I was given last night, but my father doesn't care about that. All the man wants is his breakfast. No matter how drunk he gets, he's never been one to let the sun get too far ahead of him.

Throwing back the covers, I rush to get dressed, catching a glimpse of the purple mark on my face as I hurriedly pin my wayward curls. If I'm lucky, I'll get a glare for my morning punishment. If I'm not, I may just get another mark to match.

Luck, however, is on my side after I scurry downstairs and gather the ingredients for a hot breakfast. As the fresh eggs, biscuits, and ham steaks slide in front of my father, he eyes the bruise fanning over my cheekbone. "Hmph," he grunts. "If you did what you were told, things like that wouldn't happen. Am I right, Girl?"

I nod sharply, gaze downcast as I wait by the sink. I know better than to try to speak, even if asked a question. He doesn't want to hear my voice at all. Doesn't even want to call me by the name that's too similar to my mother's. Too Puritan sounding.

When he belches and shoves his chair back after his second helping, I know he's done, which means it's my turn after I clean his spot at the table. I quietly make the table spotless and stand by the counter to eat my own food, pretending that I can't feel his hard eyes on me as I nervously chew a bite of cold eggs, heart in my throat.

I have a feeling the other half of my punishment is weighing on his mind, and if it's anything like the other times, it means I don't get to sleep in the house tonight. According to him, sleeping in the elements should make me wake up on time. He ignores me, though, and fiddles with his hat before walking out the door. Immediately, my shoulders fall with relief. Sleeping in this house isn't my favorite thing to do, but it's better than sleeping outside with no pillow or blanket.

Or the other alternative.

But I'll worry about that only if I have to. I sop up the last bite of my biscuit in the grease of the ham, then roll my sleeves up and clean the dirty dishes.

Today's washday, too, so when I'm done with the kitchen, I strip the bedding and throw it into the soapy water of the copper, stirring and poking it with the dolly before putting them through the wringer. Sometimes I wonder why the wooden stick with four little knoblike legs on the bottom is called a dolly when it looks nothing like a doll.

Then again, there's lots of things that I wonder about since my father never allowed me to go to school.

One final pass through the wringer and I feel the bedding, frowning when my fingers come away with heavy moisture. It's to be expected that they still be wet, but not this much. With a huff of air, I heft the sodden sheets with tired arms and take them outside to pin them up on the clothesline.

There.

They'll dry soon enough in a few hours, provided it doesn't rain. Wiping a bit of sweat from my brow, I lift a hand to my eyes as I survey the skies. Looks clear, so I'll bring the bedding in later. Back inside I go to put the only set of spare sheets on the beds, dust the furniture, and restock the wood for the stove.

Now it's time to go to my other job. One of them, anyway. A girl has to earn her keep to live in Clarence Crowley's house, after all. Where else would he get the money to drink and gamble if not for me?

I grab my little cloth sack and take off walking. Usually, I enjoy listening to the sounds of nature on the short journey, but the blisters rubbing my heels diminish the pleasure. Nevertheless, I'm determined not to let my late start to the morning cause me to be late all day, so I pick up the pace, hiding my pain behind a grimace.

"Girl," Mr. Collins calls as I open the door to the general store. "Just in time. There's a shipment of cigars in the back for the front display. Hop to it, child." I nod my agreement and weave between the shelves to the back part of the store. Even the townspeople don't know my name or that my father isn't my father.

No, when we moved here after my mother died, no one batted an eye at the man and his mute daughter who moved into a small, respectable house in the small, reserved town of Springwell. Most people think mute means ignorant, but I'm not stupid, even if I never did go to school. I can learn something well enough if it's explained to me and I can see how to do it.

Like cooking.

Or stocking shelves.

I just can't operate the register since I can't add and subtract when the numbers are too high. Some people buy on credit, too, so that means their names would be written down in the ledger, along with their balance and new charges. The mail and telegrams are off-limits, too. Since I can't do any of that, I'm relegated to stocking shelves. Easy enough work once I learned to put things with the same colors and shapes next to each other.

Easy enough until sometimes the designs change or the layout moves, which is how one time I accidentally filled the flour barrel with sugar. Mr. Collins only boxed my ears once for that and then showed me what I did wrong. The packets of seeds with drawings on the front are the simplest to stock because a carrot always looks like a carrot, and a tulip always looks like a tulip.

When I finish stocking the cigars, teas, and other staples, I rest against the counter and look past the weighing scale to the assorted postal letters in their boxes. I know the last two boxes belong to the Williams family and the Wright family because I've seen them come in to pick up their mail. What puzzles me here is how the first letter is the same shape but has a different sound. Williams and Wright, but they're both pronounced differently. I simply can't wrap my mind around the logic. It doesn't make any sense at all, especially since one of them sounds like what my name begins with.

The clearing of a throat catches my attention. "Don't just

stand around, Girl. Make yourself useful and sweep the floor."

Swallowing my sigh, I grab the broom from behind the counter and whisk it over the floors. There's always a thin layer of dirt because of the cracks in the slats that allow dust to fly in when the wind's blowing hard enough. And the hard-working men who come in to buy tobacco never wipe their muddy boots, so there are often boot prints that don't come off except with water and scrubbing.

I can't complain, though. If I do a good enough job, Mr. Collins pays me a little extra that I can hide from my father, so that's always incentive for me to make the store as clean and presentable as I possibly can.

When the sunlight begins to fade and heavy clouds gather in the darkening skies, I trudge wearily home on the dirt path, sack in hand and wincing again at the way the blisters rub. This time, though, I detour to the creek that runs behind the house. Our house is respectable, of course, but we still have to wash in the creek because we don't have the luxury of bathrooms inside.

Dragging aside the heavy branches that encircle the water, I head for the small wooded area that affords a bit more privacy for me to wash up. I strip down and hurriedly dip into the cold water, keeping a wary eye and ear out as I use the bar of soap from my sack. Sometimes I feel like someone's watching me, but since no one's ever actually come bursting through the tree line, I'm inclined to believe my wild thoughts are getting the better of me.

I don't have to wash my hair today, so I'm in, out, and dressed again soon, all while the sun sinks into the horizon and the clouds grow more ominous. I wonder if my luck will hold and my father will allow me to sleep inside. As I resume my journey, my house and the bedding dried on the line come into view, making my heart beat faster. If they get wet, my father won't be happy, I'm sure. I hurry to the sheets and take them down from the line, folding them into neat sections as I cast a wary eye to the house.

Luck may yet be on my side.

Cautiously walking up the crooked steps, I twist the knob to the front door.

Locked.

A niggling feeling tells me that it's not an accident, but just in case it is, I walk around to the back door. No good. It's locked as well. Useless tears begin to form, but I shrug them away. I have two options, but neither are particularly appealing.

I can wrap myself in the clean sheets and sleep outside, possibly catching pneumonia from the rain that I'm sure is coming, or I can walk back to town and beg for shelter from Madam Lulu in exchange for cleaning rooms.

At the first droplet of water that hits, I realize I have no choice.

Madam Lulu's, it is.

Tears of anger mix with the rain that falls down my face at my situation and the pain in my feet, but I steadily make my way back to town through the muddy road and knock on the door of the brothel. It swings open to reveal an older woman heavily made up and a cloud of cigar smoke behind her.

With one look at my disheveled state, Madam Lulu sighs and steps back. "Come on in, child. You'll make more of a mess than you clean, so you just get on to bed now." With a teary smile of silent gratitude, I scrape my shoes and wring my dress out as much as I can before entering the parlor.

"Who's this cute little old thing?" The voice comes from a man resting on the arm of the red velvet sofa. "Put me down for an hour with her. Or three," he adds as his dark gaze skims over my wet clothes.

I don't know what he means by that, but I don't think it's good. Alarmed, I shrink into my escort's side, but she only scoffs at him. "Not this one, Yancy. She's more innocent than even the Virgin Mary. Go pick another one."

Walking briskly to keep up with her, I ignore all the sounds and smells around me and sigh with relief when the small storage room under the stairwell comes into view.

"All right, child," Madam Lulu says in a no-nonsense voice, "get some rest and be sure not to leave the room until at least dawn. If you do get a chance to clean, make sure you don't strip the beds. That's the girls' jobs, not yours." After I agree with a small nod, she gives a soft smile in return. "Good night."

As the door closes, I fight my wet clothes off and spread them to dry. Clad in only my shift, I fall into the small bed and rest my hands underneath the musty pillow as I shiver. Earthy grunts and groans of a man and woman doing strange things to one another sound through the walls as I struggle to find my sleep. Is that the virgin Mary? And what does it mean to be a virgin?

Long minutes pass as the odd groans and squeaks keep going. I'll have to get up early in the morning and wait for my father to let me back in the house to prepare breakfast, and then I'll be going to the only restaurant Springwell has and be on my feet all day as I cook again. A jaw-cracking yawn leaves me as my eyes fall closed. I swear, I'm leaving this town if it's the last thing I do.

2

GIRL

I work my jaw back and forth as I add a bit of butter to the grits, grateful that the soreness in my cheek is almost gone. I was right. This mark didn't last much longer than three days, and the color isn't that noticeable anymore except in the sunshine.

Meanwhile, the weight of my father's stare is very noticeable.

He's quiet.

Too quiet.

If he's not bellowing at me or cuffing me upside the head, then he's ignoring my existence.

But this? This is unsettling because I'm unsure of what's going to happen. My fingers tremble, almost dropping the ladle right into the grits as I plate his food. Wary footsteps lead me to the table, and I cautiously slide his plate in front of him before stepping away to wait my turn to eat.

I watch his craggy face from under docile eyes as he tears into a biscuit. The cornsilk yellow hair he used to grease with pride is now a dingy gray, covering only half of his head. Time has not been kind to Clarence Crowley, and neither has drink. Maybe he once was a handsome man, or at least a child, but if he was, then his handsomeness faded away with every dram of whiskey he imbibed and every unkind word he spoke.

If only time would steal away a bit of his strength to lessen the force of his blows. In that regard, I suppose time has not been kind to me, either. He looks up at me, blood-shot eyes running over my form again in a calculating way. My blood quickens in my veins, and I smooth my hands over my apron. "Quit fidgetin' and stand up straight," he snaps.

Taken aback at his tone, I jolt, fingers falling flat against my plain gray dress. My only comfort is the distance between us and the fact that he's still chewing.

"How old are you now? Seventeen?"

Just because I don't speak doesn't mean my father doesn't expect an answer, so I shake my head. My counting has gotten much better since working with Mr. Collins once I learned the number patterns, but I can only go to nine hundred ninety-nine.

His eyes narrow. "Eighteen?" When I nod my agreement, he dips his eggs into his grits and talks around the mouthful of food. "Gonna have a guest for supper, so make sure you cook somethin' decent. Something sweet. Clean the floors real good. Rug, too."

I nod in assent, wondering why someone's coming for the lighter nightly meal instead of our earlier and heavier dinner—and why someone is coming at all, actually—but in the end, it doesn't matter. I'll do what I'm told. A blue-berry pie sounds good, and the rug will be easy enough to clean, too, with some dry tea leaves before I brush it.

"Outside," he tacks on.

My heart sinks in dismay. This means I have to drag the

heavy rug from the house and beat it. He's not going to help, either. Keeping my sigh to myself, I dip my chin again. When he's done eating and out the door to do God knows what, I clean his spot just in case he comes back inside. No need to set myself up for another punishment if I can help it.

An extra guest, he said.

I wonder if this means I'll get to sit at the table with them or if my father will care about such things.

Oh, well. Wondering about things won't help me clean the kitchen or the rest of the house, so I'd better get to it. My one bright spot for today is that I don't have to go to either of my other jobs, so I'll be able to rest a bit once I get the rug beaten.

Setting water from the cistern to boil so I can wash the dishes, I reach for a bowl and scrape together what my father left behind for me—a serving of grits, a few bites of eggs, and the least desirable cut of ham. Stirring everything together warms the eggs just a touch and makes swallowing the meat easier. Food doesn't go to waste in this house if I can help it. I'm not starving, but there have been nights I've gone to sleep with hunger gnawing at my belly. While I don't like being on my feet all day at the restaurant, at least I can have a hot meal a few times a week. Not just lukewarm leftovers.

But at least I'm fed. I push my woes behind me and focus on the chores I need to accomplish. I'm a little excited at the thought of a dinner guest. Also a little worried, too, because it doesn't particularly speak well of a person's character if they're willingly choosing to spend time with Clarence Crowley. At any rate, it may provide a change of pace, and maybe my father will be less inclined to get drunk.

The water's surface bubbles rapidly now, so I plug the

sink and pour it in, steam rising in front of my face. Now to add cold water and some soap flakes. Washing dishes isn't too bad. In fact, I rather like that it's mindless, and with my father gone, I can dawdle just a bit.

Within the next hour, the dishes are done, the sink is drained with the dirty water thrown outside, and the windows are cleaned. The only things left to do downstairs are the dusting, sweeping, and cleaning the rug, but I have to do the rug first.

May as well get to it.

The floor creaks underneath my feet as I roll the heavy material together and slowly drag it to the front door. That's a chore in itself, but I still have to get it down the steps and all spread out again.

By the time it's all laid out and I've gotten the wooden beater, I've broken a bit of a sweat, but not as much as I'm about to. I swing the stick behind my shoulder and bear down, coughing at the dust plumes that rise.

That actually felt pretty good, striking the rug like that. I do it again with a bit more force, pretending that it's my father.

Wham!

Take that, Clarence Crowley.

Now it feels really good. Anger builds in me at my unfair treatment, and my hands twitch on the beater. Before I realize what I'm doing, my arms lift up of their own accord and come down heavily.

Wham!

For every time he cut my neck.

Wham!

For every time he hit me.

Tears slip unbidden down my face, and I roughly wipe them away before drawing my arm back again.

Wham!

For every time he withheld food.

Wham!

For every time he made me sleep outside.

Wham!

For never loving me or my mother.

"Arghh—" Startled by the raspy noise, I raise a trembling hand to my throat and sink to my knees on the dirty ground, lungs heaving from surprise. What was that harsh braying sound? We don't have a donkey. Did it come from me? Because of my anger? That's never happened before.

Do I...do I dare try to repeat it? My father's not here, so maybe... With a glance to the yard and the empty horizon, I check to see that my father and his horse aren't in sight.

They're not.

No one is.

Gathering the courage to try again, I take a deep breath and will my heart to slow down.

Focus, Girl.

Open your mouth and just do it.

My chin drops, tongue working clumsily as I attempt to drum up a sound. Any sound. Even a whisper.

But no matter how hard I focus, it remains silent.

I remain silent.

Damn you, Clarence Crowley.

————

In the end, I decide not to chance it by assuming I'll be eating with our guest, so I gather plateware for only two under my father's watchful gaze.

"Girl," he growls at me. I freeze, body tensing and gaze

lowered to his feet that take a step forward. I should have known better. *Please don't let him strike me.* "One more."

The breath I release in relief sends a wave of dizziness through my head. I'm still unnerved by the noise that came from my throat today, and adding in my father's strange mood, I'm not sure how to process things. Not taking the time to think on it, I shakily reach for another plate, foot lifting from the floor as I stretch up to the cabinet.

"And change your dress. Somethin' a little...fancified." He almost sneers the word. "Hair, too."

My fingers lose their grasp and the plate slips to catch me on the bridge of my nose. What is going on with Clarence Crowley? Uneasiness creeps over me as I rub the sore spot, and I tighten my muscles against a shiver. This doesn't bode well.

I quietly head upstairs and to the second drawer of my vanity that holds my aprons and my one good dress. It's a few years old, but it still fits me rather well and only has one stain on it. I wonder if it'd still fit the same if I ate as much as my father does. Casting a wary eye to the door, I slip out of my work dress and pull the flowery one on, smoothing out a wrinkle or two and moving to my mirror.

All eight pieces of myself show in the broken mirror as I try on a smile, one pretty enough to match the dress. Maybe when I leave this town for good, I can find a man who will think I'm pretty and doesn't mind that I don't speak.

My smile falls.

Maybe.

Shaking my head, I loosen my braid, combing my fingers through the thick and curly strands. I think maybe a top knot will do, and perhaps some soft curls along my cheek. Mind made up, I pull my hair up and pin it carefully into place. A gentle tug on each side gives me some short tendrils that I curl around my finger to give some shape.

There we go.

The neighing of a horse sounds outside my window and sends a jolt of nervousness through me. Minding the two spots of the floor that creak when stepped on, I tiptoe closer and pull back the curtain just enough to see the top of a hat as someone steps inside the house. I turn and clutch the buttons on the front of my dress, letting the wall support me as my breath suddenly runs away from me. My father wanted me to clean the house, bake something sweet, change my clothes, and fix my hair.

But for what reason?

"Girl!" he yells out. "Get down here and give us some pie."

I suppose I'm about to find out. Giving myself a passing glance in the mirror as I leave my room, I lift my chin and force my face into a placid expression. Speculation will get me nowhere. Somehow, I nervously tread down the stairs without tripping over my feet.

At the base of the steps, boots are the first thing I see since my eyes are downcast. Slowly, I slide my gaze up, letting it catch on the legs attached to the boots. Higher to the stomach that hangs over the large belt buckle, and higher still to the bushy beard and mustache attached to a weathered face.

It's Mr. Pennington who moved to Springwell two years ago. He also lost his wife last year to sickness.

"This is her," my father states with a gesture towards me.

Oh, sweet merciful heavens.

"C'mere, child." Mr. Pennington crooks a finger, beckoning me closer. I instinctively obey, stopping when I'm close enough to smell the sweat of his horse on him. He looks at me, tipping my chin up. "Lemme see your teeth."

I bare them, stretching my lips and waiting with growing trepidation at what this means.

"She's got all her teeth," my father proudly boasts. "And she don't speak at all."

The fingers on my chin tilt my head side to side to view me from various angles. "So I've heard. Is she tetched in the head?" I am *not* touched in the head. My eyes fly to Mr. Pennington's so quickly in fury that he chuckles. "I guess that answers that question. All right, then. How about that pie now?"

Grateful when his hands are no longer on me, I find brief respite as I slice two pieces of the cooled pie and plate it. I'm unsure of where I'm supposed to eat, but my father did tell me to get another plate, after all, so I cut a third piece and just stand there.

"Sit, Girl. Right here." My father nods to the chair beside Mr. Pennington. I haltingly step to the table and ease into the chair, careful not to brush up against this man in any way.

"You were right, Clarence," Mr. Pennington mumbles around a mouthful of pie, crumbs dropping into his beard. "This pie is tasty. What else does this girl do?"

"Almost anythin' you can think of. Cookin', mendin', cleanin'. You tell her what you want her to do and she does it."

Because doing it is better than the alternative. But I don't say that. Instead, I silently bring a minuscule bite to my mouth, unsure if I'll be able to choke it down but swallowing it anyway.

"Hmm." Licking his fork, Mr. Pennington appraises me. "And what about her purity? Has she been with other men?"

What does he mean by that? I'm with two men right now.

"She ain't been touched by no man."

Touched? My chewing slows as I try to process why that matters. Mr. Pennington just gripped my chin, so I don't know what my father means. It doesn't sound good, though.

"Hmm." Mr. Pennington leans back in his chair and folds his arms over his ample stomach as he apparently mulls things over. "Truth be told, a housekeeper is more what I had in mind. Not another wife."

It takes everything within me not to spit out pieces of blueberry.

Wife?

The word trickles into my ears, making me think I've lost my hearing along with my voice. I couldn't have heard him right. My fork clanks against the plate as I put it down, unable to take another bite.

"I don't know," Mr. Pennington continues, dragging a hand through his beard to comb out the crumbs. "I'm a old man now, and the marriage bed just ain't the same. Especially at the price you're askin' with her being dumb."

Does he mean my father is trying to sell me into marriage? I don't want to share the covers with this man. He'll probably have an entire meal of crumbs from his beard in the sheets!

My father avoids my gaze as he answers. "Pshaw...look at her. Young and handsome, she'll at least warm your bed even if she don't bear any children."

The chair scrapes across the floor as Mr. Pennington pushes back with a muffled belch. "Tell you what do, Clarence. I'ma think on it a few days, and I'll let you know."

"Don't think on it too long. A wife that can cook and

don't talk back?" My father shakes his head. "That's a down-right steal at any price."

The men move to the door while I stare at a lone, shriveled blueberry. My father is getting rid of me by selling me to anyone who will pay the price and doesn't mind a mute woman. Once Mr. Pennington leaves, I calmly go through the motions of cleaning the kitchen while my father ignores me once again, muttering something about how he needs to come up with the money within two weeks.

Did he get himself in trouble with his gambling? As if it's not enough to gamble in his hometown, sometimes he'll spend a weekend in Hope's Stand at the bigger tables.

When I make it upstairs, I quietly pull out my hidden stash and count it again with trembling hands. Whether I have enough or not, I'm going to have to leave sooner than I planned.

Before two weeks have passed.

3

JEDIDIAH

The heat of the afternoon sun burns my neck as I sway to the rhythmic pace of my chestnut-colored horse. Sadie and I have been together for so long that I could fall asleep in the saddle and have complete trust that she'd still be headed the right direction when I woke up. Good horses are worth their weight in gold. We've been traveling quite a ways these past few months, the two of us, and stopping back home in Hope's Stand between trips, but it'll all be worth it in the end once I find my woman.

I reach down for my canteen, hand glancing over the coiled rope on my saddle. One coiled, buttery soft rope waiting just for her, because in keeping with family tradition, I'm on a hunt to kidnap a bride. Town after town Sadie and I've been through, but none of the women I've seen have caught my interest. Oh, I caught theirs, all right, with my tall height, decent smolder, and good-looking horse. But I'm a man on a mission, and I don't have eyes for anyone but her.

I'll know her when I see her. And when I do, she'll be mine, whether she comes easy or hard. Sadie nickers, bringing my attention to a wooden signpost standing tall in the ground.

"All right, then," I drawl. "Guess we're stopping at Springwell. Population five hundred." Must admit, it'll be nice to spend a night on a mattress instead of my bedroll and the hard ground. Following the lead of my horse, we soon make our way into the little town. Solemn stares poke holes into my back as we traipse past the places of business in the center. Huh. Real friendly folks here.

It's a typical small town with the typical small shops. Not so different from any other we've seen. Passing the barber-shop and general store, Sadie draws to a halt at the saloon. "Good guess, old girl. But we're taking care of you first. Come on." With a light nudge, I direct her to the metal water trough in front of the livery, where a scrawny boy sizes me up from under his hat as I dismount and adjust my holster and knife sheath.

"What'll it be, mister?" Pulling a knife from his pocket, the kid digs the blade underneath his fingernails. "We got three types of boardin'. Full, partial, and self."

While my horse quenches her thirst, I take him in, too, from his dirty, bare feet all the way to the hole in his hat's brim. "What's your recommendation, son?"

He rubs the back of his neck. "How long you gonna be in town for?"

"Not rightly sure yet. Maybe a night or two to begin with."

The little businessman dips his chin. "I'd go with the partial, if I was you. That comes with everything the full boardin' does, but without turning 'em out to pasture for some exercise. It'll save you some coin, too, 'cause Mr. Henry don't always remember to turn 'em out in the mornings unless I remind him before I leave. He likes to drink too much, see?"

I do. Seems this kid runs the place better than Mr. Henry. "You got another job keeping you busy?"

Folding his knife back up, he grins widely. "Nah, I just like to go down to the creek sometimes."

Bet he gets all muddy catching fish and frogs and then heads home to be scolded by his mother. I shoo a fly away from Sadie's sweaty flank and give her a little scratch. "At the creek, eh? What do you say to full boarding, and I pay you a little extra to be here to remind Mr. Henry?"

"Well," the boy draws out the word, a glint in his eyes, "I don't know 'bout that. How much extra you talking? 'Cause I really like being down at the creek."

The little manipulator. I chuckle and name a price, watching his eyebrows hike up. "Sheeyit, mister. I'da done it for half that, but a deal's a deal. Shake on it?"

"A deal's a deal," I repeat sternly as I pump his hand firmly. "And I'm trusting you to be a man of your word, understand?"

He gravely nods. "I swear, you can trust me. And since you're payin' me so much, how'd you like to go sightseein' down at the creek with me? A favor for a favor," he adds on slyly.

What the hell. I can spare a few minutes for the kid and indulge some childish whims. "After you remind him? You just let me know when, and I'll be there."

"Tonight. After suppertime and right before it gets dark. You meet me here, and I'll show you the way."

"You got it, kid. Now, I'm gonna introduce you to Sadie here so she gets to know you, and then I'm gonna need something hearty to eat. How's the chow here?"

"Depends. When it's Girl's day to cook, it's the best, but not when old man Thomas does it. One bite of that mess, and you'll be in the outhouse the rest of the night with the damn back-door shits, and that's if you're lucky." He squirms as he recalls something. "One cowpoke was walkin' funny for three days."

Damn. Youngsters are a wealth of information. Ask the right questions, and they'll give it to you honest. Tucking my lips to hold back a smirk, I reply, "You have my gratitude for the warning. So, is today Earl's day to cook?"

His head shakes as he corrects me, sending a whiff of manure my way. "Girl. Not Earl. And yeah, Fridays is one of her days."

"That her only name?" Can't say that I've ever run across a woman named Girl.

"Don't know." The boy shrugs his thin shoulders. "That's all anybody ever calls her."

"Hmm. If she cooks so good, why doesn't she have the other days, too?"

"'Cause that ain't her only job." His expression implies I'm a bit of a dolt for not understanding.

"What else does this Girl do?"

"Welp, when she ain't cookin', she helps Mr. Collins at the general store and such. And then at night..." The boy takes a look around and crooks a finger, beckoning me to lean in. "Sometimes they'll send for her at the saloon to come get her drunk pappy and take him home. 'Course, he don't always wanna leave, 'specially when he's playing cards, so he whales on her sometimes. Gave her a black eye once that lasted more'n a month."

Anger on behalf of this unknown woman stirs inside my gut. "And no one stops him from hitting her?"

"Nope. They like to watch her wrestle him outside and

bet on how many tries it'll take her. And then sometimes she spends the night at the cathouse."

Cocksucking bastards. Setting my anger at her unjust treatment aside, I raise my brow at the rest of his sentence. "How does a boy as young as yourself know about women and cathouses?"

"A'cause I'm nine and everybody knows what a cathouse is, mister! And I seen her go in there with my own damn eyes one time." The orbs in question almost threaten to pop out of their sockets with how wide he opens them.

Kids. "All right, you little peeping Tom. You treat my Sadie right, you hear?"

"Sure thing, mister, and remember about tonight!"

"No worries, kid. I'll be here." A few minutes later, I leave my horse in the boy's grubby hands and cross the street to the little wooden restaurant, each step creaking under my weight until I reach the top. Mhmm...an aroma tickles my nostrils, calling forth a small feeling of homesickness that I force myself to pocket for later. Smells like Momma's kitchen. Much better than the stench of the livery and even my own unwashed body. As much as I hate it, water has to be conserved for drinking when I'm between towns.

"Girl!" a portly man bellows from behind a newspaper when I push open the door and survey the dimly lit room. "Don't just stand there! Give the man a place to sit and bring him something to drink."

A small, aproned figure detaches from a shadowy corner and makes its way to me, head downturned. Well, well, well. This is the soiled dove that spends nights in cathouses? She's a very pretty dove, from what I can see as I tuck my hat back to see her better. Slim and with dark, outrageous curls barely tamed by the knot she's tied them into. Wild tendrils spring free and decorate the sides of her thin face, just dusting the tops of her dainty shoulders. When she stands before me, barely reaching my shoulders, her hand gestures slightly toward an empty seat at the only table in the cramped space.

"There? You want me to sit there?"

Girl gives a modest nod and turns, giving me a chance to look her over. Fragile shoulders taper down to a trim waist, and Lord a'mercy, that backside is just as lovely as her front as she walks to the chair. When she turns with a frown, I realize I'm still standing here like a dunce with his boots on his ears. "Sorry. It's a mite hot out there today. Sun musta slid inside my ears and melted my brains."

There's just something about her that has me discombobulated, even if she won't look me in the eye. Something that makes me want to learn more about her. Maybe it'd help if I could see her better, but the two small windows and oil lamps on the walls don't brighten the place up much.

I shrug the thought aside and follow her, taking a seat by a man shoveling food into his mouth, drippings falling into his unkempt beard. Sparing him a brief glance, I tilt my hat all the way back and breathe in deeply. The food smells good. Really good, even if the stench of my friend here contributes to the undertones. I throw some charm into a smile and direct it at Girl, noting how the shadows play about her face. "This is your day to cook, right, miss?"

Her chin dips in assent and then she disappears without a word. How about that? Not even a smile in return. I know mine's nice because I've still got all my teeth, and they're whiter than most other people's. I quietly chuckle at the hit to my pride, and determination settles within me. I'll get her to talk to me before I leave town.

Just a few moments later, Girl enters my view again with

a metal cup in one hand and hot plate in the other, placing the food in front of me. A hairy fist thumps heavily on the table between us, making Girl flinch and my eyes narrow. "More," the man beside me forces out through a belch. Just as she turns, he growls, "Now, Girl." A crack rings through the air and her face tightens in pain as she gingerly reaches behind her with a sharp breath.

Did he just strike her on the ass? Anger immediately rushes through me, making my fingers twitch and my teeth clench. No, not on my watch. Doesn't matter if she spends the night in the brothel. No woman deserves to be hit.

When he rears back to do it again, I block his arm with my own, holding it tightly. I don't mind getting my hands dirty. Back home, we Shays have the reputation of making an ordinary fight look like a prayer meeting. "Look at you. You ain't got manners enough to bring a bear his guts. You got a problem with giving the lady time to get back there?"

Yanking away, he sneers at me from under his gray, tobacco-stained mustache, showcasing his dirty teeth. Those he still has, anyway. "Bitch lollygags. Just givin' her a reason to step lively. And who in hell do you think you are, stranger, to start somethin' with me?" His eyes move to my hip, arm jerking as if about to reach for his piece. Girl takes a hesitant step back before hurrying to the kitchen.

Frustration threads through my sigh. "You'd better think twice," I warn. "I'm younger than you. Stronger, too, and I don't mind settling this with my fists, gun, or knife. Keep in mind, though." His stale breath hits my face as I lean closer to drive my point home. "I don't lose. With any of them. I can nick the wings from a fly, and I can clean a plow like no one's business. So, what's it gonna be?"

All eyes are on us now, eager to see how it'll play out. I'm eager, too. Ready to get this over with so I can eat this manna from heaven before it turns cold. I keep my heavy stare on him, waiting for his next move.

Turns out, I don't have to wait long. With a grunt, he grabs for his gun, but I'm faster. My fist flies up and knocks him solid on the jaw, right in the sweet spot. Spit shoots from his mouth and lands on my shirt as his face falls forward into his plate. He'd better be grateful he didn't land on *my* plate.

Raising him by his greasy hair, I take a good look. "You sure are an ugly old bastard. That can't be helped, but I reckon I oughtta at least help you wash that mess off your face. Anybody got a problem with that?" I ask the last bit to the room.

At the silence and ducked heads, I take that as a no. "All right, old fella. Up you go." Hefting his unconscious weight over my shoulder, I amble to the door, man on a mission. "Be right back," I tell the portly fellow watching me dumbfounded over his newspaper. "Hold my place."

Little peeping Tom watches me with bugged out eyes as I cross the street and dump the man into the trough. "Sheeyit, mister!" He gawks at me through the spray of water. "What'd you do that for?"

"Just teaching him a thing or two about manners, son. Never too old to learn. You just remember that." Leaving him slack-jawed, I head back to the promise of that heavenly food. Murmuring voices die away when I push open the door to the restaurant again. "Don't worry," I tell all the bastards who were content to let a man abuse a woman. "He ain't drowning, just taking a bath."

That settles the tension a bit, a few chuckles ringing out here and there. Now, finally I can eat. As my steps bring me closer to the table, I see the mess he left behind has been cleaned up. Such a shame that a lovely woman has to clean up after the likes of him.

Mhmm, food's still hot. Fork in hand, I stab a piece of the succulent, tender chicken smothered in red-eye gravy and almost whimper in pleasure at the explosion of taste that covers my tongue. My God, this woman can cook! And the snap beans and mashed potatoes are just as good, too, as I shovel them into my mouth. No wonder the old grizzly wanted more. Pushing my plate back, I down the metal cup of water and pat my stomach in contentment.

But my contentment doesn't last long. What the—? Feeling the tingling pressure of someone's eyes on me, I glance around. Can never be too careful. Any gaze I meet is swiftly dropped, but that's not what I was feeling. No, it was more like...

Ah, there she is. The beautiful dove watches me curiously from the shadowy corner. Giving her a wink, I stand and toss payment on the table. Hell, better leave something to cover the old fella's meal. "Ma'am." I doff my hat in her direction. "Excellent meal. I'd never tell my momma, but you cook better than her."

More chuckles sound in agreement at that. With another polite greeting, I take my leave and head over to the saloon. Adam's ale just doesn't quench a man's thirst like some good ole whiskey.

4

JEDIDIAH

Hazy smoke fills the crowded saloon as I toss my cards on the table in defeat for the third time. I'm not a terrible player, but a stranger showing up in town and winning hand after hand tends to make a man a mite suspicious. And I aim to keep my head right where it is—under my hat so I can find my woman.

"What do you say, boys? Another round?" Looking expectantly at the three of us other players, the grizzled old-timer rakes in his earnings and pockets them, then, with perfect precision, leans over and aims for the spittoon.

"Shit," the cowpoke closest to me drawls around his hand-rolled cigarette. "I'm out."

"Dirk?"

The other one must be Dirk, because he drops a *nope* and ambles to the bar for another drink. I glance out the windows, noting the darkening skies. It's a boon that these windows are larger than the restaurant's. I don't want to break my word to the kid because I couldn't tell time and miss out on what he wants to show me. A man's word should mean something, regardless of who he gives it to.

"And you, young fella?"

"Apologies, old-timer." I offer a half-smile even as I shove back from the table. "But I've got an appointment to keep. I may take you up on the offer later, though." With a nod, I weave through the crowded gaming tables and push through the door.

The cool, dry air is a welcome change from where I've just spent the past couple of hours, breathing in the stench of hard-working men and their vices. Spurs kicking up dust, I saunter toward the livery, coming upon a man closing up shop. Mr. Henry? Wonder if the kid remembered to remind him. "Howdy." I tip my chin in a greeting, only getting a brief nod in return. I swear, with the exception of the kid, these are some of the unfriendliest folks I've ever come across. And with the sound of Girl being slapped still ringing in my ears, it appears they don't even stand up for the defenseless. Or maybe it's just because she's used goods that they feel they can do anything they want.

Girl.

Why doesn't she have a name? She's worthy of one, no matter her profession. Here and now, I decide I'm going to name her, even if only in my head.

Lucille? Nah, that doesn't fit her. Too frilly.

Adeline? That's a bit more eloquent. Graceful like her quiet movements.

Grace? That one fits better.

Or maybe Dove, because even with her profession, she's still fragile and innocent.

"You made it!" the kid calls out. "I wasn't sure you would."

Guess I'd better learn the stripling's name, too. Sure is a likable fellow. "Told you I'd be here."

Even in the dusky light, I can see excitement brewing in

his eyes. Reminds me of all the times I begged my brothers to go down to the river with me and all the games we played. Who could catch the most frogs, who could throw the stick furthest, and whatever else bored little boys could conjure up as a competition.

"Follow me, mister. I swear, I ain't never seen what I'ma show you. Leastways, not this one."

"Okay, okay. Let's go, then." And at that, he takes off like a charging bull down a dirt pathway behind the livery. "Hold up there, son. My legs may be long, but let's enjoy the journey. What's your name?"

The boy turns and walks backward as we talk, the dying sunlight shining on his freckled face. "Abner. What's yours?"

"Jedidiah Shay. But you can call me Jed."

"I wish I had a name like that, 'stead of Abner Wright. That don't sound like a name to be remembered by, does it? Abner Wright," he scoffs through a frown. "You killed lotsa men?"

"Whoa, kid. First of all, you've got a fine enough name. Why, just think of it." I grasp his thin shoulder and throw my other hand into the air. "Abner Wright. You can win every argument, even if you lose, by walking away and saying, 'I'm right.' And you wouldn't be lying."

His look of skepticism stops me right in my tracks. I shrug. "I just think you have a very respectable name, son. Don't be tossing it out any time soon. Be proud of it, because that's the name your children are going to wear one day."

"You're a strange one, ain'tcha?"

Found out by a young'un. I may have some strange ways, I'll admit, such as not smoking, washing my hands and clothes more than the average man, but I don't want to have dirty hands or smell like pig slop when I'm touching my girl.

My Girl.

Dove.

Can't get away from thinking about her. Could she be mine?

"You didn't say how many men you've got to your name. I bet you're a curly wolf."

"Kid, having numbers behind a name isn't something to brag about. And, yeah, I can be dangerous if I need to be, but respect is greater than fear, you hear me?"

He gives a long-suffering sigh. "Yeah, yeah. I hear you, all right."

Kids. He'll learn one day. "What do you do for fun around here besides going to the creek?"

"Welp, sometimes if the harvest is good enough, Pa'll load us all up and take us to Hope's Stand and let us buy some of the good candy while he looks at supplies."

"Hope's Stand, huh? That's where I live."

His jaw drops open. "Nuh-uh!"

"Yeah-huh," I say with a grin. "You ever come to the fair?"

The kid lights up. "Yeah! 'Cept for last year on account of I was sick. But I ain't gonna let myself get sick this time."

He chatters on and on while I patiently listen, but when he stops to take a deep breath, I interrupt. "We almost there?" It's been a good ten minutes of walking already.

"Almost. Just past that tree line. But you have to be quiet when we get there, okay? Don't wanna scare her off." Now I know what he's going to show me—some kind of animal he befriended, probably. Makes me wonder if he has many friends his age.

When we get to the trees, he quietly pushes back branches, then beckons me to follow. "Remember—quiet, Jed."

"Quiet," I whisper back in a promise as my feet break a twig.

"I'm serious!" he whisper-yells. "Watch your big ole damn feet! We don't want her to know we're here."

Rolling my eyes, I step a little more lightly. It's not as if I've been here before and know all the right places to put my big ole feet. Finally, we get to one final line of trees.

"Now we feast our eyes."

Feast our eyes? "On what?"

"On her," he says with a mischievous grin as he makes an opening to peek through the branches. "Go ahead. Take a look and tell me when you see her."

Surely he doesn't mean...

Pulling back the thick greenery, all I see is a prime view to the creek. Then I do a double take.

What the hell? Is it really her? A swallow gets stuck in my throat, but I'm not worried because if my cock stretches upward any higher, it'll dislodge it for me.

It's her.

Dove.

And she's frolicking in the water like a mermaid.

Or a siren.

A quiet snicker drags my reluctant eyes away from the utter perfection in front of me and to the smirking child beside me. "Told ya, didn't I? Bet you're pleased as punch you came with me."

I come to my senses, blood returning to my head instead of pooling in my britches. "Abner! What in the Sam Hill do you think you're doing?" I hiss, grabbing him by the ear and marching him out before she hears us. Or sees us.

Damn peeping Tom. *I really like being down at the creek,* he'd said. "You're only nine years old, boy! You can't be watching women bathe like that. That's private and for when you're older." And never this one. She's for my eyes only.

"Ouch, Jed! Lemme go." Shrugging away, he pouts. "I thought you'd like watching Girl take a bath. She sure is a looker, huh?" His eyes turn dreamy as a sappy grin covers his face.

Exquisitely so. But I can't deny the sudden spurt of jealousy that lances through me and strikes me deep in the chest. Especially now when I remember that he said she frequents the brothel sometimes. Does she share her body with—

No, I can't think about it. But now I know why I came to Springwell.

For her.

My Dove.

———

AFTER I CHEW ABNER'S EAR ALMOST CLEAN OFF HIS HEAD, Dove is nowhere to be seen, so I send the boy home and head back to the small saloon. I'm feeling unsettled by what I've seen and by what it means.

The sounds of raucous laughter, bawdy women, and tawdry music fill the air, mixing with the scents of tobacco and sex as I press through the crowd to a break at the bar and signal to the bartender. Damn sure got busy in the small amount of time I was gone.

"Whiskey," I say with a jerk of my chin, sliding payment over the sticky countertop. I don't drink often, but I need one after that little encounter.

Pocketing my money, the man grabs a cloudy glass from under the cabinet and pours the amber liquid, using a damp rag to mop up where it sloshes over the edge before shoving the drink my way.

"Thank you kindly." Looking at the filmy layer of white marring the surface, I cautiously raise it to my lips. At the first sip, the prairie juice burns like the devil, and tastes even worse. Damn. This batch must have been mixed with too much tobacco. I eye it dubiously, and then the image of Dove appears on the surface of the liquid. Her soft curves and the length of her dark curls as she came up from the water...

Damn it.

Better quit thinking about her sweet body and focus on how I'm going to claim her. Maybe I could pretend to buy her favors and steal her away in the dark of night. Only question is how to keep the entire town from knowing. She'd have to keep quiet, but since I haven't heard her do anything more than gasp, that might not be an issue. Bears more mulling over, for a fact, before I do anything.

Straddling a bar stool and leaning against the bar, I nurse my drink for the better part of an hour and survey the room, watching scantily-clad women straddle the thighs of men throwing their money away with every hand they play. Dove's father is probably here. I scan their faces, wondering which one he could be, but they all look too ugly for something as pretty as her to have come from.

One fancy bird swishes her feathery skirts and heads my way, but a quick shake of my head sets her lips to pouting as she concedes defeat. She doesn't stay sullen for too long, though, once someone pulls her down onto his lap with a leer.

There's only one set of female hands that are ever going to be on me, and they're gonna belong to my woman. Turning and gesturing for another drink, I lift it to my lips, only to have the rough fabric of my shirt drink my next sip for me. Some son of a bitch just ran into my back. Irritated as hell because this shirt was my good one, I swivel to see who's invaded my space.

"Gimme 'nother one, Elias." It's an older man from one of the card tables, and he's soused to the guards and wanting more. I bite back my frustration because there's no use getting riled up at a drunkard. No reasoning with them.

The bartender frowns, wiping his hands on his rag. "Last one unless you cut your tab down." Flicking his eyes to a man who looks too young to have any hair on his chest, he jerks his chin, silently issuing a command while he pours a shot. "I mean it, Clarence."

The drunkard swipes the glass with a scowl and stumbles back to his table. What a fool, wasting his money on spirits and cards. This time, two men decked out in fine black clothing join him, and it doesn't look like they're happy with the old boy as they start up another round. In fact, they look increasingly irritated as the game progresses. Suddenly, one of them pulls him clear up out of his seat by the collar and says something I can't make out from here. Wouldn't be surprising if Old Clarence got himself into a hole and now can't get himself out. Not without money, at least. With a final shove, the two men exit as silently as they entered, leaving Clarence to stare morosely into his last drink of the night.

"Dooley brothers."

I glance at Elias from under my hat. "Say what?"

"Those were the Dooley brothers. Every fool in this town knows better than to borrow money from them."

Except Clarence. The unspoken words hang in the air between us.

"Another?" Elias tips his chin to my empty glass.

"Hey!" The drunken yell comes from Clarence and draws everyone's attention. "Dooleys say I gotta pay up, so who wants to buy a woman?"

The room falls silent, music grinding to a halt.

He walks unsteadily between tables and stops in front of a gray-bearded man lighting a cigarette. "What say you, James?"

James blows a stream of smoke directly into Clarence's face. "I'd say you better ask the wife I have."

Chuckles sound out, sending a flash of anger through both me and the drunkard but for different reasons. Is the son of a bitch really trying to sell a woman?

He stares at the man beside James. "Ira? She cooks and cleans. Won't say a word, neither."

"Yeah," Ira scoffs. "That's 'cause she ain't right in the head. Nope, you're gonna be hard-pressed to find someone to take her offa your hands."

My body tightens in fury at everything I'm hearing. A man selling a woman and her being called stupid? There's no goddamn reason for this.

"Don't be stupid, boys. Judge Grady's here, and you can walk away a married man tonight and go for a roll in the hay."

Silence.

"Fine," he bellows. "Don't wanna marry her and have to take care of her, then don't. How 'bout just paying for a hour or two? More money that way. And if I keep it up, there'll be one more cathouse in town."

The crowd buzzes at his words, but before any money exchanges hands, a small figure catches my eye. A figure too small to be in a saloon at this hour.

Dove. And coming in the door right behind her is the man Elias nodded to earlier. I quickly connect the dots.

Clarence is Dove's father, and Elias sent this man to fetch her so she could fight her old man out the door.

But now he's trying to sell her off. If not in marriage, then for an hour.

These sons of bitches.

All of them.

Not happening.

Dove places a hand on her father's arm and hesitantly pulls, but he rears back and slaps her. "Stupid bitch. I ain't goin' home yet, Girl. Tryin' to sell your lazy ass off."

Fucking hell.

That's it.

I'm leaving this town, and my little Dove is coming with me.

Placing my hat on the bar, I shove aside the people until I reach my Dove. Her shoulders are lowered in pain and probably embarrassment, but she's not going to have to worry about this any longer. I tip her head up, the red hand-print decorating her cheekbone setting my simmering blood to a boil. I ease a thumb over the tender mark, mirroring her wince.

Gently tugging her behind me, I drop my gaze to the piece of shit in front of me. His dirty eyes light up as he takes me in. "You want her, boy?"

I answer with a right hook to his filthy cocksucking mouth, fist coming away with blood and spit on it. The men roar in delight at the melee, cheering me on. All the encouragement makes me seethe because the bastards don't care one way or the other as long as they get their cheap entertainment.

Clarence shakes his head and grins bloodily, alcohol likely dulling the pain. "You do." A red ball of spit hits the floor. "She's yours for the right price."

I yank him to me, his feet dangling above the floor as I lift. "Oh, she's going to be mine, all right. Never any doubt about that. How much?" I emphasize my question with a knee to his balls. Even alcohol can't protect a man's stones.

"Wha-whatever you want to p-pay," he croaks out in a high voice, legs curling inward. "I just n-need some m-money. A-any money."

This shitlicking whoreson. I check behind me to make sure Dove is still safe, but that damn mark on her face lights my fire all over again. With a growl, I throw him to a table and let loose on the piece of shit with punch after punch until blood covers the both of us and he falls unconscious. Chest heaving like a wild stallion's, I raise my head and look for my Dove, taking in the shocked silence around me. There she is, looking small and fragile and completely unsure of herself.

It's all right, my little Dove. *I'm here now.*

With bloody hands, I take some bills out of my money roll and stuff them into Clarence's mouth. Hope he asphyxiates.

"Towel," I grit out. Someone tosses one my way, and I methodically get as much blood from my split knuckles and clothes as I can before chucking the red cloth on Clarence's face.

This was my good shirt, damn it.

Squaring my shoulders, I walk towards the bride I just bought. My pretty little Dove trembles the closer I get, but she doesn't need to fear me. I'd kill for her if I had to. I wrap my arm around her stiff form as I survey the crowd. "You people heard him. He offered, I paid, and you all bear witness to it. Now, which one of you is Judge Grady? Seems I've bought myself a bride."

5

GIRL

I can't breathe.

I'm getting married.

I've never been to any weddings, but somehow I don't think they happen late at night in a saloon with the bride's father lying unconscious on a table after he was beaten to a pulp for selling her.

"What do you mean, you don't know her name?" The big brute of a man who says he bought me furrows his blonde eyebrows in consternation. His giant hand—the hand that quite possibly knocked teeth from my father's mouth—comes up to cradle my face, the metallic odor of blood making my nostrils flare.

"You...you heard Clarence, didn't you, mister, uh...?"

"Jedidiah Shay," the giant rumbles.

"Ah. Mr. Shay. Well, Girl here don't talk, just like her pa said." Judge Grady tugs at his bow tie as he delivers the news.

"Is that your name?" Jedidiah asks me softly, voice at odds with how angry his face seems.

I slowly shake my head.

"You don't talk at all, little dove?"

My head moves again in answer, my eyes wide in trepidation even as confusion fills me at the nickname. Little dove. That's...sweet, in a way. Better than being called Girl all the time.

As if he can see the reason for my silence, his burning gaze falls to my throat, setting my heart to thumping. I lift a hand to the high collar that hides my secret, almost fainting dead into the floor as his fingers follow and trace the length of my neck over the material. When his thumb discovers my pounding pulse, his full lips stretch in a small smile, exposing his straight teeth. "Breathe, little dove."

Judge Grady clears his throat. "No matter. I can just put Girl Crowley on the paperwork and it'll do just as well."

"No," Jedidiah clips out, irritation coloring his tone as he reluctantly looks away. "That's no name for a woman, and especially not my bride." He softens as he glances back down to me. "Can you write it for me?"

Shame fills me, and I slowly shake my head, the intensity of his honey-gold gaze too powerful to hold. The back of his hand brushes over where my father slapped me. I've seen him strike a man twice now. What's to stop him from doing the same to me? He could possibly kill me without even trying too hard with as big as he is. I flinch back, a delayed reaction, but I'm caught short by the other arm he still has wrapped around me.

"It's okay, little dove," he soothes. "Don't be scared. We're not gonna stay here much longer, okay?" To the judge, his voice turns harder. "Dove. That's what you can put on the paper."

"But that's not her name!" Judge Grady splutters.

The arm around me tightens, drawing me close enough that his belt buckle digs into my stomach. Merciful heavens,

I've never been this close to a man in all my life. "It is now," he grits out.

My heart drops to my feet at the steely tone of his voice, but the judge capitulates, apparently writing down my new name on the paper. Judge Grady starts talking, but I can't hear a word he says. All I can see and smell is the powerful man in front of me. I barely come up to just below his shoulders. Shoulders that are at least the width of two and a half of me and arms thicker than my thighs.

Does this mean he'll want to share the covers with me?

My gaze travels across the sandy blonde hair that brushes the tanned skin of his neck, taking in the stubble darkening his chin and cheeks and going higher still to eyes that are locked onto mine with a fervent gleam. So caught up am I in their spell that I'm taken aback when those golden brown eyes get closer to me. What is he doing? I lean back only to meet the uncompromising bar of his arm.

"Where you going, little Dove?" he murmurs thickly. "Gotta make it official."

My eyes are wide as saucers, I'm sure, as my head tilts back and away from his approaching face.

He smiles again, but I don't think he's laughing at me. "C'mere so I can kiss you."

A kiss? Oh. Relief runs through me. For a minute, it was looking as if he was going to eat my nose. I relax a bit and offer up my forehead.

People snicker, but a growled *shut up* makes them stop. Nervously, I search to see who was laughing, but Jedidiah won't let me. No, he crooks a finger under my chin and whispers, "Don't look at them. Look at me."

So I do. I stare at his nose because it's less intense than his eyes, watching as it gets blurry the closer he gets to me. I can't stop myself from leaning back again even as I cling to his shirt for balance, but one of his hands slips up my back to grip my neck. "Hold still, Dove."

Then Jedidiah closes the gap between us, lifting me up and pressing his lips to mine so suddenly I almost choke on my gasp. My instinctive reaction is to jerk back, but the warm fingers at the base of my neck don't allow for any movement.

And, well, my feet are a good six inches above the floor, so I'm completely at his mercy.

My entire world fades away at the kiss that is nothing like my mother's. Wet heat and a hint of drink coats my lips as his mouth lightly caresses mine in a way that feels...strange.

Strange, but rather nice, I decide after a few more seconds. At the pointed clearing of a throat, he slowly breaks away and gives me the forehead kiss I was expecting before easing me down the length of his body. Goodness, I don't remember his belt buckle feeling that big earlier.

Jedidiah jerks his chin to the paper in the judge's hands. "I trust you know what to do with that?"

"Yes, Mr. Shay. Every...everything is in order and will be filed away first thing in the morning."

"Good. Let's go, Mrs. Shay." Catching my hand with his, he holds it tightly as he leads me to the door.

The men murmur around us, and I hear things that suddenly make me very nervous. Things like, "Bet she'll learn how to talk when he gets her in his bed."

A chuckle. "Yeah, she won't have a choice when he splits her in two."

An answering chuckle. "She'll be singing like Madam Lulu's girls when he's done with her."

Like Madam Lulu's girls? The weird groans and shrieks I hear through the walls when I sleep in that little room? I don't like those noises. Sometimes it sounds like they're in pain. I swallow around a knot in my throat. It appears I may now be in a situation that I have no idea how to handle. I'm not the only one who heard the men, though. My new husband stops in his tracks, hand twitching around mine before he turns around with a scowl. "Who said that?"

It was Brock and Harold, two complete hotheads who are always getting thrown out for starting fights. Even at the general store, of all places.

"Which one of you cocksucking bastards said that?" he repeats grimly. "Easy enough to say something behind someone's back. Say it to my face and see what my fists think about it. Come on," he urges at the silence. "I'll make what I did with him"—he nods toward my father who's just now coming to and choking out money—"look like a Sunday sermon."

The thumping of my heart is so strong, I can feel it in my fingertips. Brock and Harold look at each other, but don't say anything. As the silence drags on, Jedidiah gently tugs my hand. I follow beside him on shaky feet now that those words are echoing in my head.

I don't want to be hurt. I've had enough of that to last me a lifetime and more.

"I'll show you a Sunday sermon, you bastard." A sudden whoosh of air accompanying the words is the only warning I get before someone roughly shoves into me on his way to jump Jedidiah from behind.

Two someones, actually.

Brock and Harold.

I stumble to the side, almost landing in Judge Grady's lap. Harold jumps onto Jedidiah's back to pin his arms, looking like a bear cub clinging to its mother. "Get 'im, Brock!"

Jedidiah roars, shaking his back to dislodge the man on his back, but Harold holds tight.

"Keep 'im still, damn it!"

To the crowd's delight, Brock lands two punches to the face and one to the stomach. Jedidiah falls backward, bringing Harold with him. The man lets out a pained yell as his back meets the floor, arms and legs falling to the side as Jedidiah crushes him with his weight.

My breath catches, a sharp pang of helplessness unexpectedly stabbing my heart. Did Jedidiah get knocked out? I don't know him at all, but of the men here—my father included—I think I'd rather take my chances with him.

A boot kicks out, catching Brock between the legs. He sinks to his knees with a choked whine. Relief and tension mix within me when I see my husband lift from the floor with fury in his eyes. He rears a fist back—

Bang!

The entire saloon falls quiet again at the echoing gunshot. Elias pumps his rifle, looking out over the destruction and mayhem. "That's enough," he booms out. "You done made me shoot a hole in my ceiling, you idiots. Brock, Harold, get the hell out of here and don't come back for three days. Take Clarence with you."

"Dove?" Jedidiah searches for me with wild eyes, only calming once he catches sight of me.

"You, too, mister," Elias says, resting his gun on the countertop within easy reach. "I can appreciate where you're coming from, but I don't think this town is the place for you."

My husband ignores him and wipes his mouth on his shirt sleeve, frowning at the red streak that appears. "Damn it," he swears softly. "My good shirt." Swaying when he gets to his feet, he takes a few unsteady steps before righting himself and walking my way. "Are you hurt?"

I instinctively flinch back at the bloodstained hand that reaches for me, belatedly noting his faltering reaction, and shake my head. I'm not hurt. More sore and stunned than anything. With a grim smile, Jedidiah easily swings me into his arms.

"Grab my hat, will you?" he asks as we pass the bar. Not wanting to anger him, I quickly reach for the worn black covering and hold it between us as we leave. The moonlight shines over his face, highlighting the blood trickling from his lips as he tromps down the three steps and next door to the inn. "Let's get a room for the night and then we'll head out first thing in the morning."

A room.

With him.

My heart rate picks up, beating faster and faster as we enter the doorway and approach the night clerk. "One room. One bed. One tub," my husband clips out as he gently lowers me down.

Oh, no.

I'll have to share the covers with him.

Is he...leaning on me? I look up to see him swaying slightly as he reaches for his money roll.

"Number four." The clerk slides a key across the counter. "Bath won't be hot, though. Soap's extra."

Jedidiah palms the key and adds another coin or two before taking my hand. "That's fine. Let's go, Dove."

I walk beside him on hesitant feet, completely unsure of what's about to happen. Inside the room, he strips his bloody shirt off and pulls me down onto his lap while two older errand boys fill the tub and top off the oil lamps, leaving only the one by the bed lit. I hear the boys traipse in and out of the room as they dump their water buckets into the tub and leave to refill them, but all I can focus on is my husband. Specifically, the odd sensation between my legs where I rest on his thigh. I both want to stay exactly where I am and also run away from this strange feeling. Squirming to get some relief, I hold my hands awkwardly in my lap as I stare at his chest.

The tanned, hairy chest that is completely dissimilar to my father's.

Broader.

Stronger.

One of his hands—probably the bloody one—plays with the nape of my neck as I stare at him, and the other holds me securely at the waist, thumb rubbing a maddening circle over my clothes. The ticklish feelings make the tips of my breasts tighten and magnify the tingling between my legs. I wonder if I've suddenly developed a fever because my body is behaving so very strangely. He's so warm like he's running a fever, too.

Hazarding a glance up, I swallow around the massive knot in my throat when I see his honey gaze locked sleepily on me. A soft smile curves his stained lips, a smile that turns hard when he looks past me to the boys. With a slight tilt of my head, I see that one of them is staring at me.

"Tub full already?" Jedidiah growls over my hair.

Caught out, the boy sheepishly ducks his head. "Not yet. Sorry, mister."

An airy breath of surprise leaves me as my center of balance is suddenly thrown off, and I throw my hands out to catch myself as he pulls me closer. His chest hair is crisp underneath my fingers, and I marvel at the smallness of my hand compared to him. As dry as my throat is at this moment, I don't think I could get any words out even if I *could* speak. Did he not like the boy looking at me? I'm used to everyone staring at me for one reason or another.

I turn my head, intending to look behind me, but then Jedidiah tips my chin up, and all my breath leaves me at the heat in his eyes. His golden gaze is narrowed, eyelids lowered, but no less intense as he tracks over my face. Frowning when he sees the mark left by my father, he leans down only to pause at my flinch. "Never again," he whispers. "He'll never touch you ever again."

I barely have time to process the words before his thumb rests on my bottom lip. Without my permission, my tongue sneaks out in nervousness to taste his skin.

"Dove," he rasps in a low, deep voice. I feel my new name as much as I hear it. His head slowly descends, and this time, I know his intentions. He's going to kiss me on the lips instead of the forehead like my mother did. Unable to lean back, I warily eye the bloody lips that get ever so nearer. Hot breath fans over my chin, and then—

"All done, mister." Tub finally full, the boys hurry out. Relieved at the interruption, I hesitantly look up at Jedidiah.

"Do you want to wash up, Dove? You can go first." He breaks the silence between us.

I shake my head, a fleeting sense of loss flickering through my core as he stands with me. When his hands move to his gun belt, I jerk my eyes away and whirl around. He's...he's undressing in front of me!

"Ah, little Dove," he says with a lazy chuckle, "there won't be any of that tonight. Just sleep. After being on a horse for days on end and then gettin' my head spun around, I need some rest in a real bed." *Plop.* I hear his pants fall to the floor, and then a splash of water.

Wanting to afford him his privacy, I keep my back turned, listening to the occasional splash as he washes. This presents a problem, though. The only other thing for me to look at is the bed. It's not a very big one, which means we'll be sleeping practically on top of each other.

On *top* of each other.

I suddenly have a clear and vivid memory of the time I accidentally walked into a room at Madam Lulu's to clean and saw a man on top of a woman, her face pinched tight at whatever he was doing. Is that what Jedidiah meant we weren't going to do tonight?

I don't think I want to feel that way.

I'd rather feel good.

"Dove?" A yawn sounds as he climbs from the tub. "Why don't you go ahead and get in bed? We've got an early start in front of us."

His words are beginning to slur, so he must be really tired. Relaxing marginally, I pull back the covers and toe off my shoes.

"Sleeping in your clothes?" His voice is close enough to tickle my ear.

Cautiously, I turn around, my mouth dropping at the sight of him wearing only a towel slung around his waist. Merciful heavens!

"As you wish," he says with a sleepy smile and a shrug, pulling me down to the bed before blowing out the lamp and dragging the covers up over us.

Once again, my heart races. A strange, undressed man is sharing the covers with me and holding me tightly in his arms. As if he knows my thoughts, he tightens his arms further, dragging a light kiss over my cheekbone with his clean lips before burying his face in my hair.

"Ah, my little Dove," he whispers. "My wife."

His wife.

I lie stiffly in his arms, wondering if he can feel each beat of my heart. I can feel his because it hits my cheek with its pulsing cadence. But when he doesn't do anything other than hold me, my muscles lose their stiffness by degrees. And by the time I twitch my little toe, Jedidiah is fast asleep and snoring lightly.

It's time to leave.

I can't stay.

Not with him, and not in this town.

If I stay with him, he might expect to lay on top of me like I'm a brothel girl. Or worse, he might get angry with me and use his fists. He could hurt me more than my father ever did.

Oh...sweet Lord. My father. If I stay in town, he may very well sell me off again to pay off his debts.

No, I've got to go.

When Jedidiah's snores turn deep and slow, I ease out from his embrace and look down at his sleeping face that I can barely see in the dark of the night. Regardless of what he might want to do with me in the future, he defended my honor more than once today, and for that, he deserves at least a kiss of gratitude. I lean down, pausing when I remember how he put his mouth to mine. My fingers trace over my lips, the phantom sensation still so real.

No, I can't do that. I press my lips to his forehead instead and breathe in the scent of the soap from his bath. At my soft touch, Jedidiah gives a grunt in his sleep and pats around for me. Oh no! Panicking, I push a pillow close to his searching fingers. He grabs it and pulls it close, murmuring, "Dove."

That was close. He almost caught me before I even got away. With a final glance as I gather my shoes, I dig in his pants for the room key and unlock the door. In the hallway, I lock it once more and then tread lightly to the lobby. All's clear, though, because the night clerk is passed out in his chair, mouth wide open in slumber as I quietly place the key to the room on the counter.

The night air is cool on my hot cheeks on my quick trip to Madam Lulu's while the rest of me still feels aflame with the strangest fever I've ever had. Even my head feels fuzzy.

So odd.

Someone bumps into me, scaring me halfway to death. My hand flies to my chest as I gasp and look around. But there's no need to worry because it's only a boy. Abner, who is notorious for being out past his bedtime.

"Sorry, Girl." His little voice is contrite as he picks up his pocketknife that he dropped. Wiping his snotty nose on his sleeve, he earnestly asks, "You got married tonight? Where's Jed?"

Jed. I like his name being shortened like that. Nodding, I arch an eyebrow in question, pointing my finger at Abner and putting my hands to the side of my face. Surely his mother must not know he's not in bed.

"I know, I know," he says with a scowl. "I'm going home. Grownups get to have too much damn fun when they stay up." I wave good night and hurry on my way, thinking wryly on how nothing tonight was fun.

Three knocks on the little side door, and Madam Lulu answers. "Oh, child," she exclaims, eyes widening in surprise when she sees me, "what in tarnation happened tonight? Once we heard the gunshot, it was all the girls could talk about. Come in, come in." She's taken aback when I lurch forward and hug her in gratitude. This woman has extended grace to me so many times, she almost feels like a mother to me. Pulling away slightly, she looks at me. "You're going to need to get out of here, aren't you?"

I nod in desperation. The sooner, the better.

Her eyes narrow. "Do you have any money?"

My head bobs up and down fervently. I actually took a chance a few days ago and hid my money and my mother's book here in the small room just in case my father locked me out again.

"You'll stay here tonight." Madam Lulu takes my arm and leads me into the room that feels as much my room as the one at my father's house. She purses her red lips, tapping them with a long fingernail as she studies me. "And we'll get this all figured out in the morning, you hear?"

I hug her once more, tears building in the corners of my eyes. I'll miss her.

With a final pat to my back, she retreats to the doorway, a soft smile cracking her painted face. "You deserve much more than this place and this town, child. Now, you go on to sleep, and we'll talk tomorrow."

I slowly climb into the small bed and wrap my arms around myself, feeling the phantom sensation of arms holding me. As I listen to the noises around me again, a peculiar sort of melancholy comes over me as I think about Jedidiah Shay.

I almost regret not letting him lay on top of me.

Almost.

6

JEDIDIAH

"Hyah!" The sound of a reinsman driving off in his stagecoach wakes my ears up before it does my eyes. With an early morning yawn, I drag my wife closer and sniff her hair, wrinkling my nose up. Why does she suddenly smell like dirty linens? I don't say anything, though, because that isn't the best way to start a marriage. No, what she needs is a good morning kiss.

Yes, sirree.

I move my hand to her hip and freeze.

This isn't my wife.

Eyes flying open, I groan at what I see. I've been hugging and sniffing a damn pillow, which explains the less than delicate aroma. But where's my wife?

"Dove?" I call out, rolling to my back and lifting up on my elbows. The room's empty. Her shoes are gone. "The hell?"

Maybe she thought she needed to get breakfast for us. If only she had waited for me, she'd have known I was gonna take care of that. Stumbling out of bed, I put a hand to my throbbing head as the blood rushes to it. Goddamn, that sorry sucker got lucky with those punches last night.

I look down at myself, snickering when I see that the towel came off during the night. That would have been quite the sight for my little Dove. Somehow, I don't think she's as experienced as I previously thought. Not with the way she reacted to our kiss.

Mhmm...that kiss was almost too indecent to be seen by everyone. I pull my pants on, fighting my thickening shaft. I need to find her and show her the proper way we wake each other up. Giving my bloody shirt a rueful look as I don my hat, I tuck it into the back of my waistband and reach for the doorknob.

It's locked.

"What in the Sam Hill?" I mutter. There's no reason for that. Not unless... I straighten as the thought comes to me.

Not unless someone wanted to keep me in here.

If someone took her.

Last night would have been a prime opportunity since I was exhausted and my little Dove couldn't make a sound. But who could it be? Her father or those other two bastards?

Fury building inside me, I shove a shoulder against the door. "Dove," I roar when it doesn't budge. She's probably frightened out of her wits. With another forceful shove, the door gives and I stalk to the clerk's desk, scanning the empty lobby.

"Where's my wife?" I growl. If she's hurt again, I'm going to kill someone.

"I-I-I don't know...mister...?" The day clerk gawks at me, pushing his spectacles up the bridge of his nose.

Or maybe it's my bare chest he's looking at, but I don't give a damn about indecency at the moment as I loom over the desk. "Jedidiah Shay."

"And your wife's name?"

Mrs. Shay. "Dove," I grit out, eyes constantly on the lookout for her. "Dove Shay."

"I'm afraid I don't know anyone by that—"

Of course he wouldn't, because I'm the one who gave her that name. Both of them. "She's a short, beautiful little thing with dark, curly hair and hazel eyes. Probably has a small bruise on her face."

The clerk still stares stupidly at me.

"Damn it all! Her father is Clarence, and she doesn't speak—"

"You married Clarence Crowley's idiot daughter?" His mouth drops open.

"Listen here, you piece of shit." Muscles tensing with anger, I yank his collar and drag him to me. "That's my wife you just insulted. She's not a damn idiot just because she can't talk. Now, where is she?"

A pearl of sweat beads on the man's forehead and trickles down to the tip of his nose. "A-apologies. I don't know, Mr. Shay. We haven't seen anyone come out of your room—"

I don't have time to listen to him spout off things that won't help me. He hasn't seen her. "Where's Crowley's house?" I emphasize my demand with another jerk.

"Past the creek. Keep going past the last section of trees, then you'll see the house, plain as day." The clerk awkwardly falls into his chair when I release him. Storming outside, I glare at wayward passersby that have the misfortune to be in my way. To the left is the saloon. To the right is the way Abner took me to the creek.

Hold on, Dove. I'm coming for you.

This isn't quite the way I'd planned on kidnapping my bride, especially not after having just married her. But first I need my horse and a cooler head. While my heart picks up the beat, my legs swiftly carry me to the livery. "Ab—*oof!*" I just ran slap dab into the kid himself. "Need my horse."

"Ouch!" Abner gives me the stink eye as he rubs his head. "Mornin', Jed."

"Mornin'," I answer distractedly after I whistle for Sadie.

The kid props a bare, dirty foot on a bale of hay and leans an elbow onto his thigh as my horse trots over between us. "I got a question for ya." He snags some straw and threads it through his front teeth.

"Gotta make it quick, Abner. I'm real busy," I manage to say in a somewhat-friendly tone as I throw the saddle over Sadie's broad back.

"If you and Girl got married last night, how come she slept over at the cathouse?"

The cinch goes slack in my hand, and I slowly move to my horse's front to see him better. No way he said what I think he said. "What?"

"I said—" He stops to cough, little mouth spraying spit everywhere. "I said, why—" He chokes on his words again, grabbing his throat and doubling over with a coughing fit hard enough to turn out his insides.

Damn it, all I need is a kid choking to death and delaying me finding my wife. Sighing with impatient frustration, I pound on the little sprout's back to help him out. "Come on, kid. You all right?"

He comes up with a heavy gasp, fishing a long, limp piece of straw out of his mouth. "I'm good, I'm good," he breathes out choppily. "Just slipped right down my throat like a hole in a bucket."

This damn kid. Even in my urgency, my lips quirk against my will. "Tell me again, and tell me quick."

Slow as molasses, Abner pulls another piece of straw

from the hay bale and looks at me curiously. "I said..." He stops to spit. I swear, if he chokes on this one, I'm gonna wring his scrawny neck. "Why'd Girl sleep at the bawdy-house again last night if she married you? Did you get a room there, too? That why you still ain't dressed?"

Confused anger with an undertone of hurt fills me. Dove left me of her own free will and went to the brothel, of all places? "How do you know? You should have been in bed."

Abner rolls his eyes. "Yeah, yeah. Should've. But I weren't."

I turn and look at the brothel housed in an old boarding house.

Oh, Dove. That's not how this works.

"Stay here with Sadie," I order as I turn around and stride determinedly to the door. It's locked, though, so I give three short knocks. If this door doesn't open within the next twenty seconds, I'm gonna break it down. Nothing's gonna stand between me and my woman.

On the eighteenth second, it swings open to reveal a hard-eyed older woman in a rich maroon dressing gown that gapes open to reveal her ample bosom. Without care for the skin she's exposing, she gives my bare chest a lingering glance. "We're not open yet, even for someone who looks as good as you, sugar. Come back in a few hours."

"Wait." I stop the closing door with the broad side of my forearm, catching a glimpse of a fancy parlor. "I'm looking for my wife."

"Oh, honey." The older woman leans against the door jamb, her smudged, painted eyes brazenly crawling up and down my form. "What woman in her right mind would leave your bed? Your poor little heart must be broken. Tell you what." She crooks a finger. "You just come on inside and Madam Lulu will let you have your pick of all my girls.

What's your preference? You want some French love? That's Opal's specialty."

French love.

Mouths on the nether regions.

Not unless it's with my wife.

"No," I get out in a clipped tone. "I believe she slept here last night."

"Oh. Oh, dear." Madam Lulu straightens and taps her lips with a red fingernail. "I see. You drove your own wife into the arms of another. All that power and muscle and you don't even know how to use it. Such a damn shame." She claps her hands and briskly says, "No matter. You've come to the right place. A barbarian that looks like you and can't satisfy his wife? That will never do. No, you need a little help, and Madam Lulu knows just the thing."

"No, you don't under—"

The woman grasps my arm tightly as she pulls me inside. "Hush, boy. We'll start you off nice and slow with Nora. She's a good teacher, and she'll be eager to get her hands all over your cutting figure. Best of all, it'll be on the house. You just remember who taught you all these skills and mention us to your gentleman friends."

Hell, no. This is getting all kinds of uncomfortable now. "Ma'am, I don't need any assistance, but thank you kindly for the offer. I got married last night and my wife seems to have run off sometime before I woke up. I've reason to believe she may have taken shelter here."

"Oh." Madam Lulu arches a fine brow and sharpens her gaze. "Did she, now?"

"Yes. Her name's Dove. Real tiny thing with curly hair and pretty hazel eyes. You may know her by the name of...Girl." Hellfire, I hate calling her that, but not enough people know the new name I gave her.

Her hand tightens around my bicep. "Dove, you say?"

She knows something. "Yes. I've come to take her home with me."

Hand dropping from my arm, Madam Lulu crosses her own and pointedly takes me in from head to foot. "She may have come to me last night. What's it to you?"

"What's it to me?" I repeat, tamping down my frustration. "She's my goddamn wife, that's what. And I'm damn sick and tired of the way all the people in this town have been treating her just because she can't speak."

"How interesting. All the girls heard about the man named Jedidiah Shay who bought Girl's hand in marriage last night. Tell me this, Mr. Shay. If she's your wife, why did she run to me last night as she has every time her father refused to let her sleep in the house? How are you any better than him?"

I tower over the shorter woman as my impatience grows. "I'm a damn sight better than that piece of shit because I'm not gonna let anyone treat my Dove bad anymore. Especially not him."

"Is that so?" Madam Lulu asks with genuine curiosity. "And how did you come up with this name for her?"

"Because she deserves a name that's a damn sight better than Girl," I snap. "A real name." Flashing a look past the parlor, I see a hallway filled with doors.

Doors to bedrooms.

One of which is hiding my Dove.

Enough of this.

The Shay instinct in me demands I hunt my bride down, so I take off determinedly to the hallway and reach for the first doorknob, roughly calling out my wife's name. "Dove?"

The door swings open to reveal a naked feminine back and the rank scent of sex and sweat. But no...the hair's wrong. I'm looking for dark, curly tresses, not straight blonde lines. The woman whirls around at the intrusion, but I'm already moving on. If I have to tear the place apart, that's what I'll do. Down the line I go, leaving a chorus of light screams behind me, but when I open the last door and discover my wife isn't there, I cast an eye to the second floor railing. I'm not leaving until I find her and kill any son of a bitch who's in the room with her.

A sick feeling twists my stomach at the thought and makes my fists clench in anticipation. But as I stride to the stairs, prepared to take them three at a time, I see something. A shadow just moved underneath the door to the small room built into the stairwell. Why would someone be hiding here and not making a sound? "Dove," I call softly through the door. "Is that you?"

A shallow gasp answers me.

Mine.

Blood pumping in victory, I turn the knob and smile into my wife's wide hazel eyes. My shoulders immediately relax when I see her dressed in last night's clothes and standing by a tiny bed.

Alone.

I sniff the air, satisfaction curling inside when a bit of staleness without any male musk wafts through my nostrils.

All alone.

Now I'm certain that she's not the soiled Dove Abner made her out to be. "There you are, little Dove." Her pretty eyes move everywhere, darting between me, the bed, and the empty door behind me.

"Darlin'," I tsk as I slowly and deliberately move forward. "There's no more running now." My silent wife retreats another step, but there's nowhere to go in this tiny room that I could cross in one flat second. Her back meets the wall, her exquisite chest heaving distractingly as her eyes linger between my broad chest and the bed.

"That bed's not big enough for the both of us. Now c'mere." One more step brings me right up to my runaway bride. Her small pushes against my bare chest don't stop me, and I easily capture her delicate wrists and carefully move them behind her back. Relief rushes through me. She's safe now. "Hello, Dove," I murmur into her hairline.

Like a little bird, she freezes, her quiet breaths hitting my neck.

"You ran from me, Mrs. Shay," I gently reprimand. A nip to a soft earlobe produces a shiver from her. Mhmm, she smells much better than the pillow I was hugging earlier. "Left me and deprived me of my morning kiss. And I was so looking forward to waking you up today."

I move across the small discoloration on her cheekbone to those tempting lips for a feathery kiss. She tracks me with her gaze, pupils so wide I can barely see the colored ring around them. "What's going on behind those eyes of yours?" I solemnly whisper. "Don't you know you're mine now?"

Holding her hands behind her still, I can feel all of her softness pressed against me. Her legs. Her breasts. Just because I've never been under a woman's skirts doesn't mean I don't know the ways of men and women. And right here, right now...my little Dove is in more trouble than she knows.

With a low groan, I lean down and hungrily take her mouth, letting a dash of my earlier frustration leak through. "My wife," I say between breaths. Needing more of her, I lift her up against the wall, pushing my thickening cock over her core with a light thrust. Dove's mouth parts in surprise, and I seize the opportunity to dip my tongue inside. Not for long, though, because she pulls her head back and gapes at me in horror.

"What?" I ease back just a touch. "What's that look for?" When she sticks her tongue out and points at it, I nip at it, chuckling when she shrinks back and wrinkles her eyebrows at me. "Oh, darlin', when I get you in my bed, this tongue is going more places than just your mouth." Unable to stop myself, I steal another kiss from her sweet lips.

"Well," a throaty feminine voice dryly interrupts from the doorway. "It seems as if you've found your wife, Mr. Shay."

The wife in question squirms in my arms, so I reluctantly pull back, licking my lips to lock in her taste. "Sure did. And now we're going home." To my blushing woman, I say, "Got anything you want to take with you? 'Cause we're not coming back."

When she wiggles and points behind me, I slowly let her down, fighting the urge to keep her tucked under me. My fingers twitch with every second that passes as my little Dove reaches under the bed for a small bag, and when she takes a hesitant step to the door, I lose the battle with myself.

"Oh, no, you don't." Being a gentleman, I relieve my wife of the burden of her bag, then sweep her into my arms, catching sight of Madam Lulu's amused grin. "Thank you for housing my woman throughout the night"—and all the other nights when no one else cared about her—"but we'll be taking our leave now."

"Wait!" The brothel owner tightens her robe and walks up. "Dove, is it?"

Pride inflates my chest when my wife darts a glance to me and then slowly nods.

"That's a beautiful name. Your husband picked a lovely

one for you." Looking slyly at me, Madam Lulu leans in and whispers something in Dove's ear, something too quiet for me to hear as a gaggle of skirts pass by the open doorway. But whatever it is turns my bride's face ten shades of red and sends her eyes flying to mine. With a kiss to a reddened cheek, the madam backs away and gestures to the doorway. "Goodbye, Dove. Go and have the life you deserve, child."

She will. And I'm gonna be right by her side. That's a vow. I gather my bride more closely to my chest and kiss her soft hair. "Time to go home, darlin'."

Every step I take as we leave the brothel brings a sense of completion. I'd left my home on a journey to find my bride. And though she was sold to me, I still managed to follow tradition and kidnap her.

Of a sort, anyway.

Looking down at her, I smile at the top of her head. "I've caught you, and now you're all mine. And when we get home, I'm gonna teach you how to write so you can tell me your other name and why no one calls you by it." I drop another kiss to her head as we get closer to Abner and Sadie. "But between now and then, I'll have fun guessing what it is. After all, we've got quite a few miles to go before we get to my little ranch."

"Hey, Jed," the boy drawls as he saddles another horse. "Where you going with Girl?"

Girl. The name eats at me. "Dove," I correct him. "Her name's Dove now. And I'm taking her home. Hold Sadie steady, would you?"

As he holds the bridle, I put my woman in the saddle and secure her little bag. "All good?" I can't stop myself from stroking the bit of ankle that peeks from under the hem of her bland dress. Then I frown. I'm gonna have to get her some better clothes. Shoes, too.

Realizing I didn't notice if she indicated her answer, I look up at her, only to find her gaze glued to where my fingers touch her bare skin. Laughing lowly, I inch my hand higher and press a kiss to her thigh over her dress. "When we finally get a bed all to ourselves tonight, Dove..."

"Jed," Abner cuts in, letting go of the bridle to scratch his back, "you gonna come back here one day? Goin' to the creek won't be the same"—the peeping Tom throws a mournful expression to my wife—"but maybe we can do something else?"

With one last pat to my bride's thigh, I crouch down and flick the kid's hat. "Hey, chin up. And who knows? We might cross paths again one day." Injecting a bit of sternness in my voice, I add, "But just you make sure of what you do down by the creek, you hear? No more of...you know. You start getting to bed at a respectable time, too."

"Okay," Abner morosely agrees. "And bye, Dove."

I give his hat another flick. "All right, kid. We'll be going now." Turning to my sweet little wife, I note a strange gleam in her eyes as she gathers the reins. She must be as ready as I am to leave this godforsaken hellhole. And about time, too. "Ready, Sadie?" I ask my trusted steed with a pat to her thick neck. Just as I reach for the pommel to swing myself up, my bride kicks my horse into a gallop. "The hell?"

Abner whoops with glee as I stare stupefied at the figure that gets smaller with every second.

Dove left me.

On my own horse and taking the rope I meant to tie her with.

Finally stopping his laughing long enough to catch his breath, the kid slaps his knee and cackles out, "What you gonna do, Jed?"

Excitement sends the blood thrumming in my veins as I

watch my runaway wife riding for the tree line, and my answer comes easily. "What all the men in my family do when it's time for them to find a bride." I look down at him. "Need to borrow me a horse, kid. I'm going on a little hunt."

I could call Sadie back and she'd listen, but what would be the fun in that?

No, it's time to be a Shay.

7

DOVE

Madam Lulu's words set my head to spinning as a still-shirtless Jedidiah puts me on his horse. *When you're in his bed,* she'd said, *all you need to remember is this—open your legs and let him in. It'll fit, even if it hurts at first.*

Even if it hurts at first?

And let what in? His hand? Never mind the fact that he can't keep his tongue in his mouth where it belongs. I look down at his fingers on my ankle, trepidation filling me. That's a mighty big hand on a mighty big man. And if my smaller-statured father hurt me so easily, how much worse could it be with Jedidiah?

That hand of his climbs higher, burning my leg as he laughs and kisses my thigh. And then he slowly tilts his head up, a secret smile playing over his lips. "When we finally get a bed all to ourselves tonight, Dove..."

No.

Dread pools in my stomach as I watch his rippling back muscles when he squats down to speak with Abner. Those rippling back muscles are attached to powerful arms and fists. Then I remember Brock's words from last night. *He'll split her in two,* he'd said.

What to do?

Sadie nickers and shifts under me, and an inkling of a thought strikes me at the movement. Abner isn't holding the bridle anymore because he's saddling another horse.

I couldn't run...could I?

Surreptitiously, I peer down one side of the horse and frown. My feet don't even reach the stirrups. But when Jed stands and makes to get on his horse, panic hits me and I realize I have no choice now. I grab the reins, and with a kick to Sadie's flank, we take off in the direction of Hope's Stand.

I don't even look behind me as Sadie sprints away. Thighs tightening around the massive animal, I ignore the pinch of remorse that pokes at my heart. Once I get to the train station, I'll leave his horse tied up there. First, though, I've got to make it through this small thicket and over the creek. If he comes after me, maybe I can lose him.

But as I fight my way through the closely-packed trees, it's working against me, too, as they slow me down and threaten my balance, costing me precious minutes. My breathing turns ragged and I hiss as a sharp branch scrapes my leg.

Can't stop, though.

Then I hear a noise behind me...the sound of a horse crashing through the trees. Sparing a quick glance, I freeze in paralyzing shock.

Oh, no.

He's coming after me. I can only see a blur through the foliage, but I know that's him. Fear makes me kick Sadie harder than I mean to as I urge her forward. Just a bit more...

More...

"Dove."

That's his voice calling out for me, all right. He's probably angry. Angry because I stole his horse and ran away from him after he told me not to, but there was no other alternative. The creek comes into view, and premature relief runs through me.

Come on, Sadie. We can make it. Can't let him catch me.

A sharp whistle cracks through the air, and Sadie slows to a trot before coming to a standstill.

No.

No no no.

We're not even to the water yet!

A sob lodges in my throat as I click my tongue and encourage her with another kick, but it's too late. She's heard her master's voice and she's not going to budge. I shimmy down and blindly feel for my bag—and my money and mother's diary—but when Jed comes breaking through the trees on a dark gray horse, I know I'm out of time.

Scarcely ten yards from me, he dismounts with a jump and slaps the horse's rump to send it on its way back to town. Merciful heavens, but the fierce emotion on his face chills my blood.

Go.

When the shirtless savage takes a step in my direction, I instinctively gather my dress and flee, feet barely touching the ground.

Fly, little Dove, fly.

"Dove!"

Keep going.

"C'mere, little Dove. Stop that running."

Jed's getting closer. Too close. Close enough for me to hear his coaxing tone that tries to trick me into letting my guard down.

Keep going.

My shoes sink into the soft soil that's moistened by the water and halting my progress. I can't even feel my blisters now.

Water, sweet water.

I'm almost there.

Five more seconds at most.

Don't look back. Don't look back.

I hear him behind me, then, out of nowhere, arms shackle about my waist. "Gotcha."

There's no escaping the strength of his grip, but I try anyway, kicking behind me and futilely pulling at his forearms as he draws me to his warm chest. I don't know where I'm getting the courage to fight him when I couldn't do the same with my own father, but I lash out like a wild animal.

"What are you doing?" Long, masculine legs wrap around mine to hold them down, but I manage to get one last kick. "Shit!"

My aim must hit a knee, because he buckles and falls back, still holding me. If I were thinking clearly, I would notice how he landed on his back and a hand reached up to shield my head from the ground, but I'm not. Pinned in place with his bear hug from behind, my breaths turn shaky as I stare up at the sky and wait for him to unleash his anger on me. I deserve it. I disobeyed him, stole his horse, and kicked him.

I wait.

And wait.

And wait.

And through the buzzing in my ears, I think I hear him say, "Shh...it's okay now. Calm down, darlin', I've got you."

No, it's not my ears buzzing. It's the raspy sounds of my wheezing lungs and something else as I tremble atop him. A shadow looms over my face—*his hand*—making me flinch in anticipation as it draws near.

But instead of striking me, it lightly presses down on my chest. "Breathe, Dove. Calm your breathing. I'm not gonna hurt you, darlin'. Could never hurt you. Come on. Breathe with me now. Right here. In...and out. There you go. Shhh..." he croons.

Against my will, his deep voice soothes me as it travels through my back and softly commands my tense muscles to relax. The hand on my chest inches up to cup my face, rough thumb rubbing small circles on my cheek.

Long minutes drag by as he holds me and waits for my breathing to return to normal. Then, carefully placing me beside him, he rolls over me and presses his weight into me.

No! I want to cry. *Get off of me.*

My lungs begin working hard again in panic. If he's not going to strike me, then why isn't he letting me go? The pained sounds of the brothel girls rings in my head and sets my blood to pulsing all the way to my toes. He...he's going to do to me whatever it is that men do to women.

Can't let it happen.

"Ah-ah-ah, little Dove," he gently scolds as I frantically push against his bare chest with my freed hands. The man isn't even breathing remotely heavily after chasing me. "None of that now. You're okay, and I'm not going to hurt you, I swear."

I barely hear his words, barely feel his fingers threading through mine as my hands are raised over my head. All I can feel is his heavy weight sinking me into the crunchy leaves. Dark spots float in front of my eyes, blurring my vision. I can't breathe...between the man on top of me and the dirt beneath me, I'm going to suffocate.

Can't breathe.

Can't breathe.

Can't breathe.

But...I'm still breathing.

No, air is flowing over my lips.

Warm air, and something soft.

Thunder sounds somewhere.

No, not thunder, but Jedidiah's voice rumbling a refrain. "Breathe, Dove. Not gonna hurt you. Never gonna hurt you."

I take stock of myself, flexing my fingers and meeting his. He's still on top of me, forehead and lips pressed against mine while the rest of him covers me like a blanket.

"There you are," he murmurs across my lips, letting me taste his words. "Now you're back with me. Keep your breathing steady, wife. With me now." Jedidiah's chest expands and collapses, calling mine to join its rhythm until my breaths turn deep and slow. "Good girl."

Only a vestige of panic remains when his hips settle deeper into my lower half, but it rapidly dissipates as I register his warmth.

"I don't know what's going through that pretty little head of yours, but you need to throw all those thoughts out with the Monday washing. I'm not your father, and I swear to you that I am never gonna hurt you, darlin'. Not ever. Look at me." He waits for my eyes before saying with a bit of sternness, "But don't run from me again. I mean it. If you run, I'm gonna come after you. And I'll always find you, Dove—always—because I'm a Shay. Once we set our sights on a woman, she's as good as ours. And you better believe that you're forever mine since I caught you twice."

Somehow it doesn't sound as frightening as it would have a moment ago. Not with him holding me like this. And even though he punched my father, Brock, and Harold, he didn't hit me. Not even with everything I gave him reason to.

Maybe...maybe he means what he says.

Maybe I shouldn't run anymore.

Because if I do—

All my thoughts leave me as Jedidiah's mouth takes mine in a dominating kiss. Never did I think I would ever want a man's mouth on mine, but this...this is quite soothing. When our lips part the slightest bit, he murmurs against me, "Kiss me back, Dove."

Dove. The name he gave me, refusing to call me by a meaningless "Girl." That has to count for something, I would think. I don't know how to kiss, but something in me wants to learn more about kisses that don't belong on foreheads, so I hesitantly move my mouth with his.

He slowly moves his hips against mine, and though my lungs start working hard again, it's not from panic. It's from the odd sensation between my legs—the one I felt last night—that returns with a vengeance. Good Lord, but it tickles something fierce! Needing to alleviate the growing itch, I squirm a bit underneath him. Why does his belt buckle feel bigger than it did a moment ago?

"Dove," he groans into my mouth, "you need to be still. You're killing me here." Now he's the one with breathing problems. He sounds...strained, and not like himself. Unable to help myself, I wiggle again, and he breaks away to bury his face in my neck with a low laugh.

This feels surprisingly good, I decide, even if it makes him laugh. Maybe it tickles him, too. Though I should probably feel shame for doing such an indecent thing, I wiggle again, angling myself so his belt buckle sends a shiver through me like before.

"Dove..." The man atop me growls into my neck and pushes his pelvis down forcefully, his buckle scraping deliciously between my thighs. "Not how I wanted"—a grunt leaves him in rhythm with his hips—"first time to go."

Jed's hips move just a little harder and then he groans loudly into my neck before collapsing onto me. I don't like this as much, though, because I still feel...unsettled?

And surprisingly warm and...wet?

All the good feelings fade into shock when he lifts up onto his knees, though, and I see his front. The man wet his pants like a small boy still wearing cloth diapers! Did...did he wet himself on me, too? Indignant, I run a hand down my dress, relieved when it comes back dry. Now I'm confused, and by the slow and rueful chuckle he emits when I look questioningly at him, he is, too. He gestures toward his lower half. "Look what you made me do, Dove. Now I gotta get all cleaned up before we go home."

Home. The word sparks a bit of hope in me where there was only emptiness before. *Trust him,* my heart whispers.

Jedidiah pulls me up with him then frowns. "There's dirt all over you, darlin'." He works his way over my dress, wiping away the dirt and leaves, before slowly moving up to my collar. Lightly wrapping a hand around my throat, he stares at his stroking thumb as if he could see the thin scars underneath. "You were making noises before. Not words, but definitely noises."

My eyes fly to his, and I nervously swallow beneath his grip, wondering if he can feel my pounding pulse. I was? Because of strong emotion? Just like when I was beating the rug and envisioning my father.

"One day soon, little Dove, I'm gonna get you to make noises for me again. But it won't be because you're scared. No, it'll be because all the feelings inside you can't stay quiet any longer." With one more soft caress, he bends and takes his boots off.

What is the man doing? But he doesn't stop there. No, his hands move to his belt. Turning scarlet, I cover my eyes as I hear his pants fall to the ground.

"Oh, darlin'," he chuckles. "C'mere."

That's all the warning I get before I'm thrown over his shoulders like a sack of potatoes. My hands fall away from my eyes and grapple for something to hold onto as he moves into the water.

That something happens to be naked, masculine buttocks that are every bit as firm as the rest of him. A silent, nervous giggle of shock builds inside of me as I realize what I'm looking at.

Holding onto, rather.

"Here we go." Jed grunts a little as he lowers me to stand on a flat rock. "Don't slip. You stay right here, woman, because I don't feel like chasing you around buck naked, you hear? Leastways, not until we get home." Without waiting for an answer, he backs away, watching with ill-concealed amusement as my jaw drops at his nakedness.

Well, not completely naked. For what it's worth, he still has his hat on.

"Like what you see?" he asks with a smirk.

My neck jerks with how quickly my head turns around. I already knew what he looked like from the chest up since he was without his shirt, but what on earth was that dangling between his legs? I don't look like that there.

Water splashes as he washes himself, and I can't help but to sneak another peek. First with the corner of my eyes to make sure he isn't watching, then with more of my head when I see he's bent over cupping water over himself.

Drawn by a force I can't explain, my eyes run over the tanned expanse of his broad back, down the lighter skin of his buttocks with the dark shadow in the middle, and drop between his legs again. But...this looks different and nothing like what I saw from the front. Do all men look like this?

An image of my father pops into my mind, and I shiver at the comparison. No, the pasty whiteness of my father's chest and arms are the complete opposite of Jedidiah. And the men at the brothel that I sometimes saw...their hairy cheeks peeking out over their pants were saggier than Jed's, too.

The man himself turns around, a toothy grin covering that handsome face of his as he catches me in the act. Good heavens, if I spoke, I have no doubt I would have squeaked just now. Belatedly, I cover my eyes again.

"You were looking, weren't you?" I hear the laughter in his voice. "Don't deny it. It's all right to want to look at your husband, little Dove." His strong hands pull mine away from my face. "Go ahead, darlin'. Get your fill."

How did I find myself going from panicking underneath him to taking covert peeks at his nakedness? Face burning, I lock my gaze onto the middle of his chest—a safe spot—not daring to go further down. But as he patiently stands there, holding my hands in his wet ones without a word, my curiosity demands to be sated.

So, curiosity conquering shyness, I haltingly glance down and then away, bouncing my eyes off of him before trying again. I start with his belly button first, noting how it dips in, and then move to the trail of body hair just underneath. It's blonde, just like on his chest and head, and it leads to the object of my curiosity.

And I frown in consternation as I take a quick look at his discarded pants and then Sadie to confirm something.

He wasn't wearing his belt buckle, because it's currently housed in the saddlebag. I can see part of it sticking out from here. I glance back at Jedidiah with a bit of confusion.

So I was rubbing against this...this flesh-colored thing that looks like a cute little snake?

And a floppy one, at that.

If that's all he's wanting to stick between my legs like Madam Lulu seems to think he might, I don't think it'll hurt at all. It didn't earlier when he was on top of me and between my legs already. Satisfied and feeling relieved, I meet his eyes.

"You all done, darlin'?" His full lips twitch with a smile.

I dip my chin in a short nod.

"Good. Let's get going." In no time at all, he's carried me to land, gotten dressed, and swung himself behind me on Sadie.

Sandwiched between the pommel in front of me and a powerful man in the back, the tingling that never left gets stronger between my legs again.

In less than one day, I've been sold, married, and caught.

Caught twice, at that.

But I don't think I mind very much.

8

DOVE

At least, I didn't mind very much when I wasn't tied up. Now I'm bound to my husband by a rope around my waist.

Don't look at me like that, wife, he'd said with a little grin as he fastened the knots and tested the hold. *How can I keep you safe if you keep running away from me?*

Not how I foresaw my great escape happening, especially once I learned we were headed to Hope's Stand anyway.

"And that's all my brothers," he finishes telling me now. "No sisters, but I got a whole passel of nieces and nephews. How about you? You got any brothers or sisters?"

I sway with Sadie's movements and shake my head. I don't know what to make of him. Even though I can't speak, he hasn't made fun of me or ignored me. Instead, he phrases his questions so that I can answer with a gesture or an expression. Nobody else has ever done that with the exception of Madam Lulu, and never for this long.

"So it's been just you and...him? What about your momma?"

I tilt my head back, showing the deep sadness in my eyes at the mention of my mother. Sometimes I envied her death because she got to escape the nightmare that is Clarence Crowley.

But, a little voice whispers inside me, *now you have Jedidiah Shay.*

A short kiss to my downturned lips lifts my spirits. "How long ago?" my husband rumbles.

I flash my hand two times, then stick three fingers up.

"Thirteen?" he asks, probably to be sure.

I nod.

"How old were you?"

Too young. I keep one hand lifted with all five fingers showing.

His face falls before he grabs my hand and brushes a warm kiss over my knuckles. "You'll never be alone again, Dove, I promise you that. You're mine now, and we're gonna be together for the rest of our lives. Especially now that I've caught you."

He's caught me, just as he said. But why does he keep speaking about it? My face shows my question, I'm sure, as I look up at him in confusion and give my ankle a little shake.

Jed gives a faint grin when he notices my expression. "All the men in my family have a little tradition to follow. They have to catch the woman they plan on marrying. And you?" Arms tighten around me. "Now I know you're mine because I've caught you twice."

So he has. Now the rope around my waist has a completely different meaning. I turn back around, but the muscles between my shoulder blades scream at me to stop sitting so stiffly. So inch by inch, I slowly give him more of my weight, wiggling just a bit to situate myself.

His arm tightens around me. "Hellfire, Dove, you push me to the edge of my limits without even trying."

What does he mean by that? While I ponder on it, the tugging sensation by my ankle that's been bothering me for the last few minutes demands my attention. There's the problem—part of my dress is tucked underneath. Holding onto the pommel with one hand, I lean slightly to the left to free the trapped material.

Jedidiah groans softly, and when I raise back up, something pokes me in my bottom. What on earth? I know he couldn't have put anything between us in the short time I was bent over.

Surreptitiously, I give another discreet movement to see if I can feel it better.

And I do.

Something definitely feels hard.

A low, wicked laugh tickles my ear. "You know what, wife? I've dirtied my good shirt and a pair of pants for you, and I'd do it all again. But I think I've been remiss as a husband. You made me feel so good that I spent myself in my britches, but I didn't do the same for you."

Jed loosely loops the reins around the pommel, giving Sadie her head, and spreads his big hands over my thighs. Even with the heat of the day, this feels good. The laugh that tickled my ear mellows into words. "Mhmm, let me tell you what's gonna happen later, Mrs. Shay. We'll be home by nightfall so I can make love to you all properlike, but for now, let me show you how good it feels to have your husband's hands on you."

His hands? All of his words hit me at once, and I don't know which to focus on first—*Mrs. Shay* or *make love*—because his fingers creep up my thighs until they meet the slight curve of my hips.

My breath catches at this intriguing sensation. His hands move higher still, until they slip up the thinness of my ribs.

"Breathe, little Dove," he murmurs, waiting for my rib cage to expand again.

My new husband is so attentive to me, always mindful of my breathing, and I don't know what to make of it. A dash of self-doubt trickles in at what he must feel under his hands. Am I too thin? Remembering what he said, I fill my lungs with air again.

"Good girl."

At the two words that ruffle my hair, something tingly runs through my veins, like when lightning streaks through the sky on a hot summer night, and makes my fingertips burn. Hearing my previous name spoken like this...I don't mind at all.

Movement startles me as his hands reach just under the slight curve of my breasts. Where does he think those hands are going? Indignant, I push him away and cover myself.

"What's the matter, wife?" The depth of his voice sends goosebumps shooting over my arms. "Has anyone ever touched you here before?"

I shoot him a surprised glare over my shoulder. Of course not. It isn't proper!

"No?" He smiles faintly with a bit of surprise before prying his big fingers under my resistant ones. "Good. That's what I thought. You always slept alone at Madam Lulu's, didn't you? No, don't fight me. Let me touch you," he softly commands in my ear as we shift side to side with Sadie's movements.

Unsure of his intentions, I hold to his forearms and nervously swallow as he cups my small breasts.

"Mhmm...little Dove. Look at these beautiful things. Do

you know what I'm gonna do to these the first chance I get? I'm going to put my tongue right...here." At his final word, he circles both of my hardened peaks with his thumbs, eliciting a gasping jolt from me as my fingers reflexively tighten around his wrists. "That's the spot, isn't it, darlin'? Feels good, doesn't it?"

It sharpens the tingling between my legs, just as if he'd touched me there. Dazed with pleasure, I don't answer until he lightly pinches my sensitive tips, and then a harsh noise leaves my throat as I squirm.

Hips move against me from behind. "And after I've licked all around your sweet little bud, I'm gonna wrap my mouth around it and suckle like a babe."

Sweet Lord, I remember seeing a newborn calf suckling its mother's teat, tugging at it to get the milk. Is...is that what Jedidiah wants to do to me? A raspy sound escapes me as I watch his rough thumbs moving over my nipples.

"Now you do it." He takes my hands and uses them to cover my small breasts. "Keep 'em there and stroke the tips. Yeah, there you go. Still feel good?"

Surprisingly enough, it doesn't. It doesn't feel at all like before.

"No? Did it feel better when I did it?" A pained laugh erupts from his throat at my answer. "I only have two hands, darlin', and one of them has to keep you steady. You're gonna have to help me out until I get you in a bed and can use my mouth."

I look down at myself, the shadows of the neighboring trees darkening our path as we trek forward. Help him out?

With a press of his knees, he guides Sadie to a stop underneath a tree with low-hanging branches. As if I were nothing more than a doll, he maneuvers me around to face him, wrapping my legs around his waist and bunching the rope up between us. "There we go, Dove. This is better 'cause now I can see you."

Though we're still tied together, I clutch his shirt for balance. He can see me, but can anyone else? My head jerks to the side, but as if he'd heard my thoughts, he captures my chin and brings it back. "Don't worry, Mrs. Shay. I'd never let anyone look at what's mine. Now, put those sweet lips on me."

I freeze, body locked in place.

Another of those faint smiles shows his straight teeth, and when I still don't move, he leans in and thumbs my bottom lip, pressing down on it. "All right, my shy little wife. We'll get there in time."

Without giving me any chance to think, he captures my lips in a hot kiss, slipping past the barrier of my teeth to tease my tongue. I shove back and furrow my eyebrows, gesturing wildly to my tongue. Why does he insist on doing that?

"Oh, darlin', that's the way it is between husbands and wives." Jed steals a small kiss from my surprised mouth. "Just try it. We'll learn together."

When he lightly slips his tongue in again, I stiffen for a brief second before relaxing into him.

It's not my favorite, but also not that bad.

Slow, easy strokes and soft brushes of tongue and lips soon have me melting fully into him. His mouth is so warm and wet, demanding something from me that I don't know how to give. I vaguely feel Sadie shifting her weight from one leg to the other, but all I can focus on now is the man I'm wrapped around. I fist his shirt and pant into his mouth, wanting nothing more than to stay just like this.

A hand eases under my dress to caress my thigh.

My bare thigh.

I pull back, but he chases me, tongue dipping into my mouth once more as he groans again.

"Wife," he rasps, forehead touching mine, "the things you do to me. But it's your turn now. Keep your eyes on mine and don't look away."

Unable to stop myself, I immediately scan our surroundings, but he grasps my chin and firmly commands, "Don't. Eyes on me."

I stare wide-eyed at him, face burning as the hand under my dress moves to the center of my thighs. Closer to that place that feels so oddly needy. Jedidiah laughs darkly when I futilely tighten my limbs in response. "Is my woman unsatisfied? I'm thinking she is with the way she's been squirming in my lap. I'm thinking she wants me to pet her right about...here."

And when he touches me between my legs, I jolt, mouth dropping in shocked pleasure as his hooded brown eyes carefully watch me.

"Right there, yeah darlin'?" He holds me tightly, restricting my movement as his thumb strokes over the slit of my underthings. "That's my good little wife, letting her husband touch her however he pleases. Do you like the way this makes you feel?"

Yes. That's the spot and I don't want him to stop, even if he shouldn't be touching me there.

"Good girl," he roughly says. "Now put your arms around my neck and hold on. Tighter." This is indecent, but I can't help myself. My fingers run through his blonde hair, digging in when he rubs firm little circles over my secret place, and when his fingers move away, I want to cry.

But I'm introduced to a new sensation when he signals for Sadie to walk again, because our centers are completely pressed together and that thickness I felt poking my bottom is now against my front.

"You like this, too, darlin'?" The words are almost growled out. "The way your sweet spot rubs against me with each of Sadie's steps?" My lashes fall closed. I don't know how to process these sensations. "Thought I told you to keep looking at me," Jedidiah softly scolds before pinching my beaded tips, sending an icy hot sensation down to my center.

Breathless with desire, I drown in his golden gaze, our souls connecting us in a way words never could. Hips meet hips, and with every step of Sadie's rolling gait, every light twist of his fingers, the tingling inside me grows into a raging fire.

Fear rises up in me the stronger the fire roars. Something's happening to me, and I don't know what to do about it. I angle my body away, but he drags me back.

"Ah-ah-ah...don't be afraid, Dove. I know it's something new, but keep those pretty eyes on me and just move, darlin'. Move your hips while I pet these soft nipples." The soothing timbre of his voice calms me, and I do as he says. Rolling my hips with the movement of the horse, I give in to the sensation, letting it build as a gasp leaves me.

"That's it," he croons. "Look at you. It's all over you, darlin'. Cheeks all flushed with desire, pretty eyes all heavy. That's how a wife should look under her husband's hands." My eyes fall to his mouth—the mouth that's going to suckle from me—then down to my breasts. Imagining him attached to my breast and peering up at me, I begin to wheeze.

"There you go. C'mon, Dove, that's it. Keep chasing that feeling." Voice strained, Jed rocks with me in a steady rhythm even as he restricts my movement.

It's all too much.

His deep voice.

The fire in my core.

The hardness rubbing me.

The rope about my waist.

Through it all, Sadie keeps walking, feet clopping on the path.

I have no choice.

Following an unknown instinct, my toes curl within the confine of my boots, fingernails anchoring themselves to strong shoulders. The tension in my lower core releases in an explosion, sending spots in front of my eyes and a silent whimper drifting on an exhale. A whooshing floods my ears —maybe my heartbeat—while a tear tracks down my cheek at the intensity of the moment.

And underneath everything, I hear Jedidiah's soft words as I cling to him in the aftermath. "That's my girl. Let it take you, darlin'. I got you...I got you."

When I come to myself, it's to find the man who calls himself my husband staring hungrily at my mouth before swooping down to claim it with a kiss. "That, my sweet wife," he rasps as our lips separate, "is only the beginning."

———

WE STOP A FEW TIMES SO I CAN STRETCH MY LEGS AND relieve myself behind some bushes. Actually, since Jedidiah refuses to untie the rope connecting us, *we* relieve ourselves. I must say that after what he did to me, I'm very curious to what the piece of flesh hanging between his thighs does. I sneaked a peek at him through the greenery once, watching as he held himself, but I couldn't see it that well because of his hand. It seems to fit in his hand, but I'm almost certain what I felt was bigger than that.

Well, he does have rather large hands, I suppose, so maybe that's it. Another thing I don't understand is how he can apparently make it hard or soft at will. It seems men are fascinating creatures with magical abilities.

Now, as the sun dips lower in the sky, the tingling between my legs has long turned to numbness. I definitely am not used to riding for hours on end, but Jedidiah made it as comfortable for me as he could, even seating me facing him again so I could sleep against his chest if I felt like it.

I did once or twice, but whether I sat facing forward or backward, my hips and legs were still forced to straddle either a horse or a man, both much larger than me. Now I sit with arms and legs around Jed's waist, dozing off and on while his hands play at my lower back and his mouth drops the occasional kiss to my hair. I suppose if the journey had to be made like this, it's one of the more tolerable options.

My stomach rumbles, reminding me it's been a while since we ate the nuts and dried bits of meat he pulled from his saddlebag.

"Almost there, darlin'." The softly spoken words travel through his chest and into my ear, sending a fresh dash of excitement through me.

Hope's Stand.

What a fitting name for the place of my salvation.

After a few minutes more, the fence line and cattle come into view, signaling the end of our journey. I sit up a little straighter, twisting my head to see his house.

Ours, rather, according to him.

Probably twice the size of my father's, it's a lovely house, painted a crisp white with dark blue shutters and a row of rose bushes lining the front.

It...it looks like a home.

"Guess I better hurry up and get you down before you twist your head right off." Jedidiah laughs at me, but I'm too eager to mind much. "Whoa, girl."

Girl. For once, the name isn't referring to me. No, he's talking to Sadie as he guides her to a stop in front of the house.

Holding me carefully under my arms, he lowers me to the ground, making sure I've got my balance before jumping down himself. A single step is all I manage, though, before my legs give out beneath me and Jed catches me. From the safety of his arms, I scowl at the source of my soreness—Sadie.

My husband peers down at me from under the brim of his hat, looking as if he's holding back a laugh or two. "Riding too long'll sure tenderize a backside. Let's get you settled and then we'll get something to eat." The wooden steps creak under his weight, and before he can twist the knob on the front door, it opens from the other side.

"Hands in the air," a voice coolly demands over the barrel of a rifle.

9

DOVE

Jed rolls his eyes. "You knew damn well it was me, Warren. Now move it." The sensation of panic that stabbed my heart quickly ebbs away at the annoyance in his response.

The rifle disappears and the door opens further to reveal a crooked grin on the face of someone who must be related to my husband. A younger brother, perhaps? He's not as tall as Jed—but still taller than me—and with dark brown hair instead of a lighter blonde. Their eyes both match, though, with that perfect shade of honey mixed with sunlight.

"This is one of my brothers I told you about. The youngest one." My husband turns to the side to carry me through the doorway. Moving to a plush sofa with arms of oak and cushioned with a pale green silk brocade, he lets out a weary sigh as he drapes me over his lap. "Did you cook something, or you been barking at knots all day?" As if he can't help himself, he strokes my thigh mindlessly and gives my forehead another kiss. I've never been kissed this many times in a day.

Kicking the door closed, Warren ignores him as his eyes

catch on the rope that still connects us and hangs over to the floor. "Well, well, well. You went and finally caught yourself a little woman. Did you get married or do we need—what the hell is that mark on her cheek? Not from you, is it?" He glares at his brother.

"We're good and married already, and you know damn good and well that wasn't me." Jed tightens his arms around me. "Take my hat off, would you, darlin'?"

"Looks like this slip of a woman led you on a merry little chase. Can't say I wouldn't do the same if a ugly giant was thumping his big ole ugly feet after me." Warren throws a little wink in my direction as I remove Jed's hat and put it beside us on the sofa. I wouldn't call him ugly, but that's just about how it happened. And it seems Jed was telling the truth about their little family tradition. Warmth wraps around my hand, and, ignoring the silent warning emanating from his brother, Warren raises my fingers in the air. "Dear sister, allow me to introduce myself. Warren Shay, and the best looking out of all the Shay brothers."

I can't help but to smile back at his obvious charm. With mischief shining in his eyes, his head lowers to my hand. But before he can make contact, a tanned blur swallows my hand, just in time for Warren's daring lips to skim over his older brother's fingers.

"Warren, keep your fancy mouth away from my wife," my husband growls. Wariness flickers in my chest as I tense in his arms. He almost sounds like he did before getting into the brawls at the saloon earlier. I don't like that. Even knowing his anger isn't directed at me, it reminds me too much of my father.

Blithely ignorant of the imminent danger in front of him, the younger man just smacks a noisy kiss to Jed's interrupting hand and innocently bats his dark lashes. "But brother, how else am I to welcome her to the Shay family?"

Jedidiah snatches our hands away and brushes his fingers over my face when he sees my expression. "That's my job, not yours. Now get on out and put Sadie away for me. I've half a mind to make you head back to your own house for the night."

"But Jed," Warren whines on his way to the door, "I wasn't finished talking to...I don't even know her name yet! And it's gonna be dark soon. You wouldn't want them old coyotes to eat me, would you?"

Keeping his eyes on me, my husband answers, "Her name's Dove. And with all that gristle you have on your bones, the coyotes would spit you right back out. Go on with you."

Warren grumbles, but the sound of the latch tells me he's outside now. Not sure of where to look, I take in my surroundings a little more. Instead of just a rug, carpet covers the entire floor, and soft yellow wallpaper with a busy pattern lines all the walls, complementing the light green of the furniture beautifully. High above the mantle of the fireplace, an impressive rack of antlers cradles a rifle, and to the right is a wall filled with books. Empty chairs are scattered about here and there for when company comes calling, but what catches my eye most of all is the seat in the window.

Oh, it looks so comfortable and inviting as it overlooks the pasture! Maybe I'll get a chance to sit in it when Jedidiah is out in the field. Once I'm finished with whatever chores he gives me, though. When I run out of things to look at, I turn my head back and awkwardly encounter my husband's piercing gaze.

"I want you to know that I may fuss a bit at him, but I'd never lay a hand on my brother, Dove. And especially not on you. But if someone other than me touches you, you can bet your sweet little bottom I'm gonna get fired up about it. You're mine now." A small kiss accompanies the words, quickening my pulse. "I didn't tell you earlier, but welcome home, Mrs. Shay. Let me show you around."

Hurrying to stand so he can get up, I quickly regret it. Pain so harsh I can barely breathe shoots through me from my calves to halfway up my back, and I freeze in place, hunched over.

"I'm sorry, darlin'." Arms carefully pick me up again. "It's always worse after you sit still and quit moving. We'll take care of that before we go to bed."

Bed.

The very word sends a shiver through me, and I can't decide how I feel about it. But I put it aside for now and focus on what he's showing me as we leave the parlor and enter the kitchen.

Oh.

A messy one with plates, cups, and utensils overflowing from the sink to the countertop.

Now I feel as if I have a purpose, because the dishes aren't going to clean themselves. Determination settling within me, I gesture to the dirty dishes and squirm to be let down.

"What are you doing?"

I point harder to the sink and mimic washing a pot.

Jed's entire body tenses as he frowns. "Oh, no, darlin'. That's not how it works around here. Damn kid made the mess, so he's gonna clean it all up. And before he goes to sleep, too."

What?

My father would never stoop to doing women's work. I

glance up at Jed with my question on my face. Surely I didn't hear him right.

"I mean it. You didn't make the mess, so you're sure not gonna clean it. Besides, you can barely move." At that, a twinkle shines in his eyes, but he hides it as he dips his head. "So, parlor and kitchen. Got two bedrooms upstairs, but we can add on when we need to for all the young'uns we get."

Before I can think too much on what he just said, my world shifts as he ascends the staircase. "This is where Warren's gonna sleep tonight if I don't make him bed down in the barn." He nods toward a simple and modestly-sized bedroom before continuing on. "Here's the bathroom, and here's our room."

Ours.

The first thing my eyes see is a bed.

A poster bed with huge oak columns that twist up to the ceiling.

The bed is big. Much bigger than the one we slept in last night. Disappointment slowly settles in my stomach when I realize that we'll both be able to sleep in it and not even touch.

I don't like that, for some reason.

Back downstairs we go to find Warren in the kitchen, sprawled out in a chair and legs stretched out on the table.

"Warren..." The agitation in Jed's voice delights his brother. "Get your damn boots off my table and clean that mud up. Dishes too, while you're at it."

"All right, all right. Give a man a chance to catch his breath."

My husband carefully deposits me next to his grinning, mischievous brother and unties the rope, accidentally grazing my breasts as his hands pull away. He stills, looking at me with heat in his eyes and promising...something...as he casually tosses the rope onto the table.

Warren interrupts the moment between us, begrudgingly doing what his brother told him. Looking me up and down with curiosity, he says, "You sure are a quiet one."

"That's because she doesn't talk, and I don't want you pestering her about it. Now quit your yammering and get done." Jed arranges some food on a plate and brings it to the table along with a glass of water.

It looks delicious. The pinkest, best cuts of ham and thick pieces of cheese... Saliva pools in my mouth as the scent wafts over to me. Maybe there will still be some for me when he's done.

Hopefully.

Ignoring the grumbling of my stomach, I stare out the kitchen window to the darkening skies to keep my mind from the food. If I don't look, maybe I can ignore the smells until it's my turn to eat.

To my surprise, his arm cuts through my view, placing the plate directly in front of me. What? I push it back to him because surely he didn't mean to do that. He hasn't even eaten yet!

"Dove." His blonde eyebrows dip together. "This is for you. Don't try to tell me you aren't hungry. I heard your stomach just now."

For me?

"All right," he says with a rumbling laugh as he sits next to me. "Guess we get to do this my way." Tearing the meat, he pairs it with some cheese and lifts it to my mouth. "Eat."

Stupefied, I mindlessly accept his offering. He's letting me eat first. I don't know what to make of this because he's not behaving at all like my father. I slowly chew and swallow, reaching for the plate to move it closer to him just in case he changed his mind.

"Ah-ah-ah," he gently scolds before he offers up another bite. "I want to feed you."

I open my mouth, something hot rushing through me when his rough fingers brush over my lips. Something that seems to happen any time he touches me. He lets me take my time, never glaring at me or yelling at me to hurry. Even though Warren noisily cleans the kitchen—it appears my husband has a sink with its own plumbing!—all I can see or think about is the man feeding me from his hands while staring at my lips as if he wants to eat me.

When the plate is empty, he asks if I want more, and I gesture no. I'm full. I hesitantly reach for the water, half-surprised when Jedidiah doesn't stop me. Giving a satisfied grunt, he makes another plate for himself and joins me again. The heat from his thigh is both comforting and distracting, and for some reason, sitting close to him like this feels different than when we were on Sadie. I suppose because we had no choice but to be close together since we were sharing a horse.

Now, though...now he has four other chairs to choose from, yet he decides to sit in the one next to me, pressing himself against me and wearing an expression that both frightens and thrills me.

How quickly a person's circumstances can change. My gaze flits over the sharp lines of his jaw as they work together, then down his neck. When the muscles in his throat still, I glance up to see him focused on me. "Open," he murmurs.

It becomes very clear that he means my mouth once the food touches my lips. I obey, letting him carefully place the small morsel on my tongue. His fingers linger as I chew, softly brushing over my bottom lip before returning to his plate for another bite.

"One more," Jedidiah softly commands. But I simply can't eat another bite. I hesitate before grasping his wrist and nudging it aside while I shake my head. A heated smile slowly forms on his lips before he moves the food to his own mouth. When his plate is empty, he gives it to his younger brother, who gives him the stink eye but accepts it with a grumbled sigh.

As I listen to the banter of the two men, I become aware of the fullness of my belly and the way my lips throb with the memory of his touch. It's a strange feeling, but not unwelcome. Even if it makes me swallow a yawn and rub at my eyes.

"Ready for bed?" Jedidiah asks me.

Warren snickers, earning a stern look that cuts it off as quickly as it formed. Lifted in strong arms, I'm carried from the kitchen.

"Goodnight, sister!" Warren calls out over the clank of dishes. "See you in the morning."

Even though he can't see me, I give a tiny smile. One that falls away when I see blatant jealousy on my husband's face. "A smile looks good on you, little Dove," he quietly says, "even if I'm not the one who put it there." With a slow brush of his lips to my forehead that sends flutters to my stomach, he carries me upstairs and to the bathroom, kicking the door shut behind him.

I wince as he lowers me to stand by the toilet. I would have thought all the walking and standing I did for work would have lessened the effects of riding, but apparently not. But when his hands reach to lift my dress, I shimmy away. This man is always doing something improper! I move too quickly, though, because my muscles catch and pain steals my breath.

"Dove..." Jedidiah chastises, slipping an arm about my waist to support me. "Let me help you, wife. That's what I'm here for."

Aiming a glance behind me at the low toilet with the tank high above it, I know I can seat myself if I hold onto the wall. Especially if I move slowly enough. So I lightly push against his chest and shake my head, pointing to the door. Relieving myself in front of him like this is entirely different than when using the bushes on the way here! At least I didn't have his full focus on me then.

Jedidiah leans back against the wall and crosses his arms, kicking the heel of one boot out as his lips tilt in a devilish smile. "Now darlin', snubbing your husband's offer of help is no way to start a marriage."

I stand there, worrying a bit of fabric in my hands, and as the seconds tick by, it slowly sinks in that he's not going to budge.

Fine.

I'll show him that I'm tougher than I look. After all, I grew up with Clarence Crowley. Hiding my wince, I bend over just a bit to slip my hand under my dress. The higher it climbs my legs, the redder my cheeks get at the very vivid memory of Jedidiah doing the same thing, but I keep going.

I feel him watching me. His whiskey eyes seem heavier on me than the rug I had to drag outside to beat.

Almost got it...

Now time to sit.

Chancing a sneak peek at him, I see his smile growing wider and wider.

What on earth could be so funny?

I hold to the wall with one hand and slowly bend my

knees to sit. My thighs aren't having it, though. The moment I ask them to support me, they give way and I collapse onto the toilet seat.

Wait.

I pause for a moment.

The wooden lid of the toilet seat, rather.

Oh.

That would be the reason for his smile.

"Oh, Dove." Though amusement shines in his gaze, he doesn't laugh as he pushes off the wall. "I see the point you're trying to make. Pain won't stop you once you get your mind made up. But one thing that pretty little head of yours needs to learn is to accept help when it's offered. Especially from me. Now c'mere."

He lifts me with one arm and rucks up my dress with the other before lifting the lid and setting me back down. "I left the salve for your muscles downstairs. I'm gonna go get it and then I'll be right back." With a fingertip to the end of my nose, he backs away and out, leaving me to do my business.

I sigh with relief and rush as quickly as I can. Some things a lady should do on her own! By the time he thunders back up the stairs, I've managed to do a quick washing up, too, and hobbled halfway to our bedroom.

"Confound it, woman. You were supposed to wait for me," he tsks before carrying me the remaining distance to our bedroom. Easing me onto the bed, he kneels at my feet and unlaces my boots. "Let's take care of you so you're not too sore in the morning. We're gonna have to get you some new shoes so you don't blister up like this."

As odd as it is for him to be unlacing my shoes, it's even odder when his hands reach for the buttons at my waist.

Taken aback, I push his offending hand away and cover my buttons. Has the man completely lost his mind?

A certain gleam enters his light brown eyes. "Mrs. Shay," Jed begins as he casually sweeps my hand aside and resumes his task, "I'm your husband now."

One button slips through the hole.

"That means our bodies belong to each other."

Lightheaded, I watch as another button follows suit.

"You were made for me..."

Another.

"And I for you."

Another.

When he reaches my breasts, he boldly traces their shape, smiling darkly at my intake of breath. "These are for me and our babes." Continuing on, he unbuttons three more. Then he's at my throat.

My throat!

My scars.

No one's ever seen them before.

I know it will likely do no good, but a trembling hand flies up to keep my secret safe.

His big body stills as he carefully stares at me. "What are you hiding under there, little Dove?" Fresh determination settles over him and he gently forces my fingers aside for the last few buttons. Resigned, I give in. I know the moment it happens because a hard expression transforms his face into granite. At odds with his stony look, he softly tilts my chin up.

I don't need a mirror to know what he's seeing. Seven silvery lines decorate the surface of my throat, each mark made in anger by a drunken father. Shame that shouldn't be mine to bear washes over me. I close my eyes only to open them again and flinch as warm fingers touch my neck.

"Dove," Jed grits out through a tight jaw, "who the hell hurt you?" The pain in his voice brings stinging tears to my eyes. Why am I about to cry because of this? It happened long ago.

His grip inadvertently flexes around my throat. "Was it Crowley?" Anger sharpens his words, making me flinch even though I know it's not directed at me.

"Sorry, darlin'. I'm not mad at you, I swear I'm not." Now it's his turn to take deep breaths to compose himself before repeating, "Was it Crowley?"

My reply is a jerky nod.

Storm clouds gather on his face before he sweeps them away. "I know you're tired and the night's late, so we'll talk more about this in the morning. Let me go ahead and put this liniment on you."

Dragging his eyes away from my throat, Jed pulls my dress up and off with no resistance from me, leaving me in just my shift. He doesn't let me stay in that either, though, and I hastily grab a blanket to cover myself. The small motion brings a hint of a smile to his lips. "My little Dove," he murmurs. "My wife. All right, now. Over you go. C'mon...there you go."

A bit of coaxing and gentle maneuvering from him, and I'm face down on the bed with my bottom in the air as he lifts the lower half of the blanket.

My *bare* bottom.

Knowing there's no use in fighting, I lie there stiffly, muscles so sore as I wait for his touch. When it comes, along with the pungent scent of the liniment, I want to cry in ecstasy because this feels amazing. Firm pressure starts at my calves, each squeeze drawing the pain into one central spot before releasing it. Up the back of my knees, to the meat of my thighs, and higher still to the sorest part of all—my bottom.

A proper lady would never let a gentleman touch her in such a manner, but a lady is also supposed to obey her husband in all things, so I close my heavy eyes and let mine have his way.

"Good girl," he soothes as his hands run over my backside. Each stroke, each firm caress eases the soreness and pulls me further into the grip of sleep. "That's my good little wife."

Though the room is still lit with lamps, darkness falls heavily on my lashes and they drift closed as his hands slip down my legs and to my sore feet. My lungs work slowly and deeply, and as I fall to sleep, it's with the disappointment of thinking this bed is entirely too large.

10

JEDIDIAH

S even lines on her throat, each too straight and deliberate to have been an accident.

Seven reasons Clarence Crowley is going to die.

And after I'd washed up and pulled my sleeping little Dove into my arms last night, I plotted seven different ways for the cocksucking son of a bitch to meet his maker if the Dooley brothers haven't already done it for me.

Now as the sun sneaks its rays through the window and creeps up the wall, I see her scars in a different light. I could be wrong, but those lines look only surface deep. She can still make noises. If that's the case, then it's not her throat keeping her silent.

It's her mind.

And I'm gonna do whatever it takes to make her understand that she's safe with me now.

Leaning on an elbow, I look down at her wild, untamed curls and rosy lips. I can't believe she's mine. I'd have bought her and killed for her a thousand times over if that's what it would have taken to make her be mine.

My little wife.

Knowing she's wearing one of my shirts does things to me, and now I want to do things to her.

Husbandly things.

Things I didn't get to do on our wedding night or the morning after.

Easing the covers back, I roll over and position myself on top of her, the simple contact of hips to hips sending a rush of blood to my cock. A lesser man would be ashamed of having spent himself in his britches. Then again, I muse as I grind over her center, a lesser man wouldn't have a woman such as my little Dove underneath him.

Any minute now, she should be waking up. I pepper tiny kisses from the shell of her ear, across the smoothness of her cheek, and over her satiny lips in an invitation for her to join me.

Her chest lifts with a drawn-out inhale, but sleep still has ahold of her.

That's all right.

I'll just keep going until she wakes up.

Angling my head, I kiss the scars that have kept her quiet for far too long, tonguing the barely-raised lines and promising vengeance before shimmying down to reach her chest.

"Look at these little beauties," I murmur to myself. They're not big at all, but neither is the rest of her. Maybe she'll plumpen up now that she's with me. Anger stirs when I remember her surprise last night at the food I gave her. Wouldn't surprise me at all if that son of a bitch punished her with food.

Or the lack of it.

Easy, Jedidiah. Pushing my rage down, I drag my eyes back to the small mounds of her breasts. Hellfire, but I can see the darkness and beaded points of her nipples through my white shirt. Hungry for her, I dip my head and seal my mouth over one and lightly suck before moving to the other side. I lift my head and observe her slack features. Still knocked out.

I'll keep going, then.

Sitting up a bit to straddle her thighs, I lift the shirt that hides my wife's body from me. My cock pulses at the sight of slim thighs and the dark curls covering her womanhood. I smile darkly, silently promising to pay undivided attention there next and keep lifting the material. Higher and higher until I see the soft brown nipples I was petting yesterday.

One dark finger trails over the pale skin of her stomach, eliciting a small twitch but nothing more. She's so thin that my hand spans almost across the width of her waist. But not for long, and for two-fold reasoning—I'm gonna feed her all the food she could possibly want, and then I'm gonna give her my baby. One way or the other, her belly will have no other choice but to swell.

My shaft jumps at the thought, and I look at the little breasts that our babe will nurse from, almost feeling jealous that I'll have to share. But the babe's not here yet, so I have them all to myself for now.

With a groan, I lower back down to suckle, fitting the small mound almost entirely in my mouth before hollowing my cheeks and pulling off with a pop. The beaded flesh is wet and shiny, unlike its lonely companion.

That will never do.

I trail sweet kisses over the valley of her chest to lavish attention on her other little nipple. My wife stirs under me, muscles vibrating in a full-body stretch. One eye pops open, followed by the other. Never have I felt a body stiffen any quicker than hers at this moment. Her head jerks down, mouth falling open as she looks at me.

And what a sight it is, I'm sure, as I sprawl in the cradle of her legs, not letting up on the suction of my mouth. A harsh intake of breath later, and she pushes at my shoulders. I laugh as I release my treasure. "Good morning, Mrs. Shay. Now, now...none of that," I chide, catching her hands as she fumbles with the shirt to hide herself. "No need to be embarrassed with your husband."

Redness blossoms over her cheekbones, covering up the fading mark left by the man whose days are now numbered. I lean in for a kiss, but she turns her head.

"Aww...is my little wife feeling shy?" I steal a kiss anyway, nipping the corner of her mouth as I keep her hands pinned with one of mine. "This, Mrs. Shay, is the way we wake up together. Hugs and kisses and a little something extra. You still sore?" When she shakes her head, I inch back down to her naked breasts and ignore the throbbing of my cock. "Remember what I said I was gonna do to these?"

Breathing shakily, she stares at me and nods.

"Look at this, wife." I thumb slow circles over a soft nipple and watch her closely. "Do you see how it grows hard, just begging for something to suck on it?" I dart my tongue out, licking a teasing circle around it. When her lungs quiver with a breath, I smile darkly. "Watch," I growl into her chest before I pull her into my mouth again.

Wide with shock, her hazel eyes flit from my eyes to her breast. A flush of desire forms and then grows. I see it in the blush spreading over her cheeks. In the heaviness of her eyes that isn't all due to sleep. In the way her tongue peeks out to lick at her lips. Just because she's quiet doesn't mean her body isn't telling me all sorts of things.

Damn, this is working me over. I grind my hips into the bed for a bit of relief, swearing to myself that I'm not going to release early like yesterday. I come off her breast and lick my way to its twin, laughing inside at the way my little Dove's eyes jerk between my mouth and the wetness I left behind. My face nuzzles against her, breathing her in. One gentle bite to her soft flesh, then I take it into my mouth again, suckling in earnest. When I've had my fill, I pull back and reverently kiss each nipple.

Her fingers twitch in mine, but I'm not through. I cast a quick glance up at her. "Remember what else I said? How my tongue was going to go more places than your mouth?" Without waiting for an answer, I kiss the backs of her hands, one and then the other, and place them over her breasts. "These stay here, okay, darlin'?"

When her thumbs subconsciously begin to move, I hold my grin. She must be remembering how I told her to do that yesterday. Slowly extending my tongue, I let her take a long look at it before it lowers down to make contact with her chest. I lick a pattern across the underside of her breasts, learning and loving the taste of my wife. With instinct telling me to keep going, I move down. Down to her belly which jumps at every touch. Down even further to the top of her mound.

A small grunt leaves her on a push of air as she worms her hands between us and covers what's mine. "No secrets between us, darlin'," I murmur as I lift to my knees and throw her stiff legs over my shoulders. "Move your hands."

I know she heard me, but she doesn't move. In fact, she doesn't even look at me. Not at my eyes, anyway. What could she be—?

Oh.

I grin when I glance down and see my cock tenting my pants. Easing a hand down, I squeeze myself, taking care not to send me over the edge. "This is all for you, little Dove."

Concern mixed with horror twists her expression and

she moves both legs from my shoulders, but I catch one before it gets too far. "Ah-ah-ah. Put that leg back." I wait for the slight weight of it to return. "Good girl. Now move your hands."

They don't move.

"All right, wife. I'll help you out." Gently overpowering her resistance, I collect her dainty wrists in one hand and inch them higher up on her belly. "There we go...all better. Now I can see what's mine. Such a good little wife, with your legs open and showing your husband what's his. Mhmm, and look at how wet you are. How ready you are for me."

Hazel eyes track my other hand as it glides down the length of her thigh and closer to her center. She's just as pretty here as I knew she'd be. I've never seen a woman below the waist before, but my brothers told me of folds that looked and felt like flower petals and a little pearl at the top of her slit that would bring her to the heights of ecstasy when touched the right way.

That's exactly what I see in front of me right now. A beautiful flower with dewy, brown petals and a little pearl on top. They also told me a mouth to the sensitive area—a little French love—could be so intense for her that she might suffocate me with the strength of her legs.

Eyeing my little wife's thin thighs dubiously, I think I'm safe.

But I'm going to enjoy finding out.

A smile stretches my lips as the idea grows on me. Fingers first, though, to ease her into it. She tenses and jolts at my touch, so I kiss her knee. "Easy, now. This'll be like yesterday. Remember the way you rocked against me?" Dove's hands jerk under mine when I brush over her curls, but I hold them captive. "Be still, wife, and let me make you feel good again."

Breaths coming a bit faster, she throws her head back onto her pillow, mouth opening into a silent moan as my thumb meets her bare flesh without the barrier of her underthings.

"You're so beautiful," I roughly murmur. Spreading my fingers, I run them through her wetness. When the tip of my middle finger meets the entrance to her body, we both freeze. "Do you know what this is for?"

Eyes getting wider as I boldly move a little deeper, Dove shakes her head, dark hair moving everywhere.

"This, wife...is where I'm going to put myself inside of you and make you mine." Unable to help myself, I slide my finger in even more. I'm no more than two inches in, but the damn way her quim hugs my finger threatens to send my seed shooting from my shaft.

Suddenly, the harsh music of pots and pans clanging together sounds right outside our bedroom door, making Dove and me jolt in surprise. "Wake up, you lovebirds!" a boisterous voice calls cheerily. "Breakfast is ready."

Too damn cheerily.

Finger still inside my wife, I curse under my breath as I try to still the rushing of my blood from the unwelcome intrusion. If it wouldn't be such an insult to my mother, I'd call the little snot-nose a son of a bitch.

Reluctantly dragging my finger from the wet warmth it barely had a chance to discover, I cup Dove's ears to protect them. "Warren!" I roar over the cacophony of cookware. "Get the hell outta here!"

The raucous noise stops, but his laughter trails behind him as he stomps down the steps. Dove squirms under me, bringing my attention to where we were so rudely inter-rupted. Surely I have time to bring her to release before we go downstairs. Mhmm, and then she'll be glowing in the aftermath as we eat our food. "Now, wife, where were we?"

But the universe is against us, because at that very moment, her stomach rumbles, signaling its need for nourishment.

That's the way it's to be, then. I can't have my woman going hungry, especially as thin as she is. Placing a lingering kiss to her belly, I help her up. "He's leaving right after we eat, and then it'll be just you, me, and this bed. I swear."

―――――

MY WIFE'S GLOWING ALL RIGHT, BUT NOT FOR THE REASON I was wanting. Every time she lifts her chin, Warren's there with a knowing grin that sends crimson flooding her cheeks.

"Did you sleep good, Dove?" he slyly asks. "How about you, brother?"

"Shut up," I growl. My boot meets his shin under the table as I scowl at him. Thanks to him, I almost took my wife's innocence with my finger. When he winces and rubs his leg, I turn to the small woman tucked up by my side. "Here you go, darlin'. Have another hotcake." I slap one on her plate and slather butter on it before drowning it in syrup. "Eat all you want. And if you want more, I'm sure Warren will be chomping at the bits to make it for you."

Her face is lowered, but I think I see a smile there. I need to be sure, though. Hooking a finger under her chin, I lean in until she can only see me. "Hey," I murmur. "You good?"

A shy nod is my answer.

Pleased, I brush my mouth over hers and lick my lips, tasting the syrup. "Sticky."

And delicious. Just like her.

Luckily enough for his sake, Warren keeps himself in

check for the rest of breakfast, and when we're all through, I lead my wife to the parlor.

Off-key singing follows us as we leave him to clean the kitchen, but as long as he's not needling my wife, he can sing until he croaks. I shake my head at his antics. It's hard to stay mad at the damn fool. When I look to see if Dove's still smiling, I notice her eyes running over the books by the fireplace. Veering to the bookcase, I nod. "Pick one out and we'll read it together."

Delight shimmers in her pretty eyes, and she lifts a hesitant hand. It hovers a breath away from the black spine of a book before tracing the first letter of the title. "You ever read *Wuthering Heights*?" I ask, leaning on the fireplace. "Written by a woman."

Dove's head jerks up in amazement.

"Yep. A woman named Emily Brontë. Her sisters wrote, too. Charlotte and Anne were their names."

Turning back with a beaming smile, she points at that one, not even giving the others a second glance. My own smile breaks out at seeing her happiness, and I pull it down and give it to her. "C'mon, darlin'."

Once she's in my lap, she traces her fingers over the title again, her mouth silently moving. I just watch her, content in seeing the way she's raptly focused on it, especially that first letter. She doesn't seem to be saying the title, though. What else could she—?

Then it hits me.

She...she can't read.

Just like she can't write.

That cocksucking whoreson. She must feel the tension that suddenly tightens my body because she jerks her head up, wariness replacing her happiness.

"It's all right, darlin'," I soothe, smoothing my face and

relaxing my taut muscles. "Just felt a sneeze coming on." I'd love to let my gun sneeze all over the bastard. Right after I make good use of my knife. "Do you know your letters?"

She timidly shakes her head and looks down to the title again, tracing over the *W* and moving her mouth. Is she trying to mimic the sound?

"That's the letter W," I tell her. "Do you know what sound that makes?" I hear a small puff of air as her lips move, but I can't tell if she's making the right sound. I gently tilt her chin up. "Look at me, darlin', and tell me again."

Pretty hazel eyes look no higher than my throat as she moves her lips again. I have to strain my ears, but with the way her lips purse and then release, I think she's got it.

"Can you do it louder?" Immediately, her expression shuts down. Okay, that's a no. "All right, how about this? Pretend I have a word in each hand. My right hand has water." I wiggle it and emphasize the word. "And my left hand has sofa. Which one do you think makes the W sound?

Looking at me as if I'm a dunce, she gingerly taps my right hand and mouths the letter's sound.

"My little wife, how smart you are!" I plant a hard kiss on her lips. "We'll have you reading and writing in no time."

A pretty blush flowers over her cheeks again as if she's embarrassed, but I see the secret pride in her eyes at my praise. Well-deserved pride, I might add. How she lived for so long with Crowley mistreating her and still turned out sweet as pie and smart to boot, I have no idea.

"All done!" Warren announces before falling dramatically into a chair across from us. Damn man is always interrupting us at the most inopportune time. Speaking of...

"Isn't it about time for you to get on home?" My demand is clear even through the question. I stare him down, silently threatening him in advance for any wayward thoughts that might exit his mouth before his brain filters them.

"Actually, I thought I might stick around and—" Finally, he sees my expression and smothers his grin. "Oh, yes. Right. I need to stop at Momma's to...hem some dresses and darn some socks." Slapping his thighs, he stands. "Well, sister, very nice to meet you. Remember that if you ever get mad at Jed, you can always come and cry on my shoulder."

"Warren," I grit out as my arms involuntarily tighten around my new wife.

The little shit doesn't stop. "And a little kiss—"

"Warren," I bark, jealousy forming within me even though I know he's just being his annoying self.

"Alright, alright," he sighs. "I'm going. I'll tell everybody the good news. Pop'll probably send some men over since you'll be honeymooning for a while."

We will indeed. For a year, in fact.

Just like the Israelites in the Bible did.

One whole year to learn each other's bodies and let our love grow. The family picks up the slack of tending to the farm, sending men in shifts over the course of the year. My Dove and I will have all the time in the world.

"Sounds good," I reply. "Watch out for those coyotes." They're no trouble at all in the daytime, but ever since he was knee-high to a grasshopper, the boy's had a tendency to lollygag.

"Brother." Warren steps closer to slap my shoulder in a parting touch. I don't like the way he eyes the woman on my lap, though, especially with that secret smile playing over his mouth.

He's up to no good. "Warren—"

Quicker than a rattlesnake, he lunges and smacks a kiss to my wife's soft cheek. Then he takes off running for the front door, knees and arms pumping comically in the air in his haste. "Goodbye, sister, and welcome to the family. See you later!" he yells on his way out.

"That boy." I shake my head with disgust as much as I do affection before replacing the kiss on her cheek with one of my own. For good measure, I claim her mouth, too. "No part of him belongs on you, even if he's only joshing around."

The house is much quieter with him gone, but now...

Now my wife and I are all alone.

And once I finish reading to her, we're going to finish what we started.

11

DOVE

"*1*801. I have just returned from a visit to my landlord—the solitary neighbour that I shall be troubled with. This is certainly a beautiful country! In all England, I do not believe...*"* Jed's smooth, deep voice tickles my cheek as I listen to him read from the book a woman wrote.

This is the beginning of my second day with him, and I'm slowly but surely coming to realize that he's not going to hurt me, even if I still flinch at times. My mind knows it, but the other part of me, the part that was nurtured by Clarence Crowley, tells me to always expect the unexpected.

Some things are just clearly beyond my ability to expect, even for being unexpected.

For example, I certainly didn't expect to wake up to my husband's mouth upon my bare breast. And I can still feel the phantom sensation of his finger as he pushed it into me, making that strange fever, the one that I only seem to feel around him, come back.

Whatever it is, I think I like it.

I shift on his lap, prompting him to pause and softly kiss my forehead before resuming his reading. Other than when bathing or...other matters, I've never touched myself there, and never would have dreamed that there was room to stick something inside. I still can't believe I was splayed out like that...legs resting on his shoulders and showing my privates while my nightshirt was rucked up around my bosom!

I frown.

The nightshirt I didn't put on.

I frown harder.

The nightshirt that looked suspiciously like a man's shirt.

But it was the last thing on my mind because he looked so handsome as he knelt between my legs. So...so raw and even just a little bit scary because of how intensely he was staring down at me. I felt helpless, but in a good way. Like I wanted to pull him down on top of me even with that big lump he had in his pants. It looked even bigger than what I'd felt yesterday.

Puzzlement fills me as I recall the way he'd squeezed it, giving me a better idea of just how big his man part was. But it seemed to have disappeared by the time we made it down-stairs for breakfast. How does it do that?

A thought crawls into my head, daring me to find out. Am I brave enough to do so? Maybe if I just pretend to fix my dress again. That seemed to have been the starting point yesterday. Nonchalantly, I lean down and needlessly rearrange my dress over my ankles.

"'Come, come,' he said, 'you are flurried, Mr. Lockwo—'" Jed abruptly ends the word with a pained grunt when I lift back up. Did it get bigger then? I shimmy just a tiny bit and lean more into him.

It did!

The part of him that isn't his belt buckle digs into me now. He's quiet for the smallest moment before he resumes, voice deepening. "'You are flurried, Mr. Lockwood. Here, take a little wine.'"

I can't even focus on the story about a grumpy man with dogs, or whatever the book is about. But the more I think about the hardness poking me, an itching sensation forms around it, and the harder I fight to ignore it, the more fiercely it demands to be scratched. I can't very well scratch with the hand that's pressed against Jedidiah, so I inch my free hand across my waist. If I can just...

There. I manage to work my fingers in between my hip and his clothes and I furiously scratch, closing my eyes in bliss. Sweet heavens, why does it feel so good? Back and forth my short nails go, eliminating the pesky sensation.

Then I notice how quiet it is.

Why did Jed stop reading?

Right as I open my eyes again, the book drops onto the floor and a tanned hand with long fingers grabs my wrist, forcing it to be still. "Wife," my husband grits out in a strained voice.

That's all he says. Just that one word.

Braving a glance up at him, my pulse jumps. He looks...angry. No, not quite that.

Intense.

The kind of intense from this morning where his light brown eyes looked heavy with sleep. As if we were back in the bed and barely clothed and his finger pushing inside of me. Just thinking about his finger makes mine twitch.

A long, masculine groan hits the air as my finger makes contact with his hardness. "Little Dove, how you make me ache. Teasing my cock every time you move."

Cock. His big thumb rubs over my bottom lip as I mouth the word and repeat it in my mind. So that's what it's called.

"I wanted to read to you, but now"—sleepy eyes track up to mine—"I think it's time we go upstairs, wife. The book will be here when we're done, but I can't wait a moment longer to make you mine." Before I can understand what he means, he carries me up the stairs, throwing small and heated glances to me between each step. And when we reach the bedroom, he wraps my legs about his waist and presses me to the wall.

"Damn it, Dove." My silent moan of delight mixes with his verbal one when we fully touch. My husband breathes my name into my neck as he mouths my jawline. "So many things, darlin'. So many things I want to do to you to make you feel so good, I barely know where to start. But I think here's good."

Fiery heat covers my mouth as he possesses it in a claiming kiss. I can almost feel my lips swelling from his attentions. Lightheaded and breathing raggedly between his kisses, I hesitantly rest a hand on his shoulder, wanting to feel more of him.

"Yes," Jed groans with a shudder. "Touch me. No, wait." Easing back, he yanks his shirt off, exposing well-defined muscles and a trail of golden hair on his chest. "Give me your hand." Without waiting for me, he takes it and drags it over himself. "Hellfire, Dove."

For being a man, his skin is so soft. The hair on his chest tickles my fingertips, and when my short nails trip over his nipple, he hisses in response. Fire darkens the honey in his eyes as he stares boldly at me. One strong arm holds me securely to the wall while the other slips a rough hand under my dress to caress my legs. Higher, over my thigh. Higher still, where it curves around and firmly cups my bottom. He smiles faintly at my gasp, lips pulled back in a way that sends shivers running through me as he gently squeezes. "This is mine, isn't it, wife?"

Mesmerized with the sensation, I blankly nod and bring my other hand to his chest to steady myself. A light chuckle precedes his mouth as it swoops down for mine again. He kisses me with small pecks that tease when I want him to kiss harder. When his tongue moves into my mouth again, I draw back and frown at him.

"Still don't like it?" he asks, laughing huskily when I shake my head. "All right, darlin'. But a good marriage is built on compromise, so if you don't let me put my tongue in your mouth, that means you have to let me put it elsewhere."

Immediately, my mind flies back to this morning when his mouth and tongue were all over my bosom, and I instinctively cover my chest at the memory. A rogue smile tipping his lips, he shifts and carries me to the bed. "But to do this properly, clothes have to come off."

Heart pumping hard, I stand still as he unfastens the buttons at my throat. In the broad daylight, my scars are visible now, but he's not focused on them. It's my face he watches with a hooded gaze, never wavering until he reaches the last button and then slowly lowers the material over my shoulders to pool around my feet.

Now I'm clothed in only my shift, which he hastily relieves me of, too. As it drifts down, my arms tense to keep it from revealing my bare chest, but big hands catch my wrists. "No, wife," Jed rasps. "Let me see you."

Redness streaking through my cheeks, I cast my eyes to the floor as he lowers my wrists. Never having been unclothed before a man before—or anyone, really—I feel incredibly vulnerable and shy. This morning was different.

I'd woken up and found myself already that way. But now? Now I've just stood here and let my husband undress me with minimal resistance. The entire process is a bit nerve-wracking, to say the least, and I shiver even though I'm not cold.

"You're beautiful, Dove, beyond beautiful. And you're all mine." Jedidiah's fervent words deepen my blush and my desire to hide, but he tips my chin up. My nervousness grows at the hungry look he gives me, and when he steps closer, I fight the urge to run. He takes another step, a warm hand to my naked lower back encouraging me to follow his lead.

Soon enough, the backs of my knees meet the bed. Now there's nowhere for me to go.

Nowhere but back on the bed.

A gentle push, and I find myself sitting on the edge and holding onto the covers for dear life as a shirtless Jedidiah kneels before me. He lifts my leg, sliding a kiss from ankle to knee before placing it on his shoulder and doing the same to the other leg, forcing me to lean back onto my elbows.

I'm so...exposed.

Then all of his attention focuses on my center. "Look at this pretty little flower," he croons as his thumbs separate me. The sudden coolness feels odd, and a sensation of wetness even more so. "I think it needs a kiss."

A flower?

A kiss?

There?

Surely he doesn't mean to—

Before I can do anything other than twitch my toes, his lips meet the most secret part of me in a forbidden kiss. My lungs empty in a jagged sigh and my hips raise off the bed at the ticklish contact.

Rough hands slide up the length of my thighs to grip my hips and pin them down. "No, wife. Be still." His words are muffled but I understand them just the same before the hot, wet warmth of his mouth covers me again. Something—his tongue?—moves over my sensitive flesh as if looking for something. I wiggle a little, unsure of this new thing my husband is doing. It feels interesting enough now that the shock of the tickle is gone, but I honestly liked it better when he was kissing my lips and covering me with his body. At least then—

Agh!

Lightning streaks through me and the faintest whimper escapes the prison of my throat. What did he just touch? My head drops down to see what he's doing, but I can't see below his hair. Not until he lifts up and reveals a shiny smile.

"There it is." His tongue makes a pass around wet lips. Is that wetness from me? "So good. Need more." With a deep groan, he dives back down, tonguing the same spot that set me on fire.

This feeling...this is just like on the back of Sadie, but more. This time I'm naked, legs spread around my husband's shoulders as I rock back and forth on his face. Searching for stability, my fingers release the bedcovers and grip his hair.

"Yes," Jed mumbles through a mouthful of me, "hold me." As if my body is his to command at will, he forces my knees closer to my chest so he can make more room for his shoulders. The hungry licking turns to ravenous sucking, and suddenly cold flames lick over my fingers and toes.

Closing my eyes, I chase after it while his mouth has his way with me, eating at me with rough licks and sucks that send me closer and closer to an invisible edge. Barely hanging on to this side of sanity, I tumble over the edge as he wraps his lips around that sensitive part of me and releases a deep, dark groan that vibrates my entire being.

I can't fight it. Can't fight it. Can't...fight...

Back arching and mouth gaping open in a silent scream, I drown under the wave of pleasure washing over me. Jedidiah holds me tighter, refusing to let me move away from him until he's done. "C'mere, wife," he growls as he pulls me back.

Twisting my fingers in his hair, I throw my head back in ecstasy and blindly stare at the oak poster that reaches for the ceiling, just waiting for him to show mercy to me. Sweet heavens, if this is what he had in mind, I'm so glad he caught me when I ran from him!

Little by little, the pleasure wanes and I'm able to catch my breath. With a final kiss, Jed eases my legs to the bed and crawls up my naked body. He hovers over me and nuzzles his wet face into my neck. "What do you think, my little wife? Did you like that?"

Can he not hear the sound of my gasping lungs? I nod, shivering at his low answering laugh that tickles my ear. Small, teasing kisses decorate my jawline as he waits for me to catch my breath. When I do, he lifts up after a final kiss and moves off the bed. Standing like this, the bulge in his pants is clearly on display now. As a matter of fact, it seems to have grown a bit more.

Oh, my.

That doesn't look the least bit comfortable. But as if the situation in his pants were an everyday occurrence, he shifts himself with familiarity and unfastens his front. Intense curiosity eats at me the further it goes, prompting me to raise up to see it closer.

A harsh groan vibrates the air as the flap of his pants

opens. I still can't see him clearly, though, because he bends down to take them all the way off. It can't look too different from when we were at the creek. But then again, it wasn't as big then as it—merciful heavens!

He's...it's...oh, sweet Lord! What happened to the cute little snake? This swollen purplish thing looks painful! He closes his fist around it. "This is what you do to me, wife."

I...I did that. All my wiggling on his lap earlier did this to his...*cock*, as he called it. Remorse stabs at my belly as my heart sinks. I've bruised him somehow, no doubt about it. Not with his cock being so swollen and the purple discoloration on the tip there in plain sight.

I've hurt him.

Ashamed of myself, I scoot to the edge of the bed and cautiously extend a hand to trace over his length in apology. Before I can, though, he groans again, making me flinch and jerk my hand back.

"It's alright, darlin'," he soothes in a strained voice. "It's alright."

I clench the covers. No. It's not alright, because I can see the damage with my own two eyes. The poor man. First he spends his money on me, then I steal his horse, and now I've bruised him and made his cock point unnaturally upwards. I've got to make it right somehow. It must hurt something fierce, especially with his big hands around it. Hands that are too rough with calluses. He needs ones that are softer.

My heart jolts.

Ones like...mine.

"Dove." My name a low moan from his lips, he winces as he squeezes his cock even tighter. The silly man! Why on earth is he doing that? Bruises, especially those in tender areas, need a gentle touch.

Through his lowered gaze, he watches as I haltingly

wrap my fingers around—oh, no. This is more serious than I thought. I wonder if he's getting sick because he feels extremely feverish right here. Unless it's just from being swollen? I need to make sure, so I adjust my grip and slide it up towards his tip.

"Wife," Jed chokes out, throwing his head back to the ceiling as he moans in distress. Even his stomach muscles are quivering. The poor, poor man is in so much pain! I've got to do something, because if his fever gets worse, rot might set in and then we'll have to cut his man part off so the rot doesn't spread.

I don't want that to happen to him.

Sadness streaks through me as my palm rounds his bruised tip. Would it help if I kissed it better? That's what he did to my bruise on my cheek, and I felt better inside even if the outside still hurt. Maybe it will be the same for him. Very careful not to pull on him too hard, I lean forward and give his purple tip a kiss. Just a tiny one to show how sorry I am.

Wild-eyed, he jerks and wraps his fingers tightly around mine as I silently apologize with another little peck. "Dove...hellfi—"

A pained groan is my only warning before a warm liquid spurts onto my nose and mouth. I flinch backwards but I can't go too far because my hand is still trapped under his and around his cock. I...is he...the man is emptying his bladder on me!

He can keep his bruises and his rot!

Blinking rapidly in shock and keeping my mouth closed, I try to retract my hand, but he holds it too tightly. "No...wait. Just a little...more..." he gasps out, eyes tightly clenched as more liquid sprays onto me. As he gives one final drawn-out groan, I use my free hand to wipe away the mess on my face, but when I pull it back, I frown.

It's white.

And...sticky.

What on earth is wrong with this man?

"I'm sorry, darlin'." A mix of amusement and regret twists his mouth. "Let me get you cleaned up." With a lingering glance to the mess on my face, he leaves the room. I'm in a bit of shock, I think, to just be sitting here and letting it slide down my neck and onto my breasts. He quickly comes back with a wet cloth, but one thing catches my eye—he's still swollen.

Jedidiah catches me looking between his legs and grimaces as he cleans me. "I'm sorry, wife. You're the first woman I've ever been with, and you're just so damn beautiful that I couldn't hold myself back. We'll learn how to be a husband and wife together." He cups my face and smooths a thumb over my lips. "Thank you for the kiss, darlin'. I loved it very much. Give me just a few minutes to recover"—he gestures to below his waist—"and we can try again."

I eye him and his cock with wary confusion. I don't mind trying the first part where he put his mouth on me, but I can certainly do without what happened just now. That was extremely messy and I still don't appreciate it.

"C'mere, Mrs. Shay." Scooping me up, he drags us into the bed and pulls the covers around us. "Do you know what husbands and wives do?"

While I'm starting to get a pretty good idea, I'm still very unsure, so I shake my head.

"Let me tell you, darlin'." And for the next while, he does. With our heads sharing a pillow and our naked bodies pressed against each other, he tells me that I'm a woman, he's a man, and we have different parts with funny names that fit together when we make love. His part swells up and goes inside me, and even though it might pinch a little at first, it will fit.

He didn't empty his bladder on me—although he *does* relieve himself from his cock, too. That white substance happens when he reaches his "peak" and is supposed to somehow mix with something inside me and make a baby.

But it doesn't happen *all* the time. Sometimes people can do that and never have babies because it just depends on how their bodies are made up. And that's why I bleed once a month. All this information makes my head spin.

"What do you think, wife?" Jedidiah plays with a lock of my hair, warm eyes tracking over my face. "Do you want to make a baby with me?"

I stare at Jedidiah's strong throat that doesn't have any scars on it.

A baby.

With Jedidiah.

A little boy or a little girl to call my own and care for. I would never *ever* lay a hand on them like Clarence Crowley did to me. And once I learn to write my numbers and letters, I would teach them so they never get called stupid or dumb by everyone.

I want that very much, even if it means I have to have sticky white stuff inside of me. Hesitantly, I place my hand over his chest, over his beating heart, and give him my answer. *Yes.*

"Oh, Mrs. Shay," he murmurs as his eyes darken. "That's just what I wanted to hear. You and I are going to be so good together, do you hear me? So good. I'm going to take care of you and love you and all our babies. You're never going to want for anything, darlin', because I'm gonna give it all to you. But first..."

With a deliberate motion, he inches the covers down to expose my bare breasts. "Do you remember how I told you my family had a tradition of stealing brides?"

I cross my arms over my chest and nod again.

"Let me see you, wife." When I move my hands to the ropes of his muscular arms, he rewards me with soft kisses to my nipples and rolls me to my back, moving with me. "There's also a vow we say to them. One that I've been waiting to say to you. Are you ready to hear it?"

A vow just for me? *Yes.*

Lowering down on me just a bit more, my husband stares deeply into my eyes before somberly speaking. "You are my woman, little Dove, and I am your man. With this marriage, I lay a claim on you stronger than the heat of the sun"—he presses an array of warm kisses to my neck—"or the pull of the moon."

Back up he goes. "I vow to you, wife, that darkness will never fall without the press of my lips to yours"—he claims my mouth, dipping his tongue just the barest bit in—"or your body knowing the comfort of my touch."

Of their own volition, my legs spread to make room for his big body between them. My heart beats faster because now I understand what the men were doing to the girls at Madam Lulu's. They were making babies. Or at the very least, sticking their cocks inside the girls. And even though the girls didn't look like they were enjoying it, maybe it was because they didn't have someone like Jedidiah on top of them to take care of them.

A firm caress to the juncture of my thighs—my pussy, as he called it—forces a gasp from me. I hold to his thick arms, preparing myself for what I know is coming.

"Good little wife. All wet for her husband." His rough voice sounds in my ear as he fits himself to me. "Though I chased you down and captured your body, you've taken my heart. This"—a pained grunt leaves him as he slides himself over me—"this is what it means to be a Shay."

Then he moves fully forward within me, making me wince at the intrusion. He wasn't lying at all about the pinch. But now he's inside of me and shuddering above me with eyes clenched shut.

"Hellfire, Dove. You feel"—Jed draws his hips back and looks down on me in wonder—"so damn amazing."

I don't return the sentiment. The whole sensation is tight. Stinging. Throbbing. But if this is what it takes to make a baby, there's nobody else I'd rather be doing it with. In fact, as I look up at this massive man who seems to be finding the utmost pleasure with my body, I send up a prayer of thanks that old Mr. Pennington didn't want me.

"Ahh..." my husband groans out, hips jerking sharply before stilling.

Is he done? That was fast.

He buries his face in my neck, his hot breath hitting me with little puffs before he raises up. "I swear, wife," he says with a hint of regret, "I'll get better at this the more we do it. But now I'm gonna make you feel good."

A hiss of air whistles through my teeth as his cock slips out of me. Oddly enough, now that it's gone, I feel strangely empty. But with a deep kiss of promise, he moves down my body, lips worshiping every inch of me until he reaches my center.

A prideful smile plays at his lips as he caresses me. "So damn beautiful with my seed all over you and in you. And you're all mine." Not caring that his spend is still leaking from me, he falls between my legs and eats at me with an open mouth, tongue circling what he calls my clit with every pass.

Oh, sweet Lord! In an instant, the feeling that I now know to be desire rages in my belly and sends cold flames licking at every point of contact. Even if we don't make a baby, I'll be happy as long as he keeps doing this. Soft little pants hit the air as I struggle to breathe, and with every muffled groan that tickles my pussy, I find myself closer and closer to my peak. If this is what he felt when I kissed his tip, no wonder he had trouble holding himself back.

From between my legs, Jed lifts his head and licks his shiny lips. "We taste so damn good together, wife." Pressing my knees back until they almost meet my chest, he licks a line through the lips of my pussy and up to my pearl. "Let go and give me your release. Because I'm not stopping until you do."

Gasping, I clutch at the sheets, needing something to keep me steady with all the feelings rushing through me. I'm so close...so close...

My hips lift, trying in vain to get away from the over-whelming sensation and also to get even more of it. Jed pins me down, rubbing his face all over me with deep growls that tickle my folds and completely tip me over the edge.

I can't breathe.

Blackness. Stars. Twinkling lights.

I see it all as the most intense pleasure—even more than the first time he put his mouth on me—hits me harder than a mule's kick. Vaguely, I can hear him encouraging me through it as I jerk against his restraining arms.

Good wife.

There you go, darlin'.

That's my good little wife.

The low, velvety texture of his voice only prolongs my pleasure, especially with the soft kisses he places to my tender flesh. As I slowly come back to myself, gasping like a fish out of water, he crawls up to me and just holds me tight, kissing my hair and whispering that I'm his for always and forever. I cling to him in the aftermath, arms and legs trembling with all these feelings running through me. But I believe him.

I'm his.

And he's mine.

12

DOVE

A blue blur streams past the parlor window, snagging my attention. Although I love learning to write my letters, there are only so many times I can repeat them before my wrist aches or my mind tires of all the loops and swirls. Pen and paper forgotten for the moment, I welcome the interruption, hugging my knees to my chest and watching as the little blue bird fans its tail for balance while trilling a tune. It's only there for a short time, though, before it flies away.

Learning is a different sort of work, I'm finding out. Mental instead of physical, but no less demanding in its own way. Jedidiah is so patient with me, though, and never boxes my ears when I make a mistake. Instead, he prefers to dole out kisses as rewards, and I can't say that I mind that too terribly.

My cheeks heat as I remember his family walking in on a "reward" two days ago. Eyeing the two of us in our slightly compromising embrace, Warren smirked and took a deep breath, only to sputter it out when a book flew through the air and caught him in the stomach.

"Warren," Jed had threatened with a smile, tucking my face into his chest. His parents entered mere moments later. They didn't stay long, though, just enough to introduce themselves and drop off a trunk full of dresses that only needed a quick adjustment.

I'm wearing one of them now, a beautiful blue gingham dress even more fancy than the good dress that I wore when Mr. Pennington came over. No one's ever given me so many gifts before, and especially without expecting anything in return. My husband has the kind of parents I never had the chance to have. Not with my mother passing, and definitely not with Clarence Crowley.

I sneak a glance to where Jed sits on the sofa and prepares my next lesson. After only three days of him teaching me, I already know the first seven letters, both capital and lowercase, and can correctly match the sound to the letters most of the time. And once I learn to read, too, I'm going to read my mother's black book.

But for now, I roll his name through my mind, mentally sounding it out. On a burst of inspiration, I pick my pen up and turn to a fresh page. What letters make up his name? *Jedidiah* is too long, but I think I can do *Jed*.

Juh-juh-jed.

I think I know that first sound, but I need to be sure. Picking up the picture book he's been teaching me from, I flip through the first few pages until I find the one of a diamond. I know it doesn't begin with a D because I made that mistake earlier. It's actually a...

I stare harder at the word, looking at the first letter.

Gemstone! That's what it was, and it starts exactly like *Jed* does.

The E is a little trickier because it sometimes makes other sounds, like with egg and eagle, but the D is always the same. Making sure he's not looking, I copy the letters onto the paper.

G-E-D.

There. They're not all connected like I sometimes saw on the envelopes of seeds at the general store, but there's three of them. Wait...does the E have two loops or three?

"What are you doing, little Dove?" Two long arms suddenly appear on each side of me, making me jump because I didn't hear him walking up behind me. A warm kiss is pressed to my neck. "Sorry, darlin'. Just me."

I shake away the thought that I'd been doing something naughty even as I snatch the paper to my chest and hide it from view. Writing his name feels...sacred, somehow. As if by penning the letters, I now have a piece of him in my hand.

"You writing something?" A gentle tug pulls at the paper, but I don't let go. "C'mon, wife," he cajoles. "Let me see your handiwork and then we'll have a picnic outside."

When I hold fast, he playfully tugs again. I don't want him to see it, though. What if he laughs at me? What if...what if I spelled his name wrong? No, I couldn't have. I sounded all the letters out in my head and they all matched. Reluctantly, I loosen my grip and watch him study the paper.

The corners of his eyes soften. "Look at this pretty hand-writing. This is my name?"

At that, my face falls with uncertainty. If he has to ask, then I didn't get something right.

"Don't look so glum, darlin'. You did good, so good. And you're only going to get better once you know all the letters. You see this one?" He points to the first one. "This is a G, but sometimes G and J are a little tricky because they can share the same sound. So lemme show you how to do a J because that's what my name starts with."

Turning to a fresh sheet, he puts the pen in my fingers and wraps his hand around mine. "Start right here and make a loop to the left, kinda big, and then come down with a long loop that meets back at the middle. There you go! That's the best J I've ever seen a first-timer do. Now add the other two after it."

Biting the inside of my cheek in concentration, I finish his name and look at the three letters.

J-E-D.

Jed.

A soft kiss meets my forehead before he lifts me into a hug so comforting that I almost want to cry. I never knew it would feel this good to be held by someone. "My smart little wife"—a gentle squeeze—"I'm so damn proud of you. So proud."

————

Outside underneath a shady oak tree, Jed stretches and lays his head on my lap. "That was a damn good lunch, wouldn't you say so, Dove? Makes a man want to get a little shut-eye." And with those words, his black hat slides down to cover his eyes.

He's so big that one shoulder extends past my thigh and over my knee. I like it, though, this size difference between us. It makes me even more aware of him as a man and me as a woman. He's so handsome, and so gentle despite his strength. I watch the steady rise and fall of his chest, scanning down the long length of his body, past the bulge of his pants that still mystifies me even after seeing it, and to where his boots are crossed at the ankles.

My eyes travel back up to his chest where long, tan fingers interlock with each other. Those hands have done lots of things for me. Fought for me. Tied me to him. Massaged my sore bottom. Made me feel things I never knew my body could feel. How lucky I was that he happened to be passing through Springwell at the exact moment he did. Who knows where I'd be now? Underneath Mr. Pennington or another man who likely wouldn't take the time to teach me to read?

"For someone who's so quiet, I sure hear you thinking mighty hard." His hat tips up just enough for his whiskey eyes to lock onto me. "Got something on your mind?"

Smiling, I shake my head because I'm just full of my own thoughts.

"You know, I've been thinking. You're a fast learner, but I can't wait until you learn the rest of your letters. Think if I sound them all out, you can tell me which one your name starts with?"

My name.

Not Girl, not Dove, but the name my mother gave me and the one I haven't heard for thirteen years. A bit of excitement stirring in me, I shyly nod. He pats around for my hand and kisses the back before threading our fingers together. "Is it any of the ones you learned already?"

I think for a moment and answer *no*. I'm fairly certain it's none of them unless it's a tricky letter. I'd thought the book we were reading, Wuthering Heights, had a letter that started with my name, but now I'm not so sure. My mind flies back to the mailboxes at the general store. Williams and Wright. Both with the same letter but different sounds.

"Well, that narrows it down. Let's get through the rest. I'll throw out some words, and if the first sound reminds you of your name, you let me know, okay? I'll start with H."

At my nod, he begins, emphasizing the beginning sound. "Hat."

No, not it.

He tries the next. "Idea."

No.

"Jed." He laughs at the grin that accompanies my answer.

"Kill."

Isn't that what cat starts with? I thought it was a C.

Down the list he goes. "Open."

No.

"Pie."

No.

"Rabbit."

No.

No, wait! I stiffen in surprise.

"That one?" He gives a whooping holler and jolts up. "All right, darlin'. That's the letter R."

Now I'm really confused. How can that share the same sound with a W?

Jed claps his hands together, his excitement contagious. "Now we're getting somewhere. Now let's try some names. Rose?"

I twist my lips. That's a no.

"Ruby?"

No.

"Hmm..." He stares at me as if the answer is written on my face. "Rebecca?"

I shake my head. He probably won't guess it because it's not a common name.

"Rena?"

At my negative answer, he rubs his chin and admits defeat. "I can't think of any more. Not now, at least."

Meow. A gray cat with a fluffy tail slips between us and rubs its head against Jed's arm. "Well, hello there," my husband croons as he scratches between the cat's ears. "What have you been up to? Looks like you finally had those kittens."

I perk up. Kittens?

He brings my hand to the cat's nose to let it smell me. "Dove, meet Ms. Kitty."

Ms. Kitty's sides vibrate in time with her raspy purrs as her whiskers brush my hand.

"C'mon, wife." Jed stands and pulls me up with him. "She's kept her last two litters in the barn, so that's probably where these are, too. Hop on and I'll give you a ride." Stooping, he helps me climb onto his back. When he stands, I cling to him like a bear cub to its mother and fight off a short wave of dizziness. Even though I'm sitting lower than I would on a horse, I'm still a good ways off the ground.

One of his hands hitches up my feet while the other pats my thigh. "Well, well, well. That's a, uh...pretty tight grip you got there." He sounds mildly surprised, but of course anyone would have a tight grip when their feet are off the ground. Wouldn't they? "Off we go."

Whistling a jaunty tune, he carries me across the field to the big wooden barn painted a vivid red. I know I don't weigh much, but he's not even out of breath once we get inside. Closing the door, he eases me down. "Smell that? Smells like home."

My inhale isn't as deep as his, but I can still smell the earthy and comforting scent of animal and hay. Taking my hand, he leads me past the stalls for the horses, past the little storage room, and all the way to the back where an old buggy with no wheels rests. "She usually keeps them—there they are. Huh...there's only three. Last time, she had five."

There they are, indeed. Three kittens, one black and the other two gray with black stripes. One of the gray ones wiggles its tiny backside and pounces on the tail of its unsuspecting sibling, who rolls onto its back from the surprise.

How adorable!

"Want to hold them?" Jed murmurs into my ear. I eagerly nod. "Which one?"

My finger flies up to point at the black one, then falters when I hear one of the grays mew plaintively. I point to that one, but then the black one catches my eye again when it nips at its mother's foot.

How to choose? I want to hold them all!

A chuckle vibrates my back. "Oh, Dove. Sit tight, darlin', and I'll bring them all over. Ms. Kitty won't mind."

Spreading a blanket on the floor for me, Jed helps me sit and then scoops up three busy kittens and deposits them into my lap. They're so soft and fuzzy, and their tiny mews pluck at my heart. As a child, I'd always wanted a kitten but knew better than to express any interest in one. Clarence Crowley delighted too much in the misery of innocents, and what if he didn't like the kittenish noises? He probably would have cut their throats, too.

I shiver before throwing that thought behind me. Jedidiah's told me he's not going to let anything like that happen to me ever again, and it's too dark to dwell on when I'm surrounded by kittens.

Digging in with their small, sharp claws, the black one and one of the grays teeter on my knee before braving the short jump to the blanket below.

"Hey, hey, hey," Jed scolds as the gray one chews on the other's ears. Gathering them in one big hand, he plops them on his chest and scoots closer to me. "Feisty little devils, aren't they?"

They are the cutest little devils I've ever seen. Suddenly, Ms. Kitty jumps between us and onto the stacked crates, using them to gain access to the beams above. Strutting confidently across the rafters, she disappears into the loft.

"Barn cat. She's never been afraid of heights," Jed explains as one kitten bats at the stampede strings of his black hat. I love how kittens can find the most mundane things to play with and make a game of it.

A demanding mew draws my attention to the little one still in my lap. Now that they're all closer, I can see that this gray has a white tip on the end of its tail where the other one doesn't. As I give it a gentle scratch between its ears, it lifts its chin, eyes closing in bliss as a purr rumbles out.

Oh, it's just too precious. I run a hand along its back, the satin fur tickling my palm, and before too long, its head bobs heavily to the side. The little thing seems tired. It must be exhausting to be a kitten and do nothing but play all day. I glance over to see if my husband's doing the same with the two kittens he has, but he's not looking at them, even though they're practically climbing his shirt.

It's me he focuses on with a bit of heat that I know the meaning of all too well now.

He wants me. And I feel an answering heat rising in me at the intensity of his whiskey gaze.

"Dove," he says in a low voice. "I'm thinking I need a kiss, darlin'."

Blushing, I cast a look to the barn door.

"Don't you worry about anybody else. It's just you, me, and these kittens. Now, come on over here and lay one on me. Right here." He bubbles his cheek and taps it.

Giving in, I lean in and aim for the scruff of his cheek, but Jed turns his head at the last second so our lips meet, claiming my mouth in a kiss that instantly sparks the constantly simmering fire in my belly. Mindful of my wishes, his tongue doesn't stab into me but teases the shape of my mouth instead.

One kiss turns into two, two into three, and three into four. Soon, I lose count, losing myself in him instead. I love the way he kisses me. The feeling of his chest lifting with his breaths. The heat of him that surrounds me. The way my lips tingle after our kiss breaks.

A dark chuckle sounds as he tucks a wayward curl behind my ear. "Oh, you've done it now, wife."

And so I have. The swelling in his pants is plain to see.

"Do you know what I've always wanted to do with my wife in a barn? No?" Gently placing all three kittens back in the wagon bed, Jed pulls me to stand and walks me backwards. "I've always wanted"—*kiss*—"to make love"—*kiss*—"in the loft." The ladder makes contact with my back at his last word.

The ladder leading to the loft.

"C'mon, wife," my husband says with a coaxing grin as he scoops up a blanket. "Let's do some more sparking before we get to the baby-making part. Up you go." Swiftly turning me around, he pops my bottom with an encouraging smack, laughing as I jump. My father never struck me there, but I still have to force myself to relax.

"Sorry, darlin'." Seriousness pulls his face tight as he cups my chin. "That was just a playful pop. You know I would never hit you, don't you?" His earnest eyes beg me to see his sincerity.

When I slowly nod in agreement, he kisses the tip of my nose before he boosts me up. Gripping the ladder, I climb, highly aware of the fact that my bottom is now in his face, and when I reach the top, Jed's right behind me, blanket in hand. "For your hands and knees," he casually mentions as he spreads the material over the floor.

Fighting a sudden case of nerves, I rest my back against a wooden beam and throw my gaze around the piles of hay. Just because I've grown to like what we do doesn't mean getting started is any less awkward. And in a barn on my hands and knees? I'm barely getting used to sharing the covers with him in a bed!

"Wife." The low murmur is my only warning before warm hands move under my dress. He's...on his knees before me, peering up at me from beneath his hat. The shadow from his brim gives him a darker look, one that excites me and twists my stomach into knots. "Hold your dress and rest your leg on my shoulder."

Slowly lifting my dress and a leg, I expose myself to my husband. He tips his hat back and runs a line of kisses from my knee to my thigh, covering every inch of skin with his adoration before moving to the other side. "I smell your sweetness, wife." His nose feathers over the crease where my thigh meets my hip. "Smell how much you want me. How much you need me."

My head falls back with a thunk when his tongue sneaks out for a taste, and a breathy gasp leaves me when warm hands grip the bare skin of my backside. "I'm never letting you go, Dove. You know that, don't you? You're mine and I'm yours."

I nod fervently. Now that he's caught me, I don't ever want to leave. A trapped sob lodges in my throat when his mouth finds my clitoris. That's the fancy name for it, he's told me. I like to think of it as my pearl, though. It sounds softer.

But now I'm not thinking much on it because my

husband is drinking from between my legs. Drinking from me as if I'm the only thing to quench his thirst. Rolling his tongue around my pearl, fingers clenching my bottom with the force of his desire.

"Ahh..." he groans into me. "So damn good." Then his words die out as he dips his tongue inside my pussy. I jerk against his grip, but he holds me fast, leaving me open for his ardent caresses.

My leg gives out beneath me, but Jedidiah catches me before I slip too far. Standing like this, one leg around his shoulder while his hands firmly cup my bottom, I feel...free.

Uninhibited.

One hand leaves my dress to twist in his hair, knocking his hat aside. He laughs against me before burying his face further into me and sucking with little pulses onto my clit. More and more until my toes curl and blackness speckles my vision with the force of my release. Without direction from me, my hips tilt up, seeking more of this pleasurable sensation that overwhelms my senses.

Soft passes of his mouth between my legs slowly bring me back down, and with one final lick that makes me want to whimper, Jed backs away, looking at me hungrily. "You taste divine, wife. Now, on your knees."

Heart pounding rapidly from the fresh wave of desire that crashes over me, I lower down to the blanket and rest on my heels, waiting for more guidance. Heat forms at my back as he hugs me from behind and guides my hand to my lower belly. "Here. Right here is where our little one will grow, safe and warm. But first..." Soft pressure to the small of my back encourages me to lean forward, and I brace myself on my hands, breath catching with anticipation. He follows me down, covering me with his warmth as he hovers over me. "...I've got to put one inside of you."

Air rushes in as he lifts my dress and presses his hips against me, grinding in a circular motion. This...this is different. A brief image of a couple from the brothel flashes through my mind, along with a bit of hesitation, but I blink it away. Jedidiah would never hurt me.

"Look at you, my little wife." A hand sweeps my hair to the side and traces the curve of my shoulder blade. "So exquisitely beautiful. So very much mine." His weight disappears for a moment as he fumbles with his clothes, but then I feel the warmth of his bare thighs as he feeds his length into me. "Hellfire, Dove...why do you feel so damn good?"

It's still such an odd feeling for me, knowing that part of him is inside of me, but it doesn't sting anymore. Especially not when he puts his mouth on me first. Now I just feel pleasantly full.

Until he pulls out and pushes back in.

Sweet heavens.

This is...oh, Lord. I cross my arms and rest my forehead on them, lifting my bottom up to give him better access.

"That's my good little wife." A smooth thrust in. "Taking her husband's cock inside her sweet pussy." A smooth thrust out. Hands tightly gripping my hips, he picks up his pace. A little harder, but oh, so good as it makes my small breasts jostle.

Breathe, Dove, breathe.

My lungs snatch for a gulp of air and inhale his soft words of praise instead. "There you go, darlin'," he soothes. "Take all of me."

The powerful snap of his hips to my backside forces a gasp from me. Then he slowly withdraws, leaving me empty and waiting.

I widen my legs to make more room for him.

And wait.

And wait.

When he doesn't move, I wiggle my bottom.

Rough words filter into my ears. "What is it? Are you growing impatient for me?" A light pressure teases my entrance. "Show me how much you want me. Take me, wife. Push yourself back onto me."

Impale myself on his cock? My pulse thrums, the heavy beat sending a rush to my fingers and toes. Letting him have his way with me is one thing, but to actively put him inside me?

"Yes," he hisses as I arch my back and ease onto him. I feel myself stretching around him, swallowing him almost. "God Almighty, darlin', but you take me so good."

I do take him so good, don't I? Wanting to please him even more, I shift forward, then move back again.

"Dove..." He strangles my name. "Always pushing me. Always—" Hands snap onto my wrists as he leans heavily over me and ruts wildly. "Mine."

As the blanket rubs my face with his every motion, a sharp feeling forms in my belly and settles into my chest. Pride. A womanly sort of pride. Without saying anything at all, I make this big man lose control.

His deep grunts and snarls brush my ear, sending lightning to the throbbing place between my legs. He's not even touching me there, but hearing him struggle to hold back is enough to send my release hurtling through me. I claw at the blanket and clench around him in a spasm, chanting his name silently in my mind.

Jed, Jed, Jed.

Two more faltering thrusts, and a beastly growl explodes from him as he empties himself into me. Chest heaving against my back, he holds me in a tight embrace. "Don't move," he murmurs into my temple, ruffling my hair with his breaths. "Let my seed take."

His seed.

Because being with my husband like this can make a baby. A flutter of emotion hits me, and I turn to offer my mouth in a kiss.

"Wife." The word is muffled as our lips meet. "You're my every—hellfire!" At his curse, his hips jostle backward, his softened erection slipping out of me. "What in the Sam Hill...?" He tenses for a moment, then reaches behind him, bellowing in amusement as he brings out an orange kitten.

Clasped firmly by the scruff of its neck, the kitten protests with a tiny hiss that curls its whiskers. "You little devil," Jed scolds. "Did your momma hide you up here away from your siblings? You should be chasing after mice and rats, not a man's ballsack."

Is that what made him stiffen in surprise? A tiny kitten sinking its claws into his dangling man parts? I silently giggle into the blanket. Then I picture the shocked surprise on my husband's face as the little kitten innocently swatted at him, and my giggle turns into a wheezing sound.

"Dove!" Jed hurriedly places the kitten down and turns me over, worry all over his handsome face. "Are you okay?"

I can't stop. In fact, seeing him with his pants still down makes an even harsher noise leave me.

Realization dawns on his face, softening it. "Darlin', you're...you're laughing. You're laughing!"

The vibrations from my chest slowly fade away. He's right. I'm not laughing just in my head. Those ugly, croaking sounds came from me. Cringing, I drop my head.

"No...no, don't stop." A warm hand catches my chin, urging me to look up. "That was beautiful, Dove. So beautiful because I could hear *you*."

But the moment's over. I slide my fingers over my throat, stopping at the thin scars and remembering all seven of those nights when a blade woke me up. Jed's face darkens as he gently moves my hand aside to trace the lines himself. "You know what? I think you're still able to talk."

My heart stops for a jarring beat before falling back into rhythm. Fear creeps up, telling me I couldn't possibly try, but hope reminds me of the noise I made when I was beating the rug in anger.

When Jedidiah was on top of me after he caught me by the creek.

When we were on the horse and he made me feel things I didn't know were possible.

When I laughed just now.

"Whatever it was that he did to you, it wasn't permanent, Roberta."

Roberta? All heaviness leaves my mind as I stare at him in confusion.

"So," he says with a playful grin. "Not Roberta. All right, all right. I knew that wasn't it." He lifts off of me and pulls me onto his lap. "Arms around my neck, Rachel."

Scowling, I do as he says. That's not my name.

"Now give me a little kiss, Ruth."

I stubbornly evade his searching mouth, but he threads a hand through my hair, holding me still. "Don't be mad, Dove. How else am I to say that I love you if I don't know your name?"

Love.

He loves me? Wetness leaks down my cheeks, wetness that he wipes away with a tender caress as he steals a kiss that I willingly give.

He loves me.

One final kiss, then he tucks my head against him. "Huh.

Would you look at that? Got some straw in your hair. You been taking a roll in the hay or something, wife?" he asks with a wink. "Let's just fix this up right quick..." His words ease into a whistle as he clumsily unbraids my hair and picks all the loose bits of straw out before he twists it again. "There we go."

I run a hand over the lopsided braid and kiss his cheek.

Wife. *His* wife.

I think I love him, too.

13

DOVE

I can't move.

Between the heavy legs weighing me down and the long arms keeping me tucked close to a furnace of a chest, there's no getting away from my husband. Not that I would even want to try, but after sleeping alone for so many years, this is taking a little getting used to, even after a few weeks. And to think that I first thought this bed was too big. I have a feeling we could put two of these beds together and I'd still be right underneath him.

Puffs of air hit the top of my head as Jed pulls me even closer in his sleep, making my nightgown—his shirt and nothing else—ride up and expose my thigh. He's spoiling me. There's no rush to get up before the sun and quietly cook breakfast for a man sleeping off a night of drinking because my husband doesn't drink to excess. No more slaving away over a stove and cooking for a bunch of dirty men who aren't even grateful for the taste because my husband cooks with me. No more tidying up the general store because I'm too busy learning to read.

If this is how all the men in my husband's family care for their women, their chosen brides are very lucky indeed.

It's not often that I wake up before him, so I take the time to really study his features. Long, thick lashes. A strong nose. Days-old scruff on his cheeks and surrounding his mouth. He'd probably shake his head at me if he knew I thought that his lips were pretty. They're so soft, though, and combined with the roughness of his scruff, it's the perfect bit of texture when he kisses my mouth.

Or my nipples.

Or between my legs.

I shiver within the safety of his arms. So many things he's taught me beyond my daily lessons of letters and sounds. Things I never would have ever dreamed a man and woman would do to each other.

Staring at his lips again, I remember our very first night together. The night I left him sleeping and ran to Madam Lulu's. His fierceness and intensity that frightened me at first had faded away, leaving him looking much as he does now. I'd only been brave enough to kiss his forehead as he slept then, but time has passed, and now I know that kisses are for more than foreheads.

Jed is always so aware of me when he's awake, but I wonder if the same is true when he sleeps. Shrugging his too-big shirt back up from where it exposes my shoulder, I gather my courage and brush my lips over his. Just a peck. A teasing touch like he sometimes does with me.

His chest steadily rises and falls with shallow movements, so I give him another kiss, touching my lips more firmly to his. When he still doesn't wake up, I run a hand through his hair and softly nuzzle his face, the texture of his facial hair slightly abrading my cheeks. When I can't kiss any further, I trace along the sharpness of his jawline, moving down the length of his neck. There's scruff even down here, too.

I pause on his neck. His voice is perfect. So low and deep and smooth. Unlike what I'm sure mine would be if I could bring myself to speak. My finger catches on the knot in his throat as I trace over it. He always tries to make me laugh, saying he loves the rusty and dry sound. One day, I want to be able to say his name to him. To tell him my own name so he can stop guessing it.

But not today.

With one more kiss, I move on. The tanned skin of his shoulder feels so smooth, but the texture changes when my fingertips meet the golden, crinkly hair dusting his chest. A little flutter of awareness tickles between my legs when I accidentally cross over a nipple. I wonder if he likes having his sucked, too. They're a different color than my own light brown ones, which I think is odd. A shade somewhere between pink and red. And just like mine, a soft touch makes it harden. I wonder about between his legs, though, and slowly inch my hand down his stomach.

An abrupt snore freezes me in place. Is he waking up? I wasn't done discovering him yet. But no, after he sleepily mumbles my name, his breathing turns deep again. Slipping my hand under the covers, I follow the trail of hair down. Why the man insists on sleeping without any night-clothes is beyond me, but since it aids my mission at the moment, I count it as a blessing.

When the tips of my digits meet warm skin, a fresh bout of nervousness hits me. If he wakes up, I'll simply snatch my hand away and pretend that I was sleeping. As closely as we sleep, my hand is bound to wind up between his legs at some point or other, isn't it? I bite my lip as I reach downward and wrap around his cock.

Amazing! It's not as hard or as long as it usually is by the time he takes his pants off, but it still fills my hand. I tentatively squeeze it to test how hard it is, and—oh, sweet heavens, it just moved!

How on earth does it do that? My curiosity burns, daring me to lift the sheet. Glancing to his closed eyes, I inch the covers down, surprised when the material gives without much resistance. Inch by painstaking inch, more of him comes into view.

The darker hair surrounding his cock.

The hint of flesh just underneath...

Almost...just a little more and then...

Seconds pass as nervousness creeps in.

No, I can't.

I can't.

"Keep going," a sleepy voice demands in a rough whisper.

Jumping juniper trees—he caught me! Embarrassment burns in my chest and cheeks as I drop the covers faster than a jackrabbit thumping the ground and bury my face in his side. Oh, why did I do that?

I feel his deep chuckle as much as I hear it as he kisses my hair. Prying a hand between us, he tilts my chin up. "Look at me. No, not at my throat. Look at me...your husband. There you go." The low command draws my reluctant gaze because there's no ignoring a man like Jedidiah Shay. Heat mixes with amusement in his eyes as he uncurls my fist and slowly drags it over his chest, past the dips of his muscle and further down. "I believe this was right about...here." Holding my gaze captive, he wraps my fingers around his length. "Does that feel about right to you?"

I swallow my nerves and dart a quick glance down. Yes,

but it's much thicker than it was just a few moments ago. And darker, too.

A rough finger rests on my lower lip, stopping all thought. "Seems I've neglected your curiosity, wife, and that will never do. C'mere." With one sure movement, he lifts me to straddle his thighs. "Stroke me. Up and—down...yeah, darlin'. Just...just like that."

He loves my touch. That much is clear by the broken groan humming from his flexing throat. And I like sitting on him, feeling his warmth against my core with nothing in between us as I touch him. Slowing my strokes, I lower my head to see his cock better. Intimidating veins decorate his length, and at the very tip of him is the slit where his seed comes out.

Rubbing over it, I mindlessly wonder how long it will take for us to make a baby. Maybe it's already happened and I just don't know it yet. I trail a finger down to the place he was attacked by a kitten two weeks ago. A man's ballsack, he called it. It must be uncomfortable to have to keep all this contained in his pants.

Eyeing his bulge again, I correct myself. *Really* uncomfortable.

His cock twitches, reminding me of what I was doing before I got distracted. Wrapping my hand around it, I gently caress his thick length. Up from the bottom, down from the top. But what's this thin little bit of flesh just underneath his tip?

"Wife..." Jed shudders and gently pushes his rough thumb into my mouth. Did he mean to do that? My eyes cross as I look beyond my nose to his hand. "Suck."

Obediently, I purse my lips around him and suck as I tighten my grip on his cock, rolling my thumb under his tip.

"God Almighty," he curses, cupping my face. Does it

really feel that good to him? It must, because now he's leaking. I don't want it to drip down on the bed, so I swipe it up and rub it back into him, paying extra special attention to its source. His hand falls away to clench the sheets. "Hellfire—Dove!"

It feels good to me, too. Surprisingly so since I'm not the one being touched. But with his cock in my hand as I straddle his legs...I feel like a woman of the world now. Or at least more like one. My center is throbbing, and I think I'm making a wet spot on him. But I can't think about that now.

Not with his heavy cock in my hand.

For long minutes, he fights to hold back his release as I stroke up and down, the muscles in his arms clenching and showing their defined lines as he grips my thighs. "Harder." Sweat forms on his brow, but judging by the drawn-out groan, it doesn't seem to hurt too much. On the contrary.

It's affecting me, too. Hearing his sounds of pleasure and seeing him splayed out beneath me, hard length tunneling through my hand, makes me squeeze my legs together. The lower half of me burns with a maddening need, one that only my husband can sate. I shift my wet center over his bare thigh, the roughness of springy hair tantalizing my senses as instinct tells me to move.

Oh, that's...that's good.

Really good.

But I want to make him feel good like he does to me all the time, so I drag his hand to my mouth, gently kissing and licking along his palm before sucking on a finger.

"Dove..."

That sends him over the edge. Digit forgotten at Jedidiah's harsh groan, I watch in awe as sharp spasms contract his stomach and a fountain of white spews from his cock. So this is what it looks like. The first time it got all over my face doesn't really count because I had no idea what was happening then. It was sticky then, but is it always like that?

"Good God Almighty," he rasps out, watching through lowered eyes as I collect an errant drop from his tip and inspect it. A thin web forms between my fingers as I spread them.

Hmm. It's stretchy, too.

Interesting.

A warm hand grabs my wrist and slowly reels my finger into an even warmer mouth. My own mouth drops in shock. Is he...tasting himself? Or me? He hums around my flesh, lapping up the remnant. "Wife," he says in a low voice, "after waking me up like that, I'm thinking I need to repay the favor."

And with his only warning a rough, "Hold on," Jedidiah swiftly slides me up his slick stomach and over his face.

Oh no! Firstly, I'm coated in his spend, and secondly, how can he breathe if I'm covering his nose? I shift to the side, but he growls into my pussy and tightens his grip around me as his tongue does unspeakable things between my legs. Fiery heat bursts from my core and spreads across my body, erasing all thought and care except for this moment.

Delirium leaks into my head, making me dizzy. I need...I need to hold onto something or I'm going to fall. Pitching forward, my fingers grapple for purchase on the solid headboard, finding a nook in the swirls of the design.

Over and over, his tongue swirls around me, the sensation so intense that I lift up for relief. That doesn't make him happy, though. Tearing his mouth away from me, he latches onto the tender inside of my thigh and gives a warning bite that sends a trickle of wetness from my core and the faintest whimper from my lips.

"Wife," he growls against me before carefully removing his teeth, "sit still and let me have my turn." The throbbing of my thigh matches the beating of my heart as his mouth finds my pearl again, sucking this time instead of licking.

So good...

So good...

His arms are steel bands around me, refusing to give me any respite. Trapping me. His mouth taking from me.

Taking what's his.

What I freely give him.

When the edge of his teeth nips over the most sensitive part of me, I fall to pieces on top of him, dark spots dancing before my eyes and a harsh noise escaping my throat as I lose control of myself. Another sound drives from my throat as he flips us over and lays over me, pinning my hands above my head. "Say my name, Dove. Say it," he urges.

Still recovering from my intense release, I stare breathlessly at his amber gaze, mouth working back and forth on air.

"C'mon." One hand moves to encircle my neck as he fiercely watches my lips. "Just one time. Let me feel you try."

Jed.

Now my heart beats quickly for another reason. How can such a small word be so hard?

Jed. My mouth silently forms the word, but when my lips part, the sound won't leave. It refuses to. Because I'm still afraid.

Come on, mouth...speak. My tongue makes a quick pass as I try harder to get the first letter out, holding my breath until I feel the blood pounding in my temples.

Nothing.

A tear trickles down, landing in my ear. I want to say his name. I want to. But my throat still feels the phantom blades slicing into it. And suddenly, all the good feelings fade away as disappointment crushes me like sopping wet bed linens.

I can't say it.

I'm a failure.

Ashamed to look at him, I close my eyes, a river of tears running free as my lips wobble uselessly.

"Oh, darlin'."

Two words. Two simple words said with ease when I can't even say one. A harsh sob lifts my chest and comes out on a deep, guttural cry. I touch my throat in surprise and dismay at the ugly and raw sound but I can't stop it.

Lifting us up, he gathers me into his arms and rocks back and forth as my broken cries hit his chest. "Shh...I got you, Dove. It's okay now, I swear. It's just gonna take a little bit more time, that's all."

Slowly, my tears dry up as he murmurs reassurances into my hair, but I don't move. Just lean listlessly against him, my face rising and falling with his steady breathing. This morning didn't go how I'd planned for it to at all, but it's not his fault that I can't make myself talk. I'm the one who ruined things with my stupid throat that doesn't work right.

"Hey, I hear you thinking down there. Look at me." A callused finger lifts my chin. I'm sure I look quite a sight with a swollen nose and watery eyes, but all I see on my husband's face is concern. Concern for me. "I'm sorry, darlin'. Shouldn't have pushed you like that. I don't know what it is in here"—he kisses my temple—"that's holding you back, but I want you to remember two things, okay?"

Wiping my face with his shirt, I nod.

"Whatever that piece of shit father of yours did to you is in the past. I'm here now, and he's never gonna hurt you again. Ever," he vows fiercely as he traces over my scars.

"And I think your laugh and the sounds you make are beautiful."

He can't be serious.

"No, no, I really do," he firmly says when I shoot him a look of disbelief. "You have to remember that it's been thirteen years since you've used these muscles. Things are bound to be a little tight until they get used on the regular again. Does it sound a little rough now? Yeah, it does, but you could sound like an old howling polecat and it'd still be the most beautiful thing in the world to me because it's coming from you."

He tenderly brushes his lips over mine, letting me taste his soft, whispered words. "You've been silent for too long, little Dove. Far too long. I wanna hear you calling my name when we're in bed together. Hear you singing sweet lullabies to our babes when we put them to bed and hear you reading to me. And it'll happen. When you're ready here"—he gently taps my head before sliding a big hand over my chest—"and here, it'll happen. And that's gonna be the best day of my life, darlin', when I hear your sweet voice."

The picture he paints for me seems so real. I can see him over me in bed, smiling in dark satisfaction as I chant his name. And as for the rest? I want that so desperately. To sing to my wee babe and to read to my husband.

"And I'm gonna be the first one to hear it, aren't I? You're not gonna be laughing at one of Warren's jokes and decide to tell him how funny he is, right?"

A barking laugh sneaks out at the thought and I smile tearily at him. If I ever manage to speak, I can't imagine it happening in front of anyone other than my husband.

He rubs my back and gives me a soft kiss. "That's what I thought, darlin'. Tell you what. Let's get dressed and eat something and then we'll go riding, okay? Maybe even go into town."

After he helps me off the bed, I go to the vanity and pull the drawer. It's my brush I was looking for, but it's my mother's diary that makes me pause. I know the names of the first four letters now, but I still don't know enough to read it comfortably, let alone what's inside.

A warm kiss presses to my neck as Jedidiah walks up behind me. Lifting my eyes, I meet his in the mirror. "Was that your momma's?" When I answer *yes*, his smile lights up. "Want me to read it and see if your name's inside?"

No. No, I don't. I want to be the first one to lay my eyes on her last words even more than I want Jed to know my name. Hesitantly, I shake my head, hoping he'll understand, but I see the flash of hurt that crosses his face before he masks it with a cough and a quick smile.

Oh, no! Remorse twists my heart because the last thing I want to do is hurt the man who saved me.

The man I'm beginning to love.

I turn and reach for his hand, gesturing wildly between the diary and me.

"It's yours? I already know that, darlin'." At his confused tone, I realize I'm not making sense.

Calm down, Dove. One deep breath, then release. And again. Making sure I have his attention, I hold up one finger before pointing to the book and then me.

"You first?" he guesses.

Yes! He's getting it. Then I point to the book again and circle two fingers between him and me.

"Then..." His voice trails off as he tries to understand. "Then you want the both of us to read it?" I give him a tiny smile, relieved when his face softens in return. "All right, darlin'. That's what we'll do."

———

It's not far to town by wagon, and when we arrive at Hope's Stand, I realize just how small Springwell is. My mouth drops at the tall buildings, crowds of people, and more horses and wagons than I'd ever seen at one time back home. To my right are at least five different stagecoaches, and the horn of a train sounds in the distance.

Jed smiles at my look of awe. "Just you wait until Hope's Stand has its annual fair in a few weeks. A traveling show comes to town with all kinds of animals you never would think were real until you see them. Horses and people everywhere—even more than this—and the best eating and games you could ever experience."

His smile changes to a frown when we come upon a small wooden building with a line of people waiting outside and even some on the porch, leaning against the columns for support. "Make sure you stay far away from there, wife. That's for indentured folk, and the men running the place aren't always the most honest. Innocents have been known to be snatched up and forced into labor."

Ranging from children to older folks, the people wait despondently outside with a small pile of belongings. Shivering, I hug Jedidiah's arm to me, the heavy air of despair suddenly all too familiar.

Pulling up to what must be the general store, Jed helps me down. "All right, wife. Let's go shopping." Inside the store that is at least three to four times the size of Springwell's—and cleaner, too, since there are no cracks in the floor—he leads me to the ladies' section.

More specifically, to the undergarments.

"What do you think?" Two long arms reach around both sides of me as he lifts a frilly white nightgown. I run a hand wistfully over the line of satiny bows on the front. It's pretty, no doubt about it, but I can't let him spend his money on me like this. Not when I have my nightgown from home—not that he lets me wear it, of course—and his shirts. Shaking my head, I gently push it away. He won't let me, though.

"Now look here," he starts sternly, "you should know by now that I love you sleeping in only my shirt or nothing at all"—jumping juniper trees...did anyone hear him?—"but every woman deserves some finery. Especially my wife. And we're not leaving here without at least three nightgowns. And shoes, too, but we'll have to get those ordered. And maybe some hats," he adds on with a frown. "You like hats, little Dove?"

Then without giving me a chance to answer, he grabs two more nightgowns and pulls me behind him to the rack of hats with feathers sticking out every which way. "Which one you like best?"

Oh, my. I look over the bizarre display, puzzlement filling me at some of the offerings. I can't imagine why any woman would want to wear an entire bird on her head.

"Well, how do you do, Mr. Shay? Been a while since you been home, hasn't it?" A short, aproned man steps around a counter to shake Jed's hand.

"Sure has, Mr. Howell, but now I'm home to stay."

As if waiting for permission, the man glances to my husband before acknowledging me. "And who might this be?"

"This here's my wife." Jed lightly hugs me closer.

Mr. Howell dips his head in greeting. "Pleasure to meet you, ma'am. Now Mr. Shay, how's the weather been where you were traveling?"

With both men occupied as they catch up, I sneak the nightgowns from Jedidiah's slack grip, intent on putting them back. Silently promising that I'll return shortly, I back away and ease over to the undergarments section again. They really are pretty, but I don't have a need for them, and I really don't like the thought of him spending more money on me.

"Don't like 'em?"

I jerk around and flutter a hand to my chest, the rough, masculine voice startling me. It's not my husband, though. This man is about his age, though, with a full layer of grime piled on his clothes, and the air he puts off reminds me of the men in Springwell with their wandering eyes and hands.

He stumbles closer, either not noting my wariness or ignoring it. "Them night things shore is pretty. Not as pretty as you, though. You uh...you got a man?" His breath wafts into my nose, and I turn even more wary.

He's drunk.

Frozen, I dart my eyes to where Jedidiah was but he's not there any longer. Dread pools in my stomach. Did he leave me? No, no he wouldn't have done that. I know better than that.

"Hey, lady, I'm talking to you. You got a problem talking to a man like me?" My gaze flies back to his red eyes and takes in his squared up shoulders. "Must think my hands are too dirty for the likes of you, don'tcha?"

My husband's name trapped in my throat, I ease away from the promise of trouble in front of me only to be stopped by familiar heavy hands on my waist.

Jedidiah.

"Clean or not, your hands have no business on my wife," he coolly states while I almost choke at my sudden relief. "And I definitely have a problem with her talking to you. Did he touch you?" My husband directs the question to me while staring the other man down, but he must see me shake my head in reply.

"Good. Let's go, wife." Grabbing a handful of nightgowns, he tucks me into his side and walks back to the counter, not giving the man behind us a second look. Is he mad at me because I left his side? Anxiety sits heavily in my stomach. I didn't mean for any of that to happen. If only I could have called out for him—

Pulling me into a small corner out of the way, he cups my cheeks, delayed worry darkening his gaze. "You all right?"

I should have known he wasn't going to blame me for that because that's not how he is. He's shown me this time after time. At my cautious nod, his lips tighten with wry humor. "I swear, Dove. I'm gonna have to keep you tied to my side so I don't lose you, aren't I?"

I can't deny the benefit of that.

14

JEDIDIAH

Day by day and week by week, my little Dove blossoms with confidence, both in her learning and in herself. Looking over the line of letters she wrote just now, my heart pinches remembering when she tried to write my name. That one wrong damn letter and the shy hope on her face made me want to hunt that son of a bitch Crowley down and let him have a turn underneath *my* knife. He wouldn't be living long enough to try to speak.

The sound of shifting feet tears my thoughts away from that cocksucking bastard—for now, at least—and I turn to look at my wife. Her antsy gaze dips down to the paper in my hand, asking me with her eyes what her mouth doesn't say.

"These are perfect," I answer as I drop her work to the small writing desk. "Absolutely perfect. Your handwriting's getting so pretty, darlin'." Her letters are crooked, shaky, and occasionally backwards, but it's the most beautiful sight in the world to me. Next to seeing the muted pride bloom on her face at my compliment, that is. Unable to help myself, I swing her around in a bear hug, grinning to myself at the little squeak that flies out of her. Slowly but surely, she's getting used to making more noises. I'm dying for the day I hear her say more, but I'll be patient.

I'll have to be.

"How about we go take a ride so Sadie can stretch her legs out?" Sliding my hands down to her backside, I squeeze and slyly add on, "And don't worry. If you get sore this time, you know I'm more than happy to rub some salve on your hindquarters."

I kiss away the little scowl my wife gives, but I love it because it means she feels comfortable enough with me to express anything other than strict obedience.

Settle down, Jed. Quit thinking about him.

Fifteen minutes later and we're riding bareback on Sadie, the sun warming our backs as I head to a place I haven't shown my wife before. Between her lessons and keeping her in bed, there just hasn't been time. And as she settles back into me as we ride past the men working in the fields, I thank my lucky stars for the tradition of my family.

"You know what?" I muse over her head. "My ancestors sure had the right thinking when it comes to honeymoons."

Dove tilts back, soft hazel eyes looking at me in question from under her bonnet.

Flashing a toothy smile, I say, "I can't think of anything better for our first year of marriage than spending all of it with you. Learning each other in and outside of the marriage bed." Her face colors, making me chuckle. "Damn it, darlin', but that blush sure is pretty."

Naturally, that makes her cheeks darken even more. My innocent little wife is the best damn thing that's ever happened to me. When we miss the turn to go to town, she straightens and points a finger in that direction.

"Nope." I gesture to the woods in the distance, past the

grazing cattle and beyond the fence line. "I'm taking you somewhere special. A little place for just the two of us."

Curiosity brightens her gaze. I wonder if it'll be enough to make her speak, but it's not. It eats at her for the next little bit, though, evident in the way she leans forward in anticipation. It eats at me, too...the simple touch of my cock rubbing against her sweet bottom causing me to wince in pleasure. But I endure the torturous touches with a smile because seeing her like this makes me happy.

"Almost there, darlin. See that trail?" Clearing away the huskiness that roughens my words, I point to a worn path leading into the tall trees packed tightly together. "My pop used to send all us boys here to let our poor momma rest a spell. We'd play out here all the time, catching crickets and frogs and whatever else we could find. And if an old-fashioned dunkin' by older brothers counts, then I reckon all us boys've been baptized more than enough to make it into heaven."

Dove's raspy sound of amusement sends a soft smile to my lips. Her laugh has softened some, but even with its rougher edges, it's beautiful to me.

"Here we go, darlin'. Watch your head now." Approaching the dense foliage, I raise an arm up to shield her best I can. "It's thick here but it'll get better in just a bit."

Sadie snorts her displeasure at the sharp branches but steadfastly moves forward to the place she knows by heart. Gradually, the trees thin out some and a tiny log cabin situated in a field of blue wildflowers comes into view. But the sweet scent of the flowers and the earthy aroma of wet soil isn't the best part, though.

No, it's what's behind the cabin.

Easing to a halt, I dismount and give an affectionate pat to Sadie's chestnut coat. "Stay here, girl, and don't eat too many flowers. You know how they upset your stomach because they don't taste as good as they smell."

A nickering nip to my ass as I lower my wife down makes me jump, and I narrow my eyes at Dove's low giggle. "Think Sadie's funny for biting me, eh? Tell me something, darlin'—will you kiss it better if it bruises?"

Interpreting the pink blush coloring her cheeks as a yes, I interlock our hands. "We have a couple of cabins like this spread out over our land and stocked with supplies for when we're out hunting, but we don't hunt around this one. It's just for fun," I explain. As we round the cabin, I hear her breath hitch when she finally sees what I wanted to show her.

And what a sight it is.

I take it in, too, soaking in its beauty as if for the first time. Surrounding the rocky perimeter of the bank, a ring of tall trees stretches up to the sky. Along their fat trunks and branches, a family of fluffy-tailed squirrels chase each other while a chorus of perched birds scold them. And at the center of it all, an inviting clear pool of water waits for visitors.

"A spring," I offer up as we approach the gently-sloping bank. "One deep enough to dive in. I wish I'd taken you here before, but we'll come here more often, I promise you that. Now, off with those clothes, Mrs. Shay."

The double take she throws at me sends a slick grin across my lips. Clutching the buttons of her dress, she takes a step back in surprise.

"No one's gonna be looking at us, wife. It's just us here." No nosy little boys peeking through the bushes. But it doesn't hurt to be sure, so I surreptitiously give a sideways glance.

Just us.

Just as I thought.

Kicking my boots off, I counter her step backward with a forward one of my own as I untuck my blue plaid shirt. "Besides, how else are we gonna take a swim? Can't do it in our clothes because that'd be a miserable ride back home."

Rounded hazel eyes track my hands as I undo my buttons and casually spread my shirt. She loves my chest if the glazed look on her face is anything to go by, and I have no qualms in using that to my advantage. Hitching my hat back, I shrug my shirt off and toss it over a low branch before moving to the buttons of my pants.

Watching the stirrings of desire darken her cheeks, I undo the last button and hover over the flap, not separating it. "Aww..." I soothe at her crestfallen expression. "Don't look so disappointed. I know what you want, but you have to give me something first."

Two dainty feet step back.

Two bare feet follow.

A sly grin forms as we play this game of hunter and prey, and when her back finally meets a tree, I rest an arm on the rough bark and tug the ties of her bonnet loose. "Undress for me, darlin'. Show me what's mine and I'll show you what's yours."

Dove's breasts rise and fall in an unsteady rhythm when my finger leaves her chin and trails down to circle a button. One, two, three passes around the clasp, and then two feminine hands graze mine as they shakily undo the top collar button.

"That's my good little wife," I murmur thickly as the paleness of her small bosom is revealed. Good food and a steady diet have her hips filling out, but not so much has changed here on her chest except for her nipples turning a darker shade of brown. Odd, but not off-putting. I still think she's absolutely perfect. And when all the buttons are undone, two tiny motions send the dress into my waiting hands. "Now your shift."

With one more cautious glance around, Dove reluctantly shrugs off the thin material, curling her arms around her naked form as I lay her clothes atop mine.

"C'mon, darlin'. Let's go swimming." I snag her hand in mine but stop short at her rusty giggle that slips out. "What is it?"

A dark eyebrow arches as she raises a small foot with her new shoes attached.

Oh.

"Oops," I chuckle. Quickly remedying that, I reach for her again only for another giggle to leave her. "Now what?"

Her lips twitch as if she's forming words. Could this be the time I get to hear her sweet voice? My neutral expression belies the blood pounding into my fingertips and the jab of excitement that swells in my throat. But when she simply points to the hat still on my head, I force an easy smile and remind myself that she'll talk when she's ready.

Carelessly knocking my hat off behind me, I swing my wife into my arms to protect her soft soles from the rough rocks and wade into the cool, refreshing water. Deeper and deeper we go, until I'm treading water.

"You good to float?" I wait for her nod before carefully letting go of her. Good. Taking a deep breath, I dip below the surface to submerge myself. God Almighty, this coldness is some kind of refreshing. When my lungs scream for air, I resurface. "Dove?"

Where is she? A burst of alarm skitters through my veins when I look around and don't see her. If she's not above the water, then that means...

Good God, no.

I thought she could swim.

Just as I gulp an inhale and prepare to go under, the water parts behind me as my wife pops up. "Dove," I scold, "you—"

Even though she shaved about ten years off my life, I can't even scold her properly. Not with her dark hair all plastered to her head and especially not with her beaming smile that radiates pure happiness.

"You're it!" Lightly tagging her shoulder, I take off with a splash. "Come and get me, woman." Looking over my shoulder, I see determination settle onto her face as she chases after me.

We swim and swim and swim, taking turns catching each other until our legs give out, and then I drag her into a rocky recess and hold her from behind, content to just watch the thick clouds roll by.

"Huh." I kiss her bare shoulder and then point to the sky. "That one looks like a frog, doesn't it? You know, one time when Warren was about seven years old, all us boys were down here playing. It was my turn to keep an eye on him since he was the youngest and prone to finding trouble wherever he went. I did my best, but he was a sly son of a gun and sometimes I had to go looking for him. Like this time. Didn't take long, though, and I found him behind a bush with a big old toad in hand and lips puckered up for a kiss."

Dove tips her head back on my chest and laughs in disbelief.

"Oh, yes. Fool boy thought he could kiss a frog and find a princess." A peal of thunder interrupts us with a mighty clap and makes the both of us jump. I eye the skies warily. "Didn't look like there was rain in those clouds, but we'd best hurry home."

No sooner do the words leave my mouth than fat droplets pour down and bounce off the stream's surface. Thunder chasing after us, we quickly gather our clothes and dash into the small cabin. Water trickles down our bodies to puddle at our feet as I latch the door.

"I'll get a fire going while you spread our clothes out to dry." Keeping a ready supply of firewood at all of our cabins is just one of the ways we stock them. Of course, there's not much here beyond a rickety table and chair, a small fireplace, and a bit of dried food, but at least we're sheltered from the storm. Another clap of thunder rumbles angrily as I kneel and coax a fire to life. Sadie's not fond of storms, but she'll stick close by so I'm not too worried.

"There we go." Curling flames accompany the sharp scent of burning wood and its crackling warmth. Good thing, too, because the change in weather dropped the temperature a good ten degrees. Looking up, I see a folded blanket on the mantle. That'll be perfect for my little Dove to sit on as we dry ourselves and our clothes. "Look. I found a—"

My words fade away when I see her bare ass as she bends down to the floor. I don't even know what she's picking up. It doesn't even matter, because my eyes lock onto a bead of water that dances down the curve of her back and one cheek before disappearing between her legs as she lifts up again and lets her hair down in wet, cascading ringlets.

Good God Almighty.

With the rain noisily pelting the window, she doesn't even hear the low, lustful growl that stirs deep in my chest.

Doesn't see my cock thickening or the need that darkens my face.

Doesn't see me rise from the hearth and stalk her way.

Doesn't feel me behind her until it's too late.

I gather her wet body to mine before swallowing her surprise with a kiss that only serves to heighten my desire for her. Dove melts into me with a familiar ease, wrapping her arms and legs about me.

"I need you, and I need you now." The muttered words into her mouth don't even begin to describe the depths of my need for this woman. It doesn't matter that I emptied myself inside of her this morning. That was then, this is now, and I have an insatiable need for my wife.

My little Dove.

All mine.

Stumbling to the warmth of the fireplace, I blindly grab for the blanket and messily lay it down before I ease us onto it. "You're a damn goddess, wife," I rasp across her wet throat. "Luring me in with your beauty and making my cock drip with need. Open wider and let me in."

Soft thighs spread and sweet wetness coats my cock as my hips grind between her legs. I kiss all over her neck, her heavy breathing and hummed groan telling me she needs me, too. Dragging my teeth down her rain-kissed collarbone, I swallow her small breast and suck hard before carefully biting its sensitive tip. When she gives a broken groan of pleasure, I do the same to the other side and then lick my way back up to her mouth for a searing kiss that does more to warm us than the fire does. Lining my cock with her entrance, I push inside more forcefully than usual.

"There's a time and a place for loving relations between a man and his wife, but right here, right now," I growl over her stuttered gasp, "is for making you mine. You can take me a little harder, can't you, darlin'?"

Dove dreamily nods and hides her pretty hazel eyes from me. I don't like that. A rougher thrust makes them pop back open.

"Look at me." I shackle her hands above her head as I move within her tight warmth. "Good girl. You're mine, every goddamned inch of you, isn't that right? And you're going to watch me claim what's mine."

The force of my thrusts sends the tiniest of squeaks from her quiet throat as she pulls me even closer with her legs. Doesn't matter whether my head or my cock's between her thighs because they choke me just the same, and what bliss it is.

"I love you, woman, you know that? Love the way you take me so good and open yourself up to me. Love the way you smile at me. How smart you are. How you've learned to trust me." The love that I feel for her wells up inside of me, and with the glow of the fire fighting the overcast gloom of the rain, I give my wife more of my weight and say my vow to her as I bury myself deep inside of her. "You are my woman, and I am your man..."

Over and over, I repeat it to her, drilling it into her with my cock as much as my words as I maneuver her legs over each of my shoulders. "I love you, Dove, and you're going to be a good little wife and take my seed. Gonna let me make you pregnant and round with our child."

Heat sparks in her stormy hazel eyes and she licks her lips, framing them into silent words. What is she saying? Hips stalling, I move her wrists to one hand and slide the other down to rest on her throat. "I feel you talking to me, wife. Say it louder and let me hear you."

Thump, thump, tha-thump beats my heart as I wait for her voice.

But her lips press tighter, holding it in.

"No, Dove. You can't hold back with me anymore. I'm your husband, and there's no safer place than right here underneath me. Talk to me." I punctuate my command with a sudden thrust forward. "Give me your words. Every damn one of them for all the years you spent keeping them all inside. Come on, wife...start with one. Just one. I can stay inside you all goddamn day. And I will, if that's what it takes."

I see it in her eyes as she battles the ghosts of her past, but I also see a gleam of determination. Sweat beads on her forehead and I lick it away and steal a kiss from her slack lips. A puff of air hits me, along with the faintest vibration under the hand on her throat. Is she...? My temple pounds as I freeze, ears straining to hear her. "Louder, darlin'. Tell me again."

Dove's fingers grasp at the air, her face contorting as she fights to speak. When she does, it comes out in a halting whisper. *"Ch...ched."*

And suddenly I'm the speechless one.

She spoke. My quiet little wife just said her first word in thirteen years, and she said it to me. "Darlin'," I choke out in amazement.

A tear slips from her wonder-filled eyes as she tries again. *"Ched."* It's a little louder, but she clears her throat. "Ched."

"That's right, Dove." My eyes grow suspiciously wet when I realize she's saying my name. Not hers—mine. And even though the word is malformed, it's the sweetest goddamned sound in the world to me. I slowly press back inside her. "Again."

"Ched."

Thrust. "Again."

"Ched."

"Who do you belong to?" Possessiveness builds inside my chest with the need to hear her say it.

She works her hands free and cups my face. "Ched."

"Dove," I growl. I can't take it anymore, cock pounding wildly into her as I give in to the urge to claim her.

To rut her.

To breed her. "Again. Yeah, darlin', you belong to Jed. To your husband. Tell me again."

My name becomes a hoarse chant from her lips, and when she pulls my head down and breathes it in my ear, I'm done for. Blissful release seizes the both of us, refusing to let us go until we're a writhing mess on the blanket. Lifting up, I wipe sweaty strands of hair from her forehead and kiss away the salty tears streaming down her cheeks. "I love you. Love you so damn much."

"I..."—the small, simple word haltingly leaves in a raspy sob—"love you. You, too. Ched."

She's probably saying my name that way because of hearing herself speak only in her head all this time. But even if she never says it right, I won't care. It'll be my new one and I'll tell my folks to start calling me by it. "And I'm so proud of you, darlin'. So damn proud because you were so brave just now. And I want you to talk my ears plain off my head. But first"—I roll us to our sides and thread my legs between hers—"I want to know your name."

Dove runs slim fingers through my chest hair. "Re..." She stops to wet her lips. "Remembrance. Remem...brance Irons."

I repeat it in a daze, noting that she didn't claim Crowley's last name. "Remembrance Irons. Dove—I mean...Remembrance—that's so damn beautiful." And I never would have guessed it.

"Please," she begs in a choppy cadence, "call...Dove. I...you gave that...name. To me."

"Dove." I pull her to me and kiss her head, unable to process all the feelings running through me now. She wants the name I gave her. "All right, my little Dove. I don't want you to strain your voice, but I really, really want to know more about you."

And from the shelter of my arms, she tells me her story. The story of a small toddler with a loving Puritan mother who fell on hard times. The story of a cruel man who deserves the death I'm going to give him if he's still alive once I track him down. The story of a woman who's fallen in love with me.

By the time she's finished, her voice is all but gone. "Don't worry, Dove. You just need to rest your voice and drink lots of water. Thirteen years is a long time without saying a word." And I still can't believe it's happened. The empty silence has me glancing out the window. "Storm's stopped. Let's go home and get you into some fresh clothes."

After we're dressed in our still-damp clothes and shoes, I whistle for my horse, who, just as I'd expected, was nearby. Dove throws a longing glance to the cabin and the stream as I lift her up onto Sadie. *"I love...it here."*

My ears tune in on her fractured whisper as I look at where we just spent the last couple of hours. "Me, too. And we'll be back, because as special as this place was before, now it's even more—Dove?"

Alarm pulses through me as her lashes flutter and she lists to one side. *"Ched..."*

"What's wrong, Dove? Talk to me, darlin'." But she falls into my arms, unconscious, silent once again.

15

DOVE

"**N**o. Don't touch..."

Muffled voices travel in and out of my ears. Voices that I think I know. My husband and...Warren?

"*...examine...injuries...*"

No, not Warren. The voice is older than that. But who? Clarity slowly dawns as I fight my eyes open and see the fine threads on Jedidiah's gray cotton shirt. Wasn't he wearing a plaid shirt before?

Oh, right. We went swimming and got caught in the rain. Tracking my gaze slightly to the left, I see the tall oak poster of our bed. But when did we get back to the house, and why is Jed in bed with me? More importantly, why is there another man sitting in our bedroom chair?

"Dove." Relief palpable, Jed runs a heavy hand through his messy hair before caressing my cheek. "You're awake. How do you feel?"

Dragging my gaze from the older man dressed in black, I take a moment to assess myself. Other than a fuzzy head and sore throat, both probably from my wet hair and the rain, I feel fine. My mouth opens to tell him so, but the words never make it past my lips.

No! Icy dread rushes to my fingers and toes as I claw at my throat and stare at Jed in horror. I can feel the words there, just hovering in the back of my throat, but they won't come out. A tear leaks unbidden down my cheek. I can't go back to the way it was…not now that I've unburdened myself onto my husband.

"Sh-sh-sh…" Jed shushes at my silent crying. "It's okay, darlin', it's okay." He rocks me against his chest and barks at the man. "Why is this happening to her?"

The other man's placid expression never changes. "Now that she's awake, Mr. Shay, I need to examine her before I can offer up an opinion."

Jed tightens his arms before loosening them just the barest amount. "Mind where your hands wander, doctor."

A doctor. Did I hurt my head? I sniffle and feel along my head, confusion growing when my fingers touch my hair.

My dry hair.

Just how long was I unconscious for it to dry and for the doctor to have been sent for and still waiting on me to wake?

A rough hand clumsily pets my head and thumbs one last tear away. "Don't cry, Dove. Please. Everything's all right, I swear." If that's the case, he needs to do a better job at hiding his panic.

"Hello, Mrs. Shay." The older gentleman looks friendly enough as he approaches. "I'm Dr. Smith, and I'm just going to sit right here on the edge of—" At Jed's low growl that I'm not even sure he's aware of, the doctor falls back into the chair that he barely lifted himself from. "Fine, fine, Mr. Shay," he drolly states. "I'll just drag a chair up. Assuming that's alright with you?"

As he scoots closer, I grab a fistful of Jed's shirt and

burrow into his chest. I don't like having a strange man in our room even if my husband's wrapped all around me.

A pained sigh sounds and then a kiss falls on my head. "Darlin', we need to let the doctor see what's wrong. You were unconscious for too long and we need to find out why. I'm gonna be right here with you. Not gonna leave you, I swear. He'll make it fast, won't you, doctor?"

"Of course. As quickly as I can. Let me just take a listen to your heartbeat first." He rummages in his bag and produces an odd-looking contraption, looping it around his neck. "I'll, erm...just need to listen to her chest."

With two dark whiskey eyes tracking his every move, the doctor presses the black rubber piece between my breasts and concentrates for a moment before moving it to my back. "Heart and lungs sound clear. Let's just check your temperature."

Fever and other maladies are swiftly dismissed from the protection of my husband's arms. The doctor stares thoughtfully at the faint scars on my throat. "Have you been feeling well lately, and have you fainted within the last six months?"

Yes to the first and no to the second.

"Hmm. And you haven't spoken for thirteen years due to trauma, but spoke your first words only today. Is that correct?"

I lift up from Jed's chest and nod tentatively. He must have told him while I was sleeping.

"And it was just the two of you together when you spoke?" I blush and let Jed answer for me. Dr. Smith leans back in the chair and steeples his fingers together. "The mind is a fickle thing, Mr. and Mrs. Shay. I believe you're perfectly fine and healthy, and that the act of breaking your silence after so long is what shocked your mind and caused you to fall into a restorative sleep. The inside of your throat looks well enough, so with a bit of patience, rest, and fluids, I think you'll recover just fine. As for the fainting"—he looks over at my husband—"how long have you been married?"

"Three months and a few days." Pride drips from each husky word before another kiss lands on my head.

"Newlyweds," the doctor mutters with a knowing smile. "How I remember the days well myself. Forgive the delicate question, but when was your last menses, Mrs. Shay? Has it happened since you married?"

My monthly bleeding. No, it hasn't. Not since a good two weeks before I met Jed. I turn my head and meet his stunned gaze, even as hope stirs in my heart. With what he told me the first time we truly lay together, this means...a baby?

Dr. Smith chuckles. "With your permission, Mrs. Shay" —although meant for me, the words are directed to my overbearing husband—"there's one more examination I need to perform."

A muscle in Jed's tensed jawline twitches as a rumble builds in his chest.

———

"A BABY." MY HUSBAND WHISPERS IN AWE AS HE PALMS MY flat belly, just as he's done for the last ten minutes after the doctor left.

Yes, a baby.

Warm lips nuzzle my hairline. "I wonder when it happened. Our first night together, maybe? Or in the hayloft?"

At the memory of the kitten attacking his man-parts, a rusty laugh slips out of me, shocking the both of us.

"You see, darlin'? He was right. Your voice'll come back if you just relax and let it happen." His shoulders drop with relief as he reassures me. "Don't try so hard, okay?"

But I want to keep trying. Being able to voice my thoughts and feelings is more freeing than I knew it could be. Unable to stop myself, I lurch up and pull Jedidiah's mouth to mine, wanting—no, *needing*—to feel his closeness.

"Dove," he mutters into our kiss as he claims my mouth. This one is different.

Maybe because I've voiced my past to him.

Maybe because I've told him I love him.

Maybe because we're going to bring a baby into this world.

Or maybe it's all three.

With a soft pop, our lips separate. "You've got my baby inside of your belly, Dove. You're gonna make me a papa." The faintest sheen of tears brightens his eyes as he inches down my body, all the way down until his face is level with my stomach. "Hey there, little one."

Oh, be still, my heart.

"Don't worry, your momma and I won't call you that forever. We're gonna pick out a good name for you, like Ruth if you're a girl. Or maybe Rebecca." Jed kisses my stomach between names, grinning like a loon. "And if you're a boy, something like Russell. Or Ransom. What do you think, Dove?"

It doesn't escape my notice that all those names begin with an R. To match mine?

Oh, merciful heavens...I'm going to be a mother! Bitter-sweetness carves itself into a little hollow in my chest as I think about my own sweet mother who died much too young. Our situations hold a similarity even among the differences. Both basically forced into marriage, but to two very different men. My mother died a browbeaten woman with all hope snatched away from her, whereas hope, love, protection, and more have been poured on me even without my asking for it.

When I tried to run away from it.

And she'll never meet my husband or my children. Never know that even though Clarence Crowley tried to keep me silent, he didn't succeed. The unfairness of it all sends a broken sob tripping over the heavy knot in my throat.

"Hey, now...what's all this about?" Jed crawls back up and drags me into a hug. "Aren't you happy? Because this has made me the happiest man in the world."

I'm beyond happy. But sad, too, which is all too apparent as I hiccup through another sob.

"Oh, no. No, no, no, darlin'. Just...just hold tight." My forehead receives a swift kiss as Jed moves to the door. He's only gone a little bit, thundering down and then back up the stairs before climbing back in bed with pen and paper in hand. "Here. Just because your voice is worn out for now doesn't mean you can't talk. Talk to me, Dove. Draw it if you have to."

Wiping my face, I stare at the blurred paper and think of which words I can use to explain my feelings. Has to be ones I know how to spell or can get close enough. Pen to paper, I write. *"Muther."*

Jed watches over my shoulder like a hawk. I'm well aware that my handwriting isn't the perfection he says it is, but it's even shakier than usual because of the rush of emotions flooding me. A big warm hand palms my face, turning me until our eyes meet. "You're scared to be a mother?"

I freeze, heart pounding as my lungs stutter. Not until he mentioned it.

"Oh, darlin'...you're gonna be a good mother to our babies. We're gonna do this together. And my momma can help us—"

I can't help it. Pain streaks across my heart and onto my face.

"Oh...that's it, isn't it? You're missing your momma, aren't you? My sweet darlin'," he murmurs and tenderly kisses my forehead, "if I could bring her back for you, I would. But I can't. I'm here, though, me and my family. And they're all gonna love our babe and spoil him or her with whatever their heart desires. Just you wait until Warren finds out he's gonna be an uncle again."

That brings a watery smile to my face, imagining Warren taking my little one hunting for magical frogs. Pushing the pen and paper aside, I move into my husband's arms that wrap around me with no hesitation.

"I swear to you that everything's gonna be alright. You'll see."

Strong words that from anyone else would have me full of doubts, but if there's anyone who could make them come true, it's Jedidiah Shay.

16

DOVE

I stick my hand in the oven, gauging the temperature before placing a freshly assembled apple pie onto the rack. Perfect. A moderate heat. And we still have plenty of apples left over if I need to make another one. Closing the ornate door on the fanciest oven I've ever cooked in, I come back up and encounter a heavy presence at my back.

"Darlin'." The husky word ruffles my hair as two long arms wrap around me. "Should have told me it was ready for the oven so I could put it in there for you."

Eyes narrowing, I turn in his embrace. "I'm helpless, not expecting."

Oops. I mixed my words up.

And if there are too many words, sometimes I skip over them completely. I suppose that's what happens after speaking only in my head for so long. Jedidiah never makes me feel bad about it, and I love him all the more for that.

Dr. Smith was right. After being plied with fluids and rest for three days, my voice has slowly come back. The slight hoarseness with its raspy undertone isn't at all how I'd ever imagined my voice sounding, but my husband seems to love it. Along with being called Ched, too, although I try to correct myself when it happens.

"That you are." He walks backwards, taking me with him. "Pregnant with the first of our many, many children. And that means you have to let me take care of you."

Many children. No—many, *many* children. Just how many does he expect me to have? "You already care of me. Better than anyone."

"Because I love you." Ever so gently, he turns me until I feel the kitchen table at my legs. "Hop up."

"On the table? What about the apples?"

"What apples?" A slow smile is all he gives me as he settles me onto the edge. "Oh, my little inquisitive wife, I already moved them." His head dips towards the counter by the sink. "You have no idea how happy I am to hear your questions. You've already done your lessons today, I know, but I think we need to fit in one more while the pie's cooking. I'm gonna say a letter, and you tell me a word that starts with it. Ready?" The pad of his finger runs down the line of buttons on my dress. "B."

That's easy. "Button."

"No."

I frown. "Yes, it does."

"No."

"Yes," I argue, prepared to sound out the word for him. Button most definitely starts with a B.

"No." A kiss lands on the tip of my nose before traveling the length of my neck and stopping on my chest. His gaze locks onto mine. "Repeat after me: bosom."

Chills—good ones—spread over my arms as he mouths one breast, then the other. "Bosom," I whisper.

Jed smiles faintly. "Good girl. On to the next letter. N."

"Nose," I blurt out.

"Now, now...I think you know better than that." He softly tweaks my sensitive nipples. "Want to try again?"

I subtly lean into his touch. "N-nip. Nipples."

"Very good." Running his hands up my back, he urges me to lie backwards. With my legs hanging off the edge of the table and a red-blooded man between them, I have a feeling I know where this is going. Especially after three months of marriage.

Jedidiah plants his hands on either side of my head and takes my mouth in a slow, deliberate kiss, one that sends the familiar stirrings of desire through me. I run my fingers through his hair, a small moan working its way up my throat as I give in to him. "I'm not done yet, wife."

The moan stuck in my throat slips out as I feel a draft over my bare legs. When did he lift my dress up? "Ched, what are you..."

"God Almighty, but I love hearing you say my name that way," he growls as he kisses his way down my body. "C. That's the next letter."

C...C...C...

"Can't think of any?" Teeth nip along my thigh, forcing a gasp from me. "Be still. It would be a shame if you wiggled too much and made me bite this pretty little clit."

Teeth...there? I wouldn't want that. Or would I? "Clit," I choke out. "Clit."

"Very good, Dove. Very good," he says with a dark chuckle that makes my blood race. "Legs on my shoulders. There you go."

I whimper in excitement and dig my short nails into the cool wood of the table. My husband has gotten very good with his tongue since that first time, and even that felt amazing to me once we both learned where my clit was.

Spreading my lower lips, Jed blows a cool stream of air over the exposed parts of me. "Damn. I didn't know your lessons got you this needy, you naughty, naughty girl. Look at you, with your sweetness almost dripping on the table. Now, smother me with these thighs, wife."

His tongue licks a line up my wet center, making me spasm and thump my head against the table. "Ched," I groan, knowing I'm getting his name wrong but not even caring. Oh, sweet merciful heavens, my husband's mouth wipes all coherent thoughts from my mind except a fuzzy melody. Now I know what those two men in the saloon meant when they said I'd be singing like Madam Lulu's girls.

But...I'm not the one singing in a deep baritone.

And neither is Jedidiah.

The two of us freeze as the song drifts in through the kitchen window.

"Charlotte LaRue rode in on the gale,
Singing give me more of that Watkins ale.
Watkins ale, Watkins ale,
Give me more of that Watkins ale..."

With a muttered curse into my thigh, Jed hastily tugs my dress down. "Damn him. Singing a song not fit for delicate ears."

Warren.

Of course.

Who else would it be other than the man with an uncanny knack for interrupting his older brother at the most inopportune of times? And now that all of me is throbbing with unfulfilled desire, I almost echo Jed's sentiments.

"Why is it fit for delicate ears?" I ask, holding onto his strong shoulders as he lowers me to the floor. Not fit, I mean.

A pained smile flashes over his face. "Watkins ale is a man's spend."

Oh, goodness. Charlotte LaRue loves Watkins ale. Well...I'm coming to find it's not that bad, either.

Mid-verse, the singing stops. Is Warren coming up the porch? No, the deep murmuring of voices tells me he's talking to one of the ranch hands.

"Wait! Your face." He can't talk to his baby brother with my...my *wetness* glistening all over his lips and chin.

"Covered in you, is it?" He rubs his shirt sleeve over his face as he backs me against the wall. "Mhmm...I can still smell your sweetness, wife. But I need more than that to get me through this visit."

And before I can even ask what he means by that, his hand moves under my dress to sink two thick fingers into my core. "Ched," I squeak when his thumb brushes over my clit. "What you—?"

Then his fingers are gone, leaving an ache in their absence as he draws them up to his mouth and slowly licks away my essence. When every last trace of me is gone, he braces a hand on the wall behind me and leans down into my neck. "One more thing, darlin'. I'm gonna need you to adjust my pants just a little bit."

Shivering at the heat of his breath, I peek down at the obscene erection tenting the material. That's a lot of man in there, and his pants need more than just a little adjustment. Why, if Warren sees this, I can only imagine the teasing. And if three months of marriage with this man have taught me anything, it's that there's only one way to deal with his hardness—he needs release, and quickly, before his younger brother finishes talking.

And there's only one thing I know to do to accomplish this.

"Hellfire, Dove...what are you doing?"

There's a time for words, but this isn't one of them. I drop to my knees, ignoring Jed's hiss of surprise as I hurriedly unbutton his pants and pull his thick length out. Just as I said—that's a lot of man. Tucking away a dash of nervousness, I gently suck on his swollen tip.

"Dove, you—ahh." He staggers forward and catches himself on the wall behind me. Good. I must be doing this right, because now his hand is cradling the back of my neck.

Hand...hand...what to do with the one not wrapped around his heavy cock? I move my hand from his thigh to his ballsack. It's a unique texture under my fingers, one I'm going to explore again when we have more time. But for now, I palm it, matching the grip to the one in my other hand.

"Ahh, darlin'—" Jed's strangled voice makes me happy until he finishes his sentence. "Not so tight."

Oops.

I ease up and concentrate on making him feel good. I like when he licks me, so maybe he'll like it if I add my tongue?

He does. A slightly salty taste, one that's not too terribly unpleasant, fills my mouth. Watkin's ale, he called it. "Mhmm," Jed groans huskily. "We have to hurry. But it's so good, the way you fit my cock inside that sweet mouth."

Yes, so good. So good it makes my eyes close in bliss as I suckle him. The hitch in his breathing and the tenseness of his thighs tells me he's almost there.

"Oh, brother..." Warren calls out in a singsong voice as the doorknob rattles.

My heart stutters as my eyes fly to Jed's in horror. I thought he was still talking with the ranch hand. We're out of sight here in the kitchen, but I'm on my knees with my mouth stuffed full of my husband!

Time drags by, each second punctuated by the beating of my heart and Jed's ragged breaths. "Damn it all to hell," he mutters. "I was close. So close. We'll finish this later, wife. Soon as he goes back home."

No. I pop off, the both of us wincing as my teeth scrape over him. "Ignore him. Maybe he'll think outside. Door's locked." It's a wonderful plan. One that would have worked if not for his long, drawn-out moan when I take his bobbing cock back into my mouth.

Rat-a-tat-tat comes a knock at the door. "Dove? Anybody? Come on...don't leave me all by my lonesome out here. Jed?"

A foul curse leaves my husband's lips. "Just a s-second," he roars as his forehead hits the wall in an almost amusing way even with the heightened urgency. I take advantage of his weakness and hold him tightly, sealing my lips around his crown and writing his name with my tongue.

J-E-D.

That does it.

"Dove—" Jedidiah's knees buckle one beat before a hot warmth fills my mouth. I swallow every last bit of the bitter fluid like a good little wife and smack my lips up at him when I'm done. One brown eye slowly opens, then the other as he blinks down at me and struggles to catch his breath.

"So you liked it?"

"You damn vixen, you." A sleepy smile plays at his lips as he softly thumbs a stray drop of his release from my chin. "You know I did. And just you wait until I get you alone again."

Excitement for later has my heart thrumming like a butterfly as he helps me up. He liked it! My first time doing that to him and he liked it. By the time we make it to the door, we look somewhat presentable.

"Was that a bull bellowing in here or was that you, brother? And what's that red mark on your forehead? No, no...too late to rub it away. Dove must have been laying down the law on you." Warren leans against the door jamb with a smirk.

Jed lowers his hand and cuts a hard look his way. "Why are you busting up in on our honeymoon?"

"Because a whole year without seeing much of you makes me sad." He bats his eyes and clasps his hands under his chin. "You know you're my favorite brother."

"I am, huh? Even when I do this?" Jed hooks an arm around Warren's neck and drags him inside in a tangle of limbs and a fit of laughter. Is this what brothers do for fun? Wrestle each other? Arms and legs get tied up into knots, making it hard to tell which brother they belong to, but with a sudden movement, Jed pins Warren to the floor and roughly knuckles the side of his head. "Still your favorite brother?"

A small amount of amused horror fills me when I realize those fingers were just inside me moments ago. Oh, well. What Warren doesn't know won't hurt him, I suppose.

"Dove!" Warren calls out between breaths. "Don't let him do me this way. Come give him a kiss or something and make him stop!"

Jed pauses and tosses a knowing grin my way. "Yes, wife, come over here and give me a *kiss*."

Merciful heavens. Did he have to say it like that? I can feel every shade of red as it colors my face. "Ched..."

Head firmly caught in his brother's grasp, Warren's jaw is about the only thing that can move. Well, that and his eyebrows that just hiked up clear to his hairline. "What'd you just say?"

Oh, right. Only the two of us know. Or knew. Seeing the look of encouragement on my husband's face, I quietly and proudly say it again, tasting the remnant of his release on my tongue.

"Jed, she just said your name. She...you can talk! But—" he splutters, eyes darting between me and his brother.

"All right, all right. Enough staring." Jed stands and extends a hand to pull his brother up. The same hand that was—no, that was his other one. "Now, what was so damn important that you had to come see me right this minute?"

Warren's mouth is still ajar. "She can talk."

"Yes, Dove can talk now. It's nothing short of a miracle, but that doesn't mean you can pester her with your incessant questions." The mild tone does nothing to mask the firm command underneath. Then it softens as he tucks me under his arm and cups my chin. "Besides, I've been waiting a long time for her words. Stands to reason they should all be mine first."

Tears gather at the back of my eyes but I refuse to let them fall. Instead, I whisper my husband's name as his forehead dips to mine. "Ched..."

Everything fades away, leaving just the two of us in the room. Just a man and woman deeply and passionately in love with each other. It all hits me again, the wonder of how this man became mine.

"*Ahem.*" The not-so-discreet clearing of a throat makes me look to the right. "Oh, sorry. Did I interrupt? Do go on." Warren grins sheepishly.

I duck my head into Jed's chest, his rumbling voice tickling my cheek. "It'll keep. You never did say why you suddenly needed to see me right this very instant."

"I didn't, did I? Well, if you must know—" Warren stops to sniff at the air. "Pie. Pecan. Blueberry." He follows the scent into the kitchen, forcing us to follow. "Wait...that's all wrong. It's got to be apple. Is this your handiwork, sister? Because I know this big old bear couldn't make anything that smells as sweet as this. No, it could only come from a woman who—"

"Warren."

His words stop at Jedidiah's growl, but that sly smile stays on his face. "All right, all right." Snagging an apple from the counter, he collapses into a chair and throws his booted feet up onto the table.

Oh, sweet Lord.

The table I was just lying on with my dress rucked up. Is this what happens to all married folks? If we ever go visiting to any neighbors, I'll always be wondering if they've done naughty things on their own furniture. Surely they have.

"Feet," Jed booms.

Warren grumbles and drops his boots to the floor as he crunches into the dark red apple. "I was hoping to ride with the both of you on the way to the fair next week. Old Widow Hester wants me to escort her. You know I can't last a wagon ride with her!" Another bite. "She always wants to pinch my backside and tell me what a good-looking boy I've grown up to be. And then she'll say, 'Why, if I was forty years younger, I wager I'd be chasing you 'round the willow tree.' Forty?!" His voice raises in horror. "More like sixty! And not me chasing her, but her chasing me! You can't let her do this to me again, Jed. If I have to kiss her wrinkled up cheek while she pinches me one more time, I'm...I'm gonna die!"

Poor Warren, falling prey to the wiles of an elderly lady. A laugh trickles through my tight throat, causing the both of them to glance my way. "Sorry," I say with a shrug, speaking slowly to ensure I don't miss any words. "But what if she's your frog?"

"You told her," he deadpans over to Jed. "My own brother, telling all my secrets. Is nothing sacred anymore? Never mind, don't answer. On that note, I'm going to leave. Provided, of course, your answer is yes?" The chair creaks as he stands and, at the risk of losing his hand, rests the one not holding the apple on my shoulder. Goodness, he's almost as tall and broad as my husband. "Sister, I'm so very happy to hear your voice. It's very beautiful. Don't ever feel as if you have to hide it around us because we're your family now, okay?"

When I nod in gratitude, he adds on, "Now let me tell you a little secret about Jed."

Oh, this should be good. I dutifully lean in, only to falter in surprise as his lips peck my cheek.

"Warren!"

He rolls his eyes at his brother. "Oh, let the air out of it, Jed. Don't you ever get tired of saying my name like that? It's just a kiss on the cheek. Besides, I needed to make sure she wasn't my frog. You know, just in case."

Jedidiah tilts my head to the side and deliberately places his lips in the same spot. "Learn your lesson now, brother. She's my princess. Mine."

Something inside me melts just a little bit. I wouldn't want to be anyone else's.

17

JEDIDIAH

"Easy now, darlin', and up you go."

"Jedidiah," Dove protests even as she accepts my hand, "I do—can do—it myself."

Her speech has gotten so good. She misses the occasional word still but that's to be expected, as is her inability to speak for long periods of time. "I know you can. But you're in the family way now and not climbing up in the buggy all by yourself. Not while I'm here to help you—which is forever, just so you know. There you go, all nice and comfy, aren't you?"

It's actually not a buggy. It's a surrey. A real fancy black one, too, with cushiony red velvet seats and a fringed cover to keep our heads dry. The other wagon just won't cut it for my expectant wife. No, sirree. Not safe enough. Nor is riding on horseback. But Sadie and Lady like pulling the fancy surrey, I think, because they get an extra little dance in their step as if they want to show off.

I hitch a leg up and settle beside my wife. "You used my long name. Am I in trouble now?" Admittedly, I may do my fair share of egging it on simply to hear her throaty voice scolding me.

"No, you're not trouble." Her sigh tells me I came close, though. "But Warren will be unless he gets here soon. Why's he riding us—with us—again?"

I look past the fence line and see a speck on the horizon. "Because he's the baby of the family and usually gets what he wants. But if he says he's escorting you and me, Old Widow Hester will have to be satisfied riding with Momma and Pop. And"—I can't help my grimace—"because he's right. That old woman has the greediest, wandering hands. I swear I can still feel those bony pinches. Quit laughing at your poor husband!"

Dove's hidden smile spills from her pursed lips. "Does this mean you're un...un...touchable now that we're married?"

"Sure does."

I see the wheels turning in her mind. "So," she says slowly, satisfaction dripping from her raspy voice, "I saved you."

"That you did, Dove. And if Warren doesn't get his sorry hide here, neither of us is gonna save him."

She giggles a bit. "He needs get—to get—married so his wife can do that."

A short laugh leaves me. "Yeah, he does. Wonder if he's got his eyes set on anybody in particular or if he's been going around kissing frogs. Ah—there's the damn fella." Even his horse ambles along as lazily as its owner. Damndest thing.

I signal Sadie and Lady to move on out and head to the fence. After Warren sets his horse out to pasture, he climbs in the back seat, shifting the surrey with his weight. "Ahh, now this is more like it. Perfect place to stretch my legs out."

Muddy boots appear in the corner of my eye. No way. No *damn* way. "Put those damn feet back down or you'll be walking all the way to town. And wouldn't that just make Old Widow Hester's day when she comes upon you in the road. Yeah, and you'd get to sit in the backseat with her—"

A grumbling sigh, and then, "Fiiine. You've been driving too long and don't remember how painful it is to keep legs this long bent so they don't poke the seat in front of 'em."

My eyes roll so hard as I toss a look over my shoulder. "As opposed to knocking the ears off the people in that front seat? And a lady's, at that? C'mon, now. You and I both know Momma raised you better than that."

Warren just grins and props his chin on the front seat, effectively sitting between us even though he's in the back seat. "So, sister...you ready to see the fair? You've never been to one of these shindigs before, have you?"

My younger brother could charm the underthings off a girl. And who knows? Maybe he has. I know he got my woman's first smile.

She gave her first words to me, though.

All the way to town, he regales Dove with stories from his childhood, like the time he and a cousin hunkered down in a field to wait for freshly dropped cow pies to light on fire and how it exploded into their faces when they didn't scramble back soon enough. Momma wanted to tear their hides up but she figured being covered in cow shit was punishment enough.

On and on he goes, telling his tales and stealing away my time with my wife, along with her giggles. But I find I don't mind too much, especially when I feel her hand slipping into the crook of my elbow and giving me a little pat as he prattles on.

My sweet Remembrance.

My little Dove.

The crowd begins to build as we come up to town, horses and people milling about and—well, what do you know? My lips twist when I see who's two places ahead of us. "Warren, be sure and wave to Old Widow Hester when we pass."

"Damn it, Jed," he hisses as he ducks and hides. "Don't do me like that!"

I throw my head back in laughter, but it slowly dies off when we pull off to park the surrey and that damn building comes into view. The one where people's lives are signed away, both willingly and unwillingly. The latter is what sends a wave of unease rolling about in my stomach that even the drifting music from the live band can't dampen. There's not a line of people waiting outside of it at the moment, but there is a man leaning against one of the columns underneath the eaves. Other than his gray mustache, I can't see him too well with his hat dipped low, but he spells trouble just the same. Almost as if he's scoping the crowd.

I angle my shoulders to shield Dove from his view. Not a chance he's going to get my woman.

"Make sure you stay far away from that place, you hear?" My words are gruffer than I intend, but I just want to make sure she knows. Not that it matters that much since I plan on keeping her close to my side the entire time, but still.

Dove tangles her fingers with mine. "Okay," she whispers. "I will."

Relief at her quiet agreement eases the burning in my gut. Or maybe it's the soft kiss she presses to the back of my hand. "Now let me help you down so we can have some fun."

———

"Keep your fingers crossed, but we've been here round about an hour or so and still not run into any old grabby hands." Warren sounds rather proud of himself as he crams his mouth full of pie. He walks backwards and turns to the little woman between us. "Want some, Dove?"

"No, thank you," she states politely.

"You sure? It's blueberry." The pie looked better before he took a bite from it and made berries fall into his hand.

My arm flexes, pulling her closer to me. "You can tell him no with a little more force, you know. And as for you"— I widen my eyes dramatically—"you're about to walk right into an eager old lady's arms."

Warren spins around quicker than I can blink. "Where —why you little..." His words trail off when he doesn't see widow Hester. "Don't let him do me like that, Dove," he pouts as she laughs.

He's right, though. We've been here an hour and seen dancing bears walking on two legs, monkeys wearing clothes and performing tricks, and other animals that Dove had never heard of before.

We've also strolled from booth to booth and sampled their wares. Bought them, too. With much encouragement, I finally got Dove to pick out a silver pendant with an amber gemstone. *It matches your eyes,* she'd shyly informed me as I fastened it around her neck that she still hides with high collars. My cock kicked almost as hard as my heart pounded when she told me that.

Dove shivers, drawing my attention back to her. "You cold, darlin'?"

"Just little." Her thin arms cross over her chest.

"I forgot to have you bring a shawl or something." The

temperature isn't that bad to me, but I'm not a small, delicate woman either. "Oh, look—up ahead."

A booth with an assortment of scarves and shawls. Some mighty pretty ones, too, I see as we get a little closer.

"Lace for the lady?" the vendor calls out, eager for a customer. "Or perhaps a colorful shawl to match her lovely dress?"

At his sudden attention, Dove inches closer to me and says something too low for me to hear.

"Do what, darlin'?" With the way her eyes keep darting around to all the people, I think she's having trouble speaking. I lean my head to hers.

"Help me pick?" comes her soft question.

"Anything for you. And he's right." I nod in the vendor's direction. "Your dress is lovely." Even if he has no business saying so, but I don't add that last part. I drop a kiss on her nose, smiling at her slight blush. But she steals my breath away in her slim-fitting white dress with roses printed all over it. Add in her dark curls that won't stay pinned to her head, and she's just a vision of complete and utter beauty.

"All right, you two lovebirds." Warren's dry voice breaks through the moment. "Cut the smooching and get a shawl already. I saw a sign for the magic lantern show that's supposed to start soon down at the church house. The one last year was pretty fun, so this oughtta be good. We better hurry, though, 'cause it's the last one of the night. "

A few minutes later and my woman has a deep pink cashmere shawl to match both her dress and the blush in her cheeks when someone whistles at her. My eyebrows draw together in a glower. "Swear to God, Warren, I'd lay you out flat if I didn't know it was you and not some yahoo."

The fool just laughs over his shoulder. "Come on. Show's about to start any minute now."

Following the sign, we all duck into the church and let our eyes adjust to the dimness. There's a nice size gathering of people here, maybe about one hundred or so. I point to a pew that's only halfway full. "Looks like we still have a few minutes before it starts. Over there. And we're in church, Warren, so take your hat off."

Murmuring a polite *excuse us* to all the people we step in front of, we finally make it to the pew with Warren sitting on the end and Dove between us.

"Jed!" a small voice pipes up.

A small voice that sounds very familiar.

Baffled, I look down at the little pipsqueak to my right. "Abner?"

"Jed!" It's him, all right. Stowing away the pocketknife he was using to clean his dirty fingernails, the boy beams up at me, showing two empty spots in his mouth. "Look. I lost some teeth," he whistles out with a lisp.

"That you did, boy. That you did. Where's your parents?" The white-haired couple on the other side of him are most definitely not his parents.

Abner proceeds to explain, spraying spit on me through the gap. "They wanted to go to this other exhibition. One about lec..elicitry, I think it is. Only I didn't want to, so they let me come here instead."

Makes sense. Electricity hasn't made it to all these small towns yet so all the folks from there are mighty curious about it.

Abner peeks around me, mouth dropping open. "Girl! I...I mean...what's her new name again?"

"I could tell you," I say with a smile, "but why don't you ask her yourself?"

He scoffs at me. "You lost your damn mind? She can't tell me nothing. She don't speak."

"Abner! You're in...in a church!" Dove scolds in a quiet whisper as the older couple stare at him with disdain.

I offer them a shrug of apology. "Not my kid."

Abner's little jaw near about falls to the floor as he gapes at my wife. "When'd you learn how to talk?"

"Ladies and gentlemen, boys and girls," a well-dressed thin man with a booming voice interrupts as he walks across the pulpit, "welcome to the magic lantern show! I'm Bailey Boothe, and we've got lots of fun and entertainment for you this evening, and for our first segment, The Ratcatcher"—he pauses dramatically—"I'm going to need your help. Can you help me?"

"Welp, I reckon so," Abner drawls with a sigh as the crowd hesitantly offers up agreement. I hold back a laugh and realize how much I've missed this damn kid. Having him and Warren in the same room highlights just how much they're alike.

The piano plays softly as Boothe asks the audience to make snoring sounds. "There you go! Now, we'll play a movie through our magical lantern, and all you have to do is snore when the man's mouth opens." At that, a large, colorful image of a sleeping man in bed projects onto the wall behind him as the audience gasps. But it doesn't stay still like a picture. No, the man's mouth opens and closes as he snores.

"Jed," Dove whispers in awe as she grabs my arm. That's right. She's probably never seen anything like this before. Well, she's in for a real treat.

"Here's where I need your help, ladies and gents," Boothe interjects as the piano player plays a lullaby. "Snore away."

Snoring and giggles fill the church, all in time with the opening and closing of the man's mouth. Suddenly, the mellow music turns suspenseful as the pianist rolls the lower keys like thunder and a black rat appears onto the bed of the sleeping man. Dove jumps in surprise as a scream or two from a child mixes with another gasp from the crowd. I chuckle lightly and adjust my arm to hug her to me.

The rat disappears and the piano plays a lullaby again, all while the oblivious man remains asleep.

Suspenseful music signals the return of the rat, eliciting another cry of surprise as it creeps over the bed. Something feels like it's creeping over me, too. Something—or someone —behind my back. I casually turn and look around, not noticing anyone in particular that would make my back tingle like that.

Hmm. Must be the music and the darkness of the room getting to me. Subconsciously, my fingers rub over my knife and the butt of my gun, just in case.

The pianist repeats the cycle again and again with the rat getting closer and closer to the sleeping man's face, until finally, much to the shock of everyone, it darts into the man's open mouth.

The audience—including my wife and Abner—roars in laughter and disgust for at least twenty seconds before the picture transitions again and the show continues to the next segment. Dove rests a hand on my neck to tug my head down. "Thank you bringing me here."

"Oh, darlin', you're more than welcome." I brush her mouth with mine because if Abner can cuss in church, then a harmless little old kiss isn't gonna hurt anything. I don't watch much of the rest of the show. No, my thoughts are on my wife and my unborn babe. No one knows yet, not even my parents.

Not even Warren.

We've been walking around this whole time with an extra little person and no one the wiser.

I kinda like it.

"Hey, Jed." Abner tugs at my sleeve. "You gonna get up? Show's over now."

Judging by the people exiting the pews and moving to the doors as Boothe packs up his equipment, it sure is. I flip my hat back up. "I reckon so. You need to find your parents yet?"

His face scrunches up. "Nah, not yet."

"Then you stick close to us. Okay?"

"Okay," he agrees eagerly. Good. Boy can get himself in a heap of trouble by wandering around.

Outside, Abner stops abruptly and turns in a full circle. "Would you look at that? Looks like the damn stars are all fallin' from the sky and landing here."

Warren snickers at him as I shake my head. No use correcting him. But I know why he's amazed. It's not completely dark yet, but just enough for Hope's Stand to show off its electric lights strung all over town just for this. The unidentifiable yet delicious aroma of hot food from the vendor at the corner wafts through the air, making us all groan.

"You hungry, Dove?" I ask.

"Ah! That's her name!" Abner hoots with a slap to his knee like an old man. "Dove. I knew that, Jed. Just forgot."

Sure he did.

"Oh," Dove says with a shiver as she folds her arms together. "My shawl. Forgot it."

"I'll go with you—"

"I'll go with her, Jed." Abner puffs his chest out. "I'm a tough man, and I'll keep her safe while you go over there and buy her some food."

"You promise?" I arch a brow at him. "That's my woman I'm entrusting into your care. And she means more to me than Sadie does."

Abner's eyes widen comically. "She does?"

"She does." I nod solemnly with a wink at my wife.

"I'll take good care of her. Promise. Cross my heart and hope to die." In dramatic fashion, he makes an X over his chest and then turns to Dove. "Hold my arm real tight, okay, Girl? I mean, Dove."

"Straight there and straight back," I say with sternness.

"You got it, Jed."

I keep my eyes on them as they move to the church and disappear behind the doors. "Go after them," I order Warren. I don't want to hurt Abner's pride, but Dove's got my babe inside her belly. "Stay hidden if you can."

My brother's teeth flash in a quick smile. "I knew you were gonna say that. At least this means you're paying for the food, right?" he asks as he jogs backwards. "Be right back."

"Hurry up. Fireworks should be starting soon and I want her to be able to see them." I shake my head and follow the smell. Judging by the long line, the food's worth the wait. As my turn gets closer and none of them are back, a little bit of worry creeps up. I nudge it away, though. They're in a church. What could happen?

Ten minutes later, I've got three bags of pastries and meat pies and no one to help carry it. "Where the hell are they?" I mutter to myself, eyes glued to the church doors. It shouldn't be taking them this long just to grab a shawl and come right out. If Abner or Warren dragged my wife to some other exhibition and left me here with all this food, I'm gonna whoop both their hides.

Just as I'm about to put everything down and go looking for them, Warren staggers out from the church.

Alone.

And rubbing his head.

When he looks up and sees me, he runs crookedly in my direction, calling my name.

What the hell's the matter with him?

"Jed." His broken words come through winded breaths as he holds one hand to his ribs and the other to his head. "Men...took kid and Dove. Gone."

No.

My fingers lose their strength, dropping everything to the ground as ice stabs at my heart. "Dove."

Warren shakes his head and follows behind me as I storm back to the church. "Dove!" I roar like an enraged beast, throwing open the doors. "Abner!"

But it's empty. Not a soul in sight in the pulpit nor pew. I whirl around to Warren and see him collapsed in a seat. "What happened?" I don't mean to snarl at my brother, but this can't be good.

"Had 'em in my sights," he groans painfully, "and then someone walloped me a good one upside the head and then kicked me in the ribs. Musta blacked out for minute or two, 'cause when I opened my eyes again, I was sprawled out on the floor and couldn't see neither one of them."

I pace back and forth, blood whooshing in my ear. Just need to keep a cool head and think. That feeling I had earlier doing the show...as if someone were watching me. Maybe they weren't watching me.

Maybe they were watching Dove.

Maybe...

It hits Warren the same time as it does me. His face pales ten shades lighter and he audibly swallows. "We...we gotta go, Jed," he says with a pant as he scrambles out of the pew. "Now."

I don't know how he does it with a possible head injury and bruised ribs, but he keeps pace with me as I tear through the town, all manners cast aside as I shove through the crowd with only one thought in mind.

Forced indenture.

The closer we get to the wooden building on the edge of town, the stronger the sour tang of fear taints my tongue. Not fear for me, but for my woman and an innocent kid. With people milling about and a live band and screams of delight to cover any sounds of dismay, this was the opportune time for them to be snatched up.

Up the three porch steps I go, eyes fixed on the man I see digging through a desk through the small window. The door's locked, though, when my hand rattles it.

No matter. Renewed anger lends me strength as I kick the door in. Drawing my gun, I aim it at the sleazy man. "No, no, don't get up. In fact, have a seat." My easy tone contradicts my hard expression.

Hovering over his chair, he falls back in it with a plop, the drawer beside him half open, eyes locked on the barrel pointed his way. "We're closed. Gonna have to come back tomorrow when we open."

"You're closed, are you?" Leaning over the desk, I trace the barrel of my gun around his collar and over his throat, stopping when it presses under his chin. "You been closed all day? Think real hard before you answer me," I threaten when his gray mustached mouth wiggles.

Fingers clenching the arms of his chair, he licks his lips and swallows nervously. "Well, w-we might've been open for just a little bit. Just a moment."

"Jed..." Warren points to the open drawer.

No. Is that—? I dig the gun deeper into his jowls. "Don't move. Grab it, Warren." The delicate fabric snags on the wooden drawer as he pulls out a shawl.

A deep pink cashmere shawl.

Keeping an eye on the snake in front of me, I bring it to my nose and sniff deeply, inhaling her scent. She was here.

Something falls from it and lands on the desk.

The pendant I bought her.

The one that I lovingly placed around the hidden scars on her neck.

And its clasp is broken.

The devil himself takes over me as I lower the barrel and shoot the man in the thigh, both the sharp blast and his pained howl blending with the celebratory fireworks outside. "Where are they?"

18

DOVE

"Can't believe you can talk now, Girl. I mean, Dove."

I give Abner's thin arm a squeeze as he escorts me up the church steps. "Me either," I say slowly. "It's because of Jed."

Abner stops and looks up at me, a gleam in his eye so wise for someone so young. "He's a good'un, ain't he?"

"He is." So very good that my stomach flutters just thinking about him. "The very best."

"You know, your pappy ain't been in town since you left. Ain't seen hide nor hair of him. Pa said he sold the house to pay back the Dooleys. 'Course, no one's complainin', and 'specially not nobody at the saloon. Oh, lemme get that door. It's too heavy for you and Jed would wring my damn neck in half if I let you do it." Digging his heels in, Abner grunts and yanks on the door and props it open with a stone.

"Thank you, Abner." Putting all thoughts of my father behind me, I step inside. With candles extinguished and only a bit of light coming through the windows, the church is empty and dark, almost as if it hadn't held a crowd of people inside just a few short minutes ago. I shiver again, but I don't think it's from the cold. I've not been one to spook easily before, but this forces me to realize just how much Jedidiah makes me feel safe and protected. I spy my pink shawl and swiftly step to grab it when the door falls closed, dimming what little bit of light we had to begin with.

"What the hell...?" Abner nervously throws his hand around for mine. "Let's go, Dove. Don't like stirring up no spirits in a church."

We both jump when a rough voice sounds from the shadows. "You're not going nowhere."

The door briefly opens again, letting in blessed light, the sounds of the fair, and—oh, thank heavens—Warren. "Found it yet, Dove?"

Unfortunately, it also illuminates the gun in the hand of the man now in front of me, its barrel pointing directly at my belly. My hand clutches the back of a pew for support. There's a gun. I'm pregnant. And my throat suddenly refuses to work.

But Abner doesn't have the same problem. "Help! Get Jed!" he yells as he kicks the man in the leg.

"Why, you little..." The man scowls and backhands the boy with his gun, sending him crumpling to the floor. A similar sound comes from the door. Is it Warren...or Jed? Hope and fear war in my heart.

Then the darkness swallows us all up again as the door falls shut. As my eyes adjust, another man with a bushy gray mustache walks down the aisle, and with every step of his boots against the wooden floor, my stomach sinks in despair. "Took care of that one. Now let's get 'em goin'."

"But Joe, what about the kid?" The man who back-handed Abner gestures to his limp form. Oh my goodness...is that the man from the general store that got upset when I wouldn't talk to him?

"Hell, we'll toss him in with her." Joe draws his gun and aims it at me. "I know we'll get a good penny or two for this purty little thing, even with her small tits." His greedy eyes move up my chest and stop on the pendant Jedidiah bought me. "Oh, now what's this?" The gun at my stomach slides up and hooks beneath the chain. "Take it off."

A tiny whimper scratches at my dry throat. Where's Jed? I just want my husband.

"Now," he growls, pulling on the chain. My shaky fingers try to manipulate the clasp, but fear makes them useless. "Goddamn it, woman." A sharp pain pinches my neck as Joe forcefully rips it from me. "You won't be needing this where you're going, but I do have a little something for you." With the gun so close to me, I don't fight him as he forces a foul-tasting gag into my mouth. "Now let's go meet your new owner."

The end of the gun presses against my collarbone when he swings me around and drags me to his front, and through the shock and fear clouding my head, I realize what he said.

My new owner.

Oh, sweet Lord.

We're being sold.

———

ABNER LIES UNCONSCIOUS NEXT TO ME AS THE WAGON bounces over the road and takes us further away from Hope's Stand.

Further away from Jedidiah.

All while the daylight fades away into an orange sunset.

In no time at all, I was shuffled at gunpoint through the

abandoned alleyways and behind the one building Jed told me twice to stay away from. My throat had completely locked up, but even if I could have screamed loud enough, it wouldn't have made a difference. Not with the swelling music and the constant chatter of all the people. And the gag, of course.

I'd dragged my feet as subtly as I could, knowing Jed would come after us once he realized we were missing, but Abner and I were both tied up and tossed into a covered wagon filled with boxes. And without our supposed new owner setting eyes on his newest acquisitions, the wagon took off, headed for God knows where.

As I lift my bound hands and work the putrid gag from my mouth, a sudden bump jars me and my head smacks into the side of a box. Pain stabs both my heart and my head and I glare at the tightly-drawn fabric that hides the driver from view. My head will be fine, I think, but—Warren! Oh, God help him, I don't even know if Warren's alive. There's no way he would have let us be taken if he could have helped it. A salty tear of despair drips and lands in my mouth at the unfairness of the situation. Why didn't I fight? Why didn't I scream? Why didn't I do anything instead of just standing there like a shaking simpleton?

I know why. I couldn't risk being shot and endangering my baby, and I suppose part of me was just waiting for Jedidiah to charge in and save me like he did in Springwell.

He's not here, though.

And it's not just me and Abner in this wagon. Over on the opposite side, there's a girl with her hands tied in front of her just like me. Her black hair's all mussed and her brown dress is torn in places and hanging off her shoulder, but it's the lack of emotion on her face that scares me and reminds me of myself. I recognize a hurt like that, one that makes you burrow into yourself. Then she shifts, and I see her front more clearly.

She's pregnant. Heavily so. And she doesn't have a gag.

"What?" she snaps. "Haven't you ever seen a pregnant half-breed before?"

My eyes fly to hers. "I'm...sorry," I manage to say. I didn't see the color of her skin, but now that she mentioned it, I take note of her light brown complexion that contrasts with her icy blue eyes. She has no accent, though. "Do you know we're going? Where we're going?"

A hard, jaded smile stretches her chapped lips. "Does it matter? We've been bought by a man. Don't worry, though. All men's hands and cocks are the same after a while. You learn to take what they give you and be grateful you're still alive. Day in and day out, everything the same. Until one of them gives you a baby and makes you wish for death." At odds with her words, she cradles her belly and hums a broken melody.

My baby. I move my tied hands over my still-flat belly. "I'm Dove. What...what's your name?"

She lazily turns her head to the slits of the canvas where I can just make out the silhouette of the driver. Looks like it's just one man. "It depends on what my new owner wants to call me. I've had lots of names over the last four years, but the one given to me was Mara."

"Mara." The name is heavy on my tongue. "How old are you, Mara?"

"Seventeen. I was broken in young, passed around to whoever paid the most."

Seventeen. Just a year younger than me. So she was only thirteen when... Oh, no. I swallow hard and look at her again. She looks at least five years older, maybe more. Imagining the horrors she's endured only strengthens my resolve.

"We've got out of here. To get...out." My whisper is harsh, but Mara just closes her eyes and ignores me. I don't think she'll be much help, especially as far along as she is, but I can't say that I blame her too much. Hopelessness is a heavy burden to bear alone.

I lean down and dig the gag from Abner's mouth. "Abner!" I hiss and poke him with my elbow. "Wake up." Head injuries can be deadly, and he's already been unconscious for far too long. "Wake up!"

"Dove?" His voice is all groggy as he comes to, blinking rapidly.

"Oh, praise be." I trip over my words in my relief. "Are you okay?"

"Just my head's pounding somethin' fierce." Another forceful bump pulls a moan from him. "And I'm thirsty. Not hungry anymore. It stinks in here." He sniffs the stale air, taking in our surroundings before stopping on Mara. "They...the bad men got us, didn't they?"

Panicking will do us no good. Jed will come for us, I know he will. I just hope we can hold on until he gets here. If he even knows where here is. *Stop it, Dove.* "They did, but we stay calm. Have to stay calm."

"Just tell him the truth. We've been sold and—"

"We stay calm." I interrupt Mara before she can frighten him to death.

But I think he already knows it can't be good. Poor Abner. His lower lip trembles as he squirms his little body closer to me. "I gotta tell you somethin', Dove. In case...well, just in case." Oh, my heart. A child his age shouldn't have to worry about what's going to happen once this wagon stops. I brush his sweaty hair back, shushing him, but big fat tears pool in his eyes as he begins to bare his soul to me. "One time...one time I snuck out the window after my momma put me to bed. I stayed out playin' all night long and lied to her when she asked me if I slept good."

"Oh, Abner, I'm sure—"

"And then one time, I stole a piece of candy when Mr. Howell wasn't looking." A quiet hiccup bubbles his voice when he pauses. "Actually, it was more like five pieces 'cause I stuffed 'em in my pants. I only got to eat two, though, 'cause Momma hadn't fixed the hole in my pocket yet and some fell out. And then—"

Mara rolls her eyes our way. "For the love of—"

"And then," Abner continues obliviously as I frown at her, "one time I left the barn door open and all the horses got out and I blamed my brother even though it was me. He's the one Pa whooped when it was me who done it."

"Listen me." The knotted fabric digs into my wrists as I cup his cheek. "It's okay, Abner. It's okay."

The poor child is utterly miserable and ashamed as he meets my eyes. "Got two more things, Dove. I...I'm sorry for all the times I spied on you down at the creek when you was bathin'. It was a lot. Almost every week, and sometimes twice a week. And for that time I brought Jed along with me. Didn't mean no harm by it, just wanted to show him how pretty you were. A-a-and I'm sorry I couldn't protect you"— he stops to rub his tears and God knows what else on my dress—"in the church. Do...do you forgive me?"

"I do, Abner. I do." Tears of my own begin to fall, but I sniff them back and stare at Mara's swollen stomach. Jed would want me to be strong, so that's what I've got to be. Strong for Abner, my baby, and even Mara. After knowing what it truly means to lay with a man—with the man I love —I can't imagine hands that aren't my husband's touching me. And I can still feel the way Joe's gun traced over me and between my breasts. A shiver of disgust wracks my frame.

No, I can't let this happen to any of us.

The wagon runs over another deep rut, and this time when my head hits the container next to me, the wooden box tumbles over, spilling its contents onto my leg. I grit my teeth in pain. Good Christ, I've never wanted to curse, but whatever landed on my leg sends a sharp, stabbing pain knifing through my entire body. I glare at the cast iron skillet that—merciful heavens!

Pain knifing...knifing...knifing...

Abner's pocketknife.

And the skillet!

An idea forms in my head. Perhaps a bad one, but an idea nonetheless. "Abner, your pocketknife! You still...have it?" Dear Lord, please let him still have it.

The boy sniffs. "Yeah. It's in my pocket."

"Cut me. Loose," I add when he looks at me strangely. "Here."

Understanding dawns on his face. "Lemme get it out...Momma sewed the hole up in these ones." With his hands tied together, he contorts and twists as he digs it out from his pocket that his blessed mother mended. "Got it!"

"Cut," I urge, casting a glance to the front of the wagon. Whoever this man is, I refuse to let him take me away from the one thing I ran to—hope.

Hope's Stand.

When Abner's fingers slip and the knife drags against my skin, I hold back my hiss of pain. "Hurry!" He awkwardly saws faster.

"Well, look at you. You've freed your hands, but now what?" Mara asks sharply, a gleam of interest belying her tone. "It's only going to be a harsher punishment for you when we stop."

"No," I rasp. "We're turning around. Not going with

him." Under the weight of her disapproving gaze, I cut Abner free, too, and then almost tumble back with the force of his hug. "It's okay. Just a little bit longer." Then I look at Mara. "What about you? Your choice."

Long, tense seconds pass with only the fast-paced clip-clop of hooves and an occasional belch from the driver as I wait for her decision. "Fine." She huffs and stretches out her hands. "What are you going to do?" she asks as the knife works back and forth.

"Hit him in the head. Skillet," I calmly tell her with a nod to the cooking pan. "He falls off...we go back."

"Are you crazy? That will never work!"

"My husband is there. My baby's here." I press a hand to my belly. "We need him." Mara rubs the soreness from her wrists and doesn't say anything else, but that's okay. I'm doing this with or without her. There's too much at stake. I heft the skillet, pleased with its weightiness. This is perfect. "If you pray, now's time."

Throwing up a quick prayer myself, I walk on my knees to the flap of canvas separating the driver from us. My fingers are almost numb with heightened urgency, but I quietly and cautiously loosen the drawstring, the scent of unwashed man and strong drink assaulting my nostrils.

There he is, the man who thinks he can buy innocent women and children and get away with it.

Not today.

It's a shame that the beauty of this sunset on the empty road is marred with the ugliness of our circumstances, but hope and determination swell within my heart, giving me courage to do what I must. With the noise of the horses and the wagon, he doesn't even hear me as I slowly stand and hunch over. Clenching the handle tightly, I say another prayer that I can fell him in one swing and grab the reins so the animals don't run wild. Every muscle in my body tightens, my heart sending blood to revive my numb fingertips.

One breath.

Raise my arms.

Two breaths.

Focus on the back of his head.

Three breaths.

He suddenly throws a glance over his shoulder, then does a double take. "Shit. It's you, Girl."

Oh, sweet Lord.

I haven't been called Girl in that tone of voice since Springwell.

It's Clarence Crowley.

My father bought us?

Jaws dropped, we both stare at each other in surprise for tense seconds before his eyes catch on my hands. "Girl, what in the hell are you—? Get back in there, bitch." He pushes me with a growl and knocks me off balance. I fall back, landing on—no, I'm still standing!

"I got ya, Dove." Abner grunts and pushes me up. "Now knock him a good'un."

Pushing down my shock, I lunge forward and swing with all my might, elated when the skillet connects with a resounding crack and my father tumbles off the wagon and onto the ground.

I...I did it.

Merciful heavens, it worked.

"Dove! The horses!"

The urgency in Abner's voice wakes me from my stupor. I scramble onto the bench and grab at the leather reins. Thunder sounds in the distance, causing the two animals to run faster. Flooded and muddy roads are the last thing we need. But when the thunder doesn't die down and gets even closer, my fingers twitch. "Not thunder," I whisper to myself. "Horses."

But...Jed talked about bandits. What if we've gotten the attention of someone worse than Clarence Crowley?

"Dove!"

I strangle on a gasp when I hear my name being called. That wasn't Mara, it wasn't Abner, and it sure wasn't my father because I left him about one hundred feet back.

It comes again in a roar. *"Dove!"*

"That's Jed!" Abner hollers into my ear.

"Ched," I sob, tears bursting out and clouding my vision. He came after me!

And suddenly my husband appears in my blurry vision, riding low and furiously on Sadie as he gets neck to neck with us. "Pull back on the reins," he yells and grabs for the bridle closest to him.

Right. The reins. Why am I still heading away from Hope's Stand? I give them a good yank, throwing up a blessing when the dusty gray horses slow their pace and then stop completely. Before I can even sigh in relief, I'm snatched off the seat and suffocated in the strong arms of my husband.

"Dove." The roughness of his voice when he says my name against my neck makes me cry because it's him. It's really him. This isn't some rescue I dreamed up. "I've got you, darlin'. I'm here now. You're safe."

I chant his name over and over while tears of happiness pour from me. "You came. Love you, Ched." I'm safe now. Only my husband is touching me.

Jed feathers kisses all up my neck until he reaches my lips, and this time when his tongue invades my mouth, I find that I don't mind it as much. Not when I came so close to losing it forever. "Of course I did, woman," he says between breaths. "How many times do I have to say I'm always gonna catch you before you start believing it?" Without letting me answer, he pushes me back to look at me. "Are you okay? Did they hurt you? You're bleeding!"

I am? My mind goes blank as he rolls my sleeves up to inspect my bloody wrists and then I remember. "Okay. I'm okay. It was Abner's knife. He cut us free."

Jed hugs me again. "How did you come to be in the driver's seat? We saw him fall off."

My words scarcely leave my throat for how tightly he squeezes me. "Hit his head a skillet. With a skillet."

"What?" Jed stares at me in shock, a smile slowly growing. "You used a skillet and knocked him off? You little genius, you."

"I couldn't let him take us. Any of us." Then I realize what he said. *We saw him fall off.*

We.

Do I dare to hope... "Warren. Is he—?"

"Y'all lose something?"

"Warren!" Never in my life have I been so relieved to be interrupted by that slow drawl. I spin around in Jed's arms and see Warren riding up through the tall field of grass next to us and dragging something behind him. Something that spits out curses in between the mouthfuls of dirt and grass when Lady comes to a stop.

"Shut him up, would you?" Jed asks his brother.

He must not recognize him. "My father. He bought us," I inform Jed as Warren dismounts and pulls a bandana from his back pocket. And while my husband's face twists with anger, a hogtied Clarence Crowley's eyes bulge in surprise at hearing me speak.

Warren stands and wipes his hands. "There you go. You just lay there nice and quiet. And as for you"—his eyes grow suspiciously shiny as they fall on me—"I thought...thought we'd lost you. Jed, you're gonna have to keep yourself together because I need a hug from my sister right now." And with two long steps, he wraps his arms around me. "No more getting kidnapped. Only Shays can do that to you, you hear?"

"Warren!" I shouldn't be surprised that he could make me laugh even in a situation like this. Brushing more tears away, I stand on my tiptoes and kiss his cheek. "So happy you're alive."

"You didn't see that, did you, Jed?"

My husband looks like he wants to smack the smug expression from his younger brother's face. "Guess there's always exceptions."

"Hey, Jed?"

Ignoring my father's muffled grunts, we all turn at the quiet little voice that's completely unlike the boy who's always so blunt and outspoken. A forlorn figure, he stands dejected by the back of the wagon.

"Abner." Jed crouches and opens his arms. "C'mere, kid. It's all okay now." Abner runs into his embrace, tears falling on the way. His thin arms wrap around Jed's neck as he buries his face into a broad shoulder and blubbers nonsensically. "Hold up, now, I can't hear you. Take some deep breaths." Jed's big hand almost completely covers Abner's back as he rubs up and down. "It's all over and we're gonna get you back to your parents."

"But Jed..." He wipes his face all over the shirt in front of him and looks up with abject misery. "I didn't keep her safe like you said. And you told me she was more 'portant to you than Sadie and I still let the bad guys take her. After I crossed my heart and hoped to die. I'm sorry, Jed." Water wells up again in his puffy eyes and his lower lip trembles. "I tried. I yelled for Warren to get you and then I kicked the man, but—"

"Hey, hey, hey...I need you to listen and listen to me good." Jed shushes him and cups his wet cheeks. "A man—a real man—knows when to fight and when to bide his time. When to use his fists and when to use his head. And that's exactly what you did. It's because of you that Dove was able to knock old Clarence down. I don't like that either of you were taken, but I'm glad that you were there with her because she needed your help, Abner. She told me you used your pocketknife to cut her free."

He perks up, but then a wince draws his face back down. "I did. But I accidentally cut her when my fingers slipped."

I lay a hand on his shoulder. "I'm okay." And it's true. The sting is long gone and all that's left is a dull ache and some dried blood. "You saved me."

Jed snakes a long arm over my waist, squeezing me tightly as if to reassure himself that he still has me. "Remember what I told you that day we first met? Abner Wright is a good, strong name to be remembered by. I know I'll never forget it."

A watery smile covers Abner's little face before he throws his arms around Jed again.

"Uh, guys? That's all sweet and stuff, but we've got a problem back here." Warren stares into the back of the wagon and then back at us, face more serious than I've ever seen it. "I think we've got a baby who wants to come into the world in the next little bit." As if on cue, Mara groans in pain and rolls her head to one side.

"I'll go with you." I throw Jed a worried look. As much as I want to be with him, I can imagine Mara won't want to be around many men.

But Jed's not having any of it as he pulls me back. "Oh, no you don't, wife. You're not leaving my sight," he growls.

"Ched," I whisper before his lips take mine in a hard kiss.

"Right." Eyes softening, Warren reaches for Mara. "It's gonna be okay."

Even in pain, she jerks her head away, teeth bared like a wild animal. "Don't touch me."

Hand hovering uselessly, he flinches as if she'd stabbed him in the heart. Pasting an easygoing smile on his face, he says in a soothing voice, "I'm not gonna hurt you, but I am gonna take care of you whether you like it or not." Not releasing her wary gaze, he slowly leans in again and gently brushes his knuckles over the hollow of her cheek before dropping his hand. "Now you sit tight and let me get you to a doctor. Come on, Abner. Here's your pocketknife. You must have dropped it."

Warren looks stunned as he hands Abner back the tool that set us free. Not just stunned because of being knocked on the head or because a baby is about to be born. I think...I think he's taken with her. I also don't think he could have picked a pricklier person, even if she has a legitimate right to be like that.

"But Jed," Abner says as Warren helps him up, "what are you gonna do?"

Jedidiah's face turns cold as his fingers flex on my waist. "I'm gonna show Clarence Crowley how a Shay man avenges his woman."

19

DOVE

T he orange rays of the sun tint the wagon's canvas as Warren drives back to Hope's Stand swiftly but carefully because of Mara's condition. Oh, how I pray both she and the baby will be alright. But what will she do afterward and where will she and the baby stay? Having been sold and resold for four years, she must not have anyone to care about her, and with as much as she's gone through, she needs someone to chase away her bitterness before it eats her up inside.

"Darlin'?" At Jed's low voice, I turn. His face is guarded as he jerks his head to where my bound father is still tethered to Lady and futilely trying to escape. "You know I'm going to kill him, right?"

My heart skips a beat. "Kill...my father? You told Abner you'd...avenge me." Death is a steep punishment, one that there's no coming back from. Does he really deserve it? When my eyes dart to Clarence Crowley's angry ones, I see pure hatred reflected at me.

Always my protector, Jed angles his body between us, blocking me from view. "Oh, Dove." His thumb smooths over my hidden scars. "A man who would cut a grieving child's throat and abuse her isn't a father. Hell, he's barely even a man. And one who goes on to abuse her for thirteen years and then tries to sell her for his debts? First in marriage and then by the hour? Despicable. He doesn't deserve to live. Besides, I already vowed to myself that if the Dooleys hadn't taken care of him, I was going to. No man lays a hand on my woman and lives to tell the tale."

"No man? What about ones who took us? Two of them."

"Dead. I shot one of them in the thigh and that made the other one come running into the room. And once I found out where you were, there was no need for either one of them to walk the face of this earth anymore."

He means it. It's written all over his face. I can't deny my relief that Joe and the other man will never have the chance to do this again. And he thinks my father—Clarence, I mean—deserves the same fate. Honestly, when I think of all the things that have happened to me, I could move past them. I want to, actually. But knowing what I do now, that Clarence has no hesitation in buying people to do God knows what with...there's no telling what he would have done to me once that wagon stopped. "You're right," I whisper hoarsely. "But...here?" I wave my hand to the tall grass. And what about the bodies he left in town?

"Damn it." His fingers plow through his hair in frustration. "What am I doing? You shouldn't be here for this. Maybe I should have let you go back with the others just long enough for me to take care of this and then catch up."

"No." My husband's big body stills at my hand on his arm. "I think...I think need this for me."

His face tightens. "I'm not going to just shoot him. No, the bastard's neck has an appointment with my knife. Listen to me." Big hands gently grasp my arms. "The minute you can't take it, and I mean the very second, I want you to turn your back and plug your ears. You may think you want to watch, but you might change your mind once things get a little messy. And that's okay. Now are you ready?"

Ready to watch my husband exact vengeance on Clarence Crowley for his transgressions? I lock eyes with Jed. "Yes."

Another hard kiss is my reward. "All right. Let's get this done so we can get home and get a bath." The thought of hot water and clean soap to wash the blood and filth from me almost makes me cry, but I focus on Jedidiah as he straddles Clarence. "Do you want to ask him anything before I get started? If not, the gag stays on."

Grim satisfaction sends a small smile to my lips when Clarence bucks in protest, but with the ropes and my husband's heavy body holding him down, he's not going anywhere. I study the panicking man, remembering the first night he crawled onto my bed and put his knife to my throat. Do I want to ask him anything? Why he couldn't love me as a child? Or where he went after he sold the house and where he got the money to buy people?

No, I don't.

It won't change the past, and he certainly has no place in my future. And while part of me craves to hear his response to me breaking the silence he imposed on me all these years, I'll be satisfied in knowing that he's powerless to stop my words any longer. "No." It rolls strongly from my tongue. "But I do...want to say something."

Five steps and I'm standing above him, feeling no fear at being this close to the man who once tormented me. Not with Jedidiah by my side. Where his eyes held such hatred for me only moments before, now they're filled with a silent plea.

But he's had his chance to make things right several times over. I breathe deeply, letting my words form in my mind and then releasing them in a loud and strong voice. "I don't know why you couldn't love us. My mother and me. She was a kind and gentle soul who tried her best to please you. You could have had a wonderful family with us, but you didn't want it. And when she died, you made me hold the pain of it in. It's your turn now, Clarence. Your turn to be silent and hold the sounds of your pain inside. May God have mercy on your soul, because my husband is about to deliver it to Him."

By the end of my little speech, my voice is nothing but a whisper. Strangely enough, I feel lighter inside with all those words gone. Free.

Jedidiah's face has a mixture of pride and lust. "Damn, woman. I love this vicious side of you. And you didn't even miss a word." Then he draws his knife, letting each inch of the blade catch the glint of the dying sun as it leaves the sheath. "You heard my wife. But you can't meet the Almighty looking as you do now. No, you're missing some things." He scratches his chin with the blunt edge of the blade, grinning at Clarence's slowly dawning horror. "Christ, man, but you stink to high Heaven. I'm thinking you need a blood bath to wash away your stench. How many scars do you have on your neck, Dove?"

"Seven." My hand lightly touches them.

"Exactly what I thought. Hold your breath, Clarence, as I make right what you did to a little girl thirteen years ago." The weakness of a man given to drink is no match for the strength of a man set on exacting revenge, and soon a thin line of blood trickles down the rolls of Clarence's neck as Jed's knife cuts the skin. "Tell me something, Dove. If a cocksucking son of a bitch is expecting seven cuts and I only give him one, how many does he still need?"

A nervous giggle slips through my lips. Never let it be said that my husband neglects my education. "Six."

"How smart you are, my pretty little wife. Six, indeed. Remind me to kiss you later." And over muffled screams, he delivers on his promise of six more cuts, making me do the math after each one.

To the relief of his victim, Jed straightens and surveys his handiwork. Both the grass and Clarence's neck are now stained red, making me think that his cuts are deeper than the ones he'd given to me. Somehow, I can't bring myself to care.

"Aww...does it hurt?" my husband mocks. "I imagine it didn't feel so good to an innocent little girl, either. Ah, that reminds me." A calculating gleam enters his eye. "You didn't like to call her by her name, did you? No, you didn't. You didn't even have the decency to call her a real name. And it's such a shame that you won't have a chance to say her real name again. But don't worry. When you get stopped at the pearly gates and St. Peter asks why you're there, you won't have to say a word."

Clarence glares at him, growling from beneath his gag, but Jed ignores him. Whistling a cheery tune, he drags the sharp blade down Clarence's dirty shirt, stopping to nick all the buttons so the fabric falls away. "There we go. A broad, white canvas for the final masterpiece. Nope, you won't have to say a word because it's going to be written on your chest."

With that ominous warning, the knife strikes. Clarence twists and bucks, but Jed's knees hold him securely as he works. What is he doing? The blood runs in rivulets as the knife moves, coloring everything in its path. Even Jed's hands.

My hand covers my mouth. Is he...?

Oh, sweet Lord.

"Remembrance. That's the name you couldn't be bothered to call her."

Remembrance. Oh, my. If I tilt my head this way and squint, I suppose that's what it says. A swell of emotion pricks my eyes and makes me sniff. How ironic. All these years, this man refused to call me by my name because he didn't like the sound of it. Now it's being carved into his chest.

Jed sharply glances up. "You all right, darlin'? Was that too much for you?"

"No." Oddly enough, I want more, even as I find myself stepping away. "Can you add my...my mother's name, too?"

"Of course I can." His bloody hand tightens in preparation. "Temperance, right?"

He remembers from the very first time I told him. I stare directly into the pained eyes of the man I once called Father until he looks away. "Yes. Temperance Irons."

The knife goes to work again and by the time it's through, Clarence's chest is drenched in blood and he's panting like a dog. "Wake up, man. Just a little bit longer and you can sleep all you want." To me, Jed says, "Do you want to turn away for this part? This is it."

It. One small word marking the end of a man's life. I press a palm to my stomach, mindful of the beginning life within me. "What...what are you going to do?" I'm both curious and a little queasy now that it's here.

"Truth be told, I'm torn between giving him a short death or a long one. Do you want to decide?"

"No," I whisper and draw my arms around myself. "I don't." I just want him gone.

Jed's eyes narrow at my shiver. "You're cold. Damn it,

darlin', I'm sorry I took so long. All right, a short one it is. I'm gonna put a bullet in his head and leave him for the coyotes. If you don't want to watch, you go stand over there by Sadie and wait for me, okay?"

Not sparing Clarence another glance, I let my weary feet take me to Sadie, who's waited patiently all this time. When her whiskery lips nip at my hair, I hug her tightly and let the tears fall into her chestnut coat. I was so close to losing everything I'd ever wanted today. "Thank you, Sadie. Thank you bringing Jed so quickly to me. You deserve all carrots you could eat, and when we get home—"

A sharp crack rings out, making me flinch. It's done then. Clarence Crowley is gone for good, never to lay hands on me in anger again.

Never to lock the door and make me sleep outside.

Never to buy innocent women and children.

Gone.

I don't turn around until I hear footsteps behind me and then I see my husband stalking my way, blood and vengeance giving him a fierce edge as he unbuttons his shirt and wipes his hands. "Let's go home, Dove."

The trip home passes in a blur. Jed doesn't want to touch me with blood on his hands, but he also won't let me ride alone. Hence the bloody handprints seeping into the waistline of my dress as he holds me now on the back of Sadie, Lady following closely behind. I somberly stare at the darkening horizon and rest my head on my husband's bare chest. Between the kisses he constantly presses to my hair and the rhythmic sway of the horse, I find my eyes are too heavy for my eyelids.

The next time they open, I'm soaking in hot water as Jed washes me. "Mind your eyes." With that quiet warning, warm water pours over my head and washes away the foamy lather.

"So tired," I whisper. I just want to sleep.

"I know, darlin'." Soft lips brush a kiss over my wet forehead. "Just one more rinse or two and then we're going to bed." It takes three to satisfy him, and then he towels me off and dresses me in one of his shirts. "C'mon. Under the covers with you."

Protected in his arms and warmed by his body, I fall fast asleep. I don't know how long I stay that way, though. An hour? Maybe two?

Something wakes me up, though. And it's the last thing I ever expected. Cloaked in moonlight, my husband is thrusting inside of me, face drawn tight as if in pain.

"Tried to let you sleep," he groans as his hips move harder, "but I need you. Need to feel you around me." When my hands reach for him, I find they're already shackled with his. "I almost lost you today. Both you and our baby." He pounds me into the mattress, raw emotion roughening his words. "Almost...lost you. But I swear to you, woman, I'll always find you. Always. Nobody can take you from me."

There's fear under his voice. Abner and I weren't the only ones afraid today. Jed was, too. He needs me now. And I need him.

"Let me hold you," I beg. As soon as my hands are free, I pull him down to me and throw my legs around his to open myself up further. "I'm yours. Always yours," I promise between his thrusts. "Never leaving you, ever." I don't think I can reach release like this, but this isn't about that. I give him my submission, reassuring him the only way I know how. Offering up my heart and my body as I whisper his name in his ear. I needed him to come after me and save me, and he needs to lose himself in my body.

Our tears mingle together as he claims my mouth in a kiss so passionate, one that tells me what he can't put into words.

Love. Devotion. Protection.

And when his heavy body presses me even further into the bed as he releases himself into me on a long, low groan, I thank God above that I was lucky enough to be bought by Jedidiah Shay.

Still inside me, he rolls to the side and clumsily brushes my hair from my face. "I love you, Dove. So damn much. I think your mother would be proud of the woman you've become."

Tears spring up again. "Thank you saying that. And I think...I think she would love you, too. Just as much I do."

Jed nuzzles my neck, inhaling the scent of our bath. "Dove," he breathes. "I need you again. Why can't I get enough of you?" He makes sweet, beautiful love to me this time, almost as if in apology for how rough he was before. And with his low murmurs of his love for me ringing in my ears, I find my release.

Again. And again. And again.

20

DOVE

How much is left of a body after coyotes eat their fill? When we make it to the outskirts of Hope's Stand the next afternoon to check on Warren and Mara, part of me is tempted to hide under Jedidiah's arm so I don't have to find out. Of course, I'm already tucked safely away next to him with not even an inch between us, so all I'd have to do is turn my head the slightest bit to the side. In the end, though, I can't bring myself to look, so I flatten a wrinkle in my dress with my free hand. Jed wants to burn the other dress and shawl and throw away my new pendant, concerned that they'll only hold bad memories.

Maybe he's right. Even if I could get the bloody handprints cleaned from it, I wouldn't be able to wear that dress again without feeling the barrel of Joe's gun as it skimmed my front. The way it hooked under the pendant and—I shiver. Yes, he might be right.

"It's okay, darlin'. There's nothing to see."

I peek up at him over his shirt. "Nothing at all?"

"Nope. Lots of times coyotes will drag their prey away to a secluded area. I imagine they didn't feel comfortable eating so close to the road where lots of wagons drive by so they either buried the rest for later or another pack member decided to help them out."

I almost wish I hadn't asked because now bile bubbles up at the image of animals feeding on a body. "What about town?" I'm back to skipping words again unless I speak very slowly. But at least I was able to tell Clarence exactly what I was thinking without missing any of them. "Joe and the...the other one."

"Don't you worry about them." A big hand squeezes my thigh in comfort. "General consensus around town was nobody liked them much, so I'd wager that it'll get called an argument between them that got out of hand and that'll be the end of it."

Still, I give that wretched building the side eye and sigh in relief as we pass it. It sure would be nice if lightning struck and burned it to the ground. And if Clarence, Joe, and the other man were still in there. Alive. To be burned to death.

Good heavens! I mentally shake myself, shocked at the sudden turn of my thoughts. It seems marriage to my husband has unleashed things in me I never dreamed were ever in there to begin with.

"Here we go," Jed says as we pull up to a modest two-story home. "Now you just stay right there and wait for me to help you down."

He's hovering. The man is constantly touching me and trying to anticipate my every need. But after the experience we just had, I'm not complaining at all. When I think of what could be happening to me right now—no, I need to stop. That was then and this is now. I throw a sweet smile on and kiss his cheek when he lowers me down. "Thank you."

"Anything for my woman. You know what I think we

need to do after this?" he casually offers up as we make our way to the house.

"Knowing you, I have idea or two," I wryly state. "But what are you thinking about?"

"I'm thinking you, me, and a nice dip in the spring. Without clothes." He whispers the last in my ear as his knuckles rap against the door.

Oh, yes. The spring that we had to leave abruptly because of the sudden storm. And who could forget the little cabin where we made mad, passionate love in front of the fire while our clothes dried? "You know," I slowly say with a teasing glance, "Abner told me something in wagon. Something about you and—" The door opens before I finish, and once we announce ourselves, the housekeeper politely ushers us upstairs.

"Me and what?"

I look at him as we climb the last step. "Tell you later." There. Let him wonder exactly what Abner told me. I can almost feel the burn of his curious gaze as he gestures me inside the room the housekeeper directs us to.

"Dove Shay, you tell me right—"

"Oh, Jed." I grab his arm and shush him. I don't know what I was expecting to see when we walked in, but it certainly wasn't this. Propped up on pillows and in a fresh nightgown, Mara is fast asleep, hair in a sloppy braid over her shoulder. The poor girl. I don't know how her birthing experience went, but she looks troubled still, even in her sleep.

But the part that makes my heart absolutely melt is Warren. He's sitting straight up next to her with his neck crookedly angled to the side and a newborn baby cradled perfectly against his broad chest as they both sleep.

"How utterly adorable," I whisper with a soft smile as I

glance back at Jed. Something presses on my belly and when I look down, I feel the prickle of tears. It's my husband's big hand cradling the place where our own child grows.

"We'll get our turn soon," he murmurs back as he spreads his fingers.

Mara's baby gives the tiniest and quietest of grunts, but Warren's eyes fly open as if it had been a full-blown wail. "Shh," he soothes as he pats the tiny back with his free hand. "I've got you, little one. Pap—oh, hey." He gives us a tired but proud smile as he nods to his chest. "Look who I've got here. Little Emmaline. Emmaline Hazel Shay."

"Shay?" That was unexpected. Then again, from the proud smile on Jedidiah's face it might not be so unexpected for a Shay.

Warren's proud smile fades away as he looks next to him. "Mara doesn't have anybody. Not a single person in the world who cares about her. And I couldn't let the child be born a bastard and leave Mara on her own, so I did what I had to do," he says with a shrug. "Called for Judge Ballard to marry us before she gave birth. She didn't like it then—hell, probably still won't like it once she wakes up—but she's got a husband to take care of the both of them now. They need me." His low chuckle ruffles Emmaline's hair. "Not quite the same as snatching her up in the middle of the night, but she's mine now just the same."

Right. Because these Shay men see nothing wrong with capturing and stealing a bride. I'm glad Warren married her, though. She's had more than enough suffering in her life, but if anyone can make her smile, it'll be him.

Mara twitches at Warren's voice, making him speak more quietly, but then he freezes. "I don't believe it," he faintly says as he stares at his hand. So faintly that I have to strain to hear him. "She's...she's holding my finger."

Oh, sweet Lord. He's right. Mara's pinky is hooked around his as she sleeps. While she had said that all men's hands and cocks were the same, I don't think she ever thought the touch of a Shay would be any different. Somehow, though, I have a feeling that Warren's going to prove her wrong.

Mara jolts awake with a stuttered gasp, eyes darting about the room. When she realizes where she is, she relaxes slightly.

Until she lifts her hand.

The one with Warren attached.

"Why are you touching me?" she snaps and snatches her hand back with a wince.

Unfazed, Warren answers dryly, "Since you're the one who reached for me, I should be asking you that."

"No." Mara frowns at him suspiciously and rubs away his touch. "I did not."

Warren holds a smile back and shrugs. "Suit yourself. Truth is truth, though, and reaching for your husband is nothing to be ashamed about. Here. Emmaline slept good on me, but now she needs the touch of her mother."

The fierce scowl on her face is swept away by a curtain of blank emotion at the mention of the baby in his arms. Her head jerks to the side as she stares stoically at the wall. "No. I...I don't want to see—"

"Here you go," he smoothly interrupts as he gently forces her to take the child, wrapping a long arm around her stiff shoulders. "Don't turn away, Mara. Look at this little girl. See how beautiful she is with her mother's eyes and hair." When his knuckles brush over her thin cheek, Mara roughly swallows at his touch. "She's got my nose and chin, though, and you can't tell me otherwise."

Mara reluctantly tilts her head to the baby in her arms as if testing the truth of Warren's claim. And when she looks at Emmaline's face—truly looks—a lone, single tear treks down her cheek only to disappear as Warren tenderly wipes it away.

Recognizing the newlywed couple's need for privacy, Jed and I quietly ease out of the room and close the door. We'll visit them once they get settled in their new home.

My emotions are a bit of a mess as we bid the house-keeper a good afternoon and head back toward our own home. I press a palm to my stomach and just imagine holding our little baby. Mara was afraid to look at Emma-line. Because she'd see too much of the man who got her pregnant? Or were there too many men for her to know which one it was?

"Don't worry, darlin'. She and that little one are gonna be okay now that Warren's looking after them."

I slide my hand around his arm and tug him down for a kiss. "I know. He finally claimed his frog." If she lets him kiss her, that is.

"Yep." Jedidiah smiles broadly. "And a little tadpole, too."

———

"Mhmm," I moan into my husband's mouth as he pins me to the tree. "But I want...want to swim now." The clear water behind him just begs for me to dive right into it.

"That presents a problem, darlin', because I want *you*. But I think I know of a way for us to both get what we want." A bite that stings in the best of ways accompanies his answer.

"You take off your pretty dress while I take off my pants. You let me have my way with you." Teeth drag down my neck, making me shiver. "Then we'll take a swim. And then..."

A thought sparks. "But Jed..." I push back and cross my arms over my chest. "What if...what if someone's watching us?" I'm almost proud of how much nervousness I inject into my voice.

"I'm not gonna let anybody see you without your clothes on." Still, a brief hint of worry crosses his face as he quickly scans the area.

I watch him closely, unable to hide my smile. "Not even Abner?"

"Especially not—wait a minute," Jed blusters. "What do you mean by that?"

I don't want to miss any words, so I take my time in answering. "I mean"—my hand slips down his chest—"you've been had, Mr. Shay. He confessed to watching me. And he admitted to bringing you." Now my fingers rest on his stomach.

"Well," he coughs out. Up until now, I'd harbored some doubts on the truth of Abner's claim, but when a bit of red chagrin colors my husband's cheeks, I know it to be fact. "If you must know, it was only once. For me, at least. And if you recall, I warned him about watching women bathing. Especially my woman. But if it bothers you so much, I can make it up to you."

Giving me a heated look, he drags my hand down to his rapidly hardening cock, encouraging me to stroke him. I coyly glance upwards, loving the mix of wariness and lust on his handsome face. "How?" I tighten my grip, loving the low groan he gives.

"You, my little Dove"—his hands come to rest on either

side of the tree behind me—"can watch me like I watched you. Oh, you like that idea, don't you?"

"I do." So much so that we both felt my legs tighten at the thought just now.

Jed snags my hands and places them on my breasts. "You take care of these for me. Rub those little nipples for me good, okay?" Leaving me holding myself, he takes a step back and reaches for his buttons. Sweet heavens, the man has a beautiful chest. He tosses his shirt over a branch and moves to his pants. When they drop to his boots, he straightens back up with a sinful smile and takes his hard cock in hand.

Oh, my. It's getting a little hard to breathe now. Needing support, I lean back on the tree as I keep my fingers working in little circles over my dress. "You're hard," I say unnecessarily.

"I am." One slow upstroke. Palm over the swollen head. One slow downstroke. "Because I have my wife tempting me with her sweet body. Tell me, Dove. Do your fingers feel good?"

"Not...not as good as yours," I manage, still mesmerized by his hand and the magnificent erection it holds. "Or your mouth."

His cock jerks in his grip as he winces. "Damn, woman, you know how to get to me."

"What about you?" I give one tip a little pinch like he does sometimes. Oh. *Oh.* I felt that. "Does your hand feel good?"

A low, pained laugh. "Not as good as yours. Or your mouth. Or your pussy. But it'll do well enough."

My mouth waters at the possibility of tasting him again. Of running my lips all over his cock, from length to tip. "I want you," I boldly say, dropping my hands and taking a step forward.

"Ah-ah-ah," he tsks, almost strangling his cock with his fist. "You stay right there, woman, and do what I told you to do. Sometimes release is all the sweeter when you make yourself wait for what you want."

That's not an option. Not with this fire licking through my bones and setting my core aflame with desire. My feet itch with the urge to disobey him. Do I dare? "But Jed," I whimper as I throw a look over my shoulder to the little cabin. It's not far. Maybe...just maybe if I can make it up the small incline. One foot steps to the side as my legs tense.

He stills, eyes narrowing. "Dove, what are you doing?" At his warning tone, a flash of excitement quickens my heartbeat. Should I push him further? I answer my own question with another step to the left.

"Sometimes..." I stop and lick my suddenly dry lips, all the moisture having diverted to between my legs. I don't know what's come over me, but I'm really doing this. "I think sometimes...it's all the sweeter when"—oh, merciful heavens, the heat in his eyes as they track my every move!—"when take what you want. Now catch me!" And leaving him with his pants around his ankles and his cock in hand, I whirl around and sprint for the cabin.

"Dove!" Jed roars, making me whimper in nervous excitement. Then he charges after me, sounding like a wild animal. "Run while you can, wife. Because I'm right behind you."

I stumble at his low growl, wetness trickling down my thighs at the promise in his voice. He's going to catch me, just like he did the first time I ran from him. With as long as his legs are, he could overtake me at any moment. But I think

I've bought some time for myself since he has to pull his pants up. Hazarding a glance back, I almost trip over my feet at the sight of my beastly husband chasing me with a massive cock bobbing between his legs. A slash of fear spikes my blood even as my lips split in a wild smile to match his.

Foregoing the cabin, I run into the thick foliage instead, weaving in and around the trees before hiding behind a random tree. Birds chirp overheard, their cheery sound at odds with the predatory hunt happening on the ground. The thumping of my heart echoes like a drum in my head while my fingertips throb. I can't even hear myself breathe over the blood rushing through my ears.

Then I freeze, lungs laboring as I quiet my breaths. This means I can't hear him, either. Is this how prey feels when it's being hunted? Good Lord, I've never felt so alive! A twig snaps, the sound barely audible, and a gasp escapes before I can keep it in. The tree bark scrapes my hands as I instinctively flatten my palms.

He's close.

But how close?

When I turn my head to peek around the trunk of the tree, a nose touches mine. "Hello, wife."

Too close.

I scream in surprise and backpedal, but it's no good. Satisfaction shining in his dark eyes, he steps around with a wicked grin as he palms his heavy cock that strains towards me. Oh, my. It seems as if I'm not the only one who enjoyed the chase.

"You're all mine now." Strong arms shackle my waist and spin me around so my back is to his front. Hot words in my ear send more wetness between my thighs. "No more running. Now you pay the price, woman."

For as rough as his threat is, he's gentle as he guides me

to the ground. My fingers dig for purchase into the grass and dirt as he nudges me to my hands and knees, and with one swift motion, my dress is tossed up over my backside. Finally! "Do you know what happens when a woman runs from her man?" he rumbles.

"She...she gets to feel him inside her?" I'm shaking, but not from fear. I think it's just my body doesn't know it's been caught yet.

"Oh, my little Dove." Jed's dark chuckle makes my thighs clench. "She does, but it'll be harder. Rougher. Because she ran."

His name leaves my lips on a girlish moan as he thrusts between my legs without entering me. "Jed...so empty. Need you."

"I know," he soothes, rubbing my clit and giving me the tiniest bit of relief. "And you'll have every bit of me until you can't take any more. Until my seed drips down your thighs and onto the dirt. And then you'll keep taking me like a good little wife so I can get what I need, won't you? Even when the pleasure hurts so good."

"Yes, yes. Please," I beg. How can he make my body rage with desire using only his words? "Please. Please."

A hand presses to my lower back as he positions his cock. "Who do you belong to, wife?" He teases me by shallowly pushing the head in and out.

"Y-you." I push back onto him and make him groan. His powerful answering thrust knocks me off-balance, but he follows me down, not letting me loose. Pinned to the dirt, I tighten my pussy around him.

"Naughty little wife, trying to force me to stay inside you," Jed chastises over me as his hips move back. "But if that's what you need, then I'm more than happy to give it to you." He fills me so quickly and suddenly and fully that a whimper is pushed from my throat. And then he moves. Hard, raw thrusts that punish as much as they reward as he tightly grips my wrists where they rest by my head.

In, out. In, out.

All while the earthy scent of dirt and wildflowers tickles my nose. A tingling sensation settles in my neglected clit as my husband unleashes himself and has his way with me. "Please..." I whimper again, fingers curling around blades of grass. "Need you."

"You want more of me, wife?" Another thrust forward. "Tighten your legs. More."

Why does he...? Oh, I see why. The closer my thighs and knees are together, the more I feel him inside me. Sweet heavens, he's— "So big," I brokenly blurt out. So full with him inside me.

And then he slips a hand between us to cup my pussy as he moves again, short thrusts that drive me higher and higher to the edge of release. The harder he moves, the more his trapped fingers squeeze my folds and tickle my clit. I submit myself to my husband's hunger as an icy hot sensation spreads from my center to my fingers and toes. So close...so close...

"Let go for me," Jed orders before latching onto my neck in a claiming bite. Stars and white specks decorate my vision as my entire body explodes in sweet release. "There you go, darlin'. Give it all to me."

He doesn't let up. If anything, he rides me harder, forcing me to stay in this heightened state of arousal as his fingers never stop. "S-sensitive," I moan, fighting just to breathe through the pleasure. "So sensitive."

"More," Jed growls. "Not stopping." Then words between us are lost as his ballsack and thighs slap against me, prolonging my painfully sweet release. Time fades away, leaving only foggy bliss as my husband holds me down and has his way with me. Is it minutes? Is it hours? All I know is that he's rutting me like he never has before.

Then with one deep groan that reverberates along my back, he empties himself inside of me as my barely audible whimpers of pleasure hit the ground and disappear. Our heavy breathing is the only sound in the woods as we struggle to fill our lungs. Jed recovers before I do and tenderly eases my mussed hair to the side to lick over the bite he gave me. "Are you going to run from me again?"

I drag my heavy head up and fight to look at his sated eyes over my shoulder. "Only if you catch me."

"Oh, wife," he purrs on a promise. "Always."

EPILOGUE

DOVE

ONE YEAR LATER

"**C**omfortable?" Jed shifts me closer on his lap. I pull his face down for a slow kiss before I rest my head back on his chest and play with his collar. "Yes, thank you." And how could I not be? With the way he uses one foot to rock the wooden cradle and the other for our rocking chair, I'll probably fall asleep before our son Ransom does.

It's so hard to believe I have a baby now. Jed was so thoughtful and sweet when my figure changed, always rubbing a hand over my belly or pressing kisses from side to side. And once the baby started moving? Oh, the man's hand was attached almost every minute for fear that he'd miss something. The birth was scary, no doubt about it, and my screams of pain had Jed swearing up and down to me that we weren't going to have any more babies. We'll see how long that lasts because neither of us can stay away from the other for too long.

Ransom grunts, his tiny fists waving in the air and

stealing my attention. I'd thought Mara's baby girl was beautiful, but that was before I met our sweet Ransom. Could a child be more perfect? With his fuzzy brown hair, deep blue eyes, and tiny chin, he's stolen our hearts.

Was this how my mother felt about me? I still haven't opened her diary yet even though I know I'm more than capable of reading the words now, thanks to Jedidiah. My heart wasn't ready. But now I think it is. "Can you...can you pass me the diary?"

He stills, concern warming his face as he studies mine carefully. "Of course, darlin'. But I thought you wanted to read it by yourself first."

"I did." Not anymore. "Will you do it with me?"

A soft caress of my cheek is his answer. Then he stretches one long arm over to the dresser and brings back the worn black book. "Here you go, darlin'."

I'm not prepared for the flood of bittersweetness when I run my fingers over the cracked letters on the front. How many nights did I stand in front of my tiny mirror in Clarence Crowley's house and imagine the words inside? Too many. But now it's time to read them for myself. Carefully turning the page, I study the handwriting I've seen so many times but couldn't decipher. I blink away the sudden tears that appear, but the words are still blurry. "I...I can't. Will you read it?"

Jed kisses my forehead, just like my mother used to do. "Of course." And then he begins to read in his low, soothing voice. The first few pages are prayers and poems, but when he reaches the seventh page, I lose my breath at the words.

My darling Remembrance,

I watch over you in the glow of the firelight as you resist the pull of slumber. It was a busy day for you today, one filled with chasing butterflies and picking flowers to brighten up the kitchen. And now, with the night coaxing your heavy eyes to close, you still fight, dreading the moment you finally give in.

How I wish I could fight as well as you! You are my hope, Remembrance, and what lifts my spirits. If not for your gracious smile as you gift me with bouquets of wild-flowers and your dirt-smudged hands that hold my cheeks as you press a kiss to them, my days would be very miserable, indeed.

Things were not always as they are at present here with Mr. Crowley, but neither will they stay the same, my sweet child. Life is not fair, but God is just, and when time grants a change for you, I pray that it is because you have found a love so great that you are overwhelmed by its strength.

Fight for it, child, and never lose hope.

Your mother for now and forever,
Temperance Irons

"Oh, Jed." My lips tremble, and before I know it, I'm sobbing brokenly into my husband's shirt while he pats my back. "She was so sad. No hope left."

"Hey, hey...that's not true." He squeezes me tighter. "She had you, and she loved you very much. Times may have been tough for her, but you helped her cope"—he pauses for a moment—"Remembrance."

Remembrance. The name I silently held near and dear to my heart for thirteen long years. Remembrance is who I was then, but Dove is who I am now. All because of this man holding me. I straighten and let him wipe my face with the handkerchief he magically produces. "You were my change."

Softness spreads over Jed's face as he cups my cheeks. "I was, and your mother was right. The love I have for you, Dove, you can never escape it."

I give him a teary smile in return. "Because you'll always catch me."

"Always, wife. Because this is what it means to be a Shay."

A NOTE FROM THE AUTHOR

As always, I just have to say thank you SO MUCH to Alexis, Ashley, and Veronica for letting me throw my chapters at you and wait for your insight. The books just wouldn't be the same without these three women. There are only so many ways to thank them before it turns repetitious, but they deserve it.

During the release of Tamed, I posted a sneak peek of Named and asked peeps in the Breeder Readers (yes, that's a legit and AWESOME Facebook group) to tell me some things they'd like to see in an erotic Western. If things worked out and I was able to use their ideas, I'd give them a shout-out in the Author's Note here.

Without further ado, I present to you:

1. Sex in a barn - Alisha Shipley

2. Spicy time while riding a horse - Bianca Williams, Mandi Gottfredson, Samah Elsayed (although it wasn't full-on sex, Samah)

3. Smexy time while she's sleeping - Brianna Stubble-field (even though I couldn't make it as clinical as you suggested)

4. Washing her, reading to her, carrying her around, & making it his mission to get noises from her - Sarah Emerson-Blackwell

5. Walking around with just his hat while she peeks at him - Helen Lee

6. Storm scene - Mandi Gottfredson

So...isn't Jedidiah Shay just the sweetest man to his Dove? I can't tell you how many times I cried writing the two of them together. Ack—the scene where she wrote his name wrong and he told her how smart she was??? Oh, the tears that fell. When he was desperate for her to say his name??? Oh, even more tears that fell. And I won't even mention how much her mother's diary made me cry. Poor Temperance Irons.

On a lighter note, how'd you like Jed's...ahem...hair trigger? Or poor Dove getting an unexpected facial from Jed's cute little snake? If ever there were two characters meant to be together, it's these two.

Who's next? Well, I fully intended for it to be Isaiah and his woman, but I kinda accidentally created another couple in this book. Totally not on purpose. I tried and tried not to have to write another book in this time period and setting, but the words just came out. Before I knew it, Jed had a really funny baby brother who would be the perfect man to love this bitter and jaded girl named Mara.

So there you have it.

Warren and Mara are next, and let me just say that this one will probably be pretty heavy. Mara's not had an easy life, so she needs someone like Warren to make her smile.

I learned my last lesson in thinking I could make Named a novella, but it wound up being around 71k words (on the higher end, novellas are no more than 40k-50k). Point being...I have no idea how long Warren and Mara's story will be. I don't even have a title or cover yet because they were COMPLETELY unplanned. Welllll...I'm toying with a title but I'm unsure if it's going to be the perfect fit. So we'll say it's untitled for now and I don't have an estimated date of release.

Speaking of Warren...he was singing a song about Watkins ale. Now, Charlotte LaRue was completely made up by me, but there IS a bawdy ballad entitled Watkins Ale. And omg...the innuendo is there. Look it up and be amused.

Until next time!

ALSO BY M. L. MARIAN

ABOUT THE AUTHOR

M. L. Marian has no clue what to put here. She sees other authors with really cool bios, but there's nothing cool about M. L. Marian. She's just an antisocial hermit who comes out of hiding long enough to put a book into the world and then scurries back into seclusion.

She would like to remind you, however, that kindness doesn't cost a thing (except for when it does) and loose lips sink ships. Whatever that means.

Subscribe to her newsletter at https://mlmarian.com/newsletter/ for all the latest updates!

facebook.com/mlmarian
instagram.com/m.l.marian
tiktok.com/@m.l.marian

Made in the USA
Columbia, SC
07 July 2025